Dark Journey

By the same author

Portrait of a Turkish Family

Cooking With Yogurt

The Young Traveller in Turkey

The Caravan Moves On

The Land and People of Turkey [under the pseudonym Ali Riza]

Phoenix Ascendant

Turkish Cooking

Atatürk [jointly with Margarete Orga]

Cooking the Middle East Way

Dark Journey
The legend of Kamelya and Murat

İRFAN ORGA

with an afterword by Ateş Orga

ELAND
London

First published by Eland Publishing Ltd
61 Exmouth Market, London EC1R 4QL in October 2014

ISBN 978 1 906011 81 9

Cover Image: *The Exile: 'Heavy is the Price I Paid for Love'*
by Thomas Cooper Gotch (1854–1931) © Alfred East Gallery,
Kettering Borough Council/Bridgeman Images

Text set in Great Britain by James Morris

Printed in Spain by GraphyCems, Navarra

Foreword

I first heard the legend of *Kamelya and Murat* when I was a child. My grandmother, who was born in Tırnava, Kamelya's own village, used to tell the story with considerable variations to my brother and I when more childish material bored her and we still clamoured for entertainment.

I have taken great liberties with the old story and have brought the period to my own generation; therefore most of the incidents are imaginary. I want to emphasise particularly that all the characters, excepting Kamelya and Murat, are fictitious and bear no relation to any person or persons living or dead.

The original version told by my grandmother may have held a germ of truth – the present version is entirely my own.

İrfan Orga
London

Publisher's Note

A glossary of foreign words and a lexicon of people and places can be found at the back of the book, for clarification.

Chapter 1

THE YEAR WAS 1915 and the boat-station at Eyüp Sultan was a raw place on a chilly spring morning with dawn barely established in the sky. The dusty jetty, heaving on the water, was empty save for the figures of a woman and a boy of about five, who stood listlessly with the first of the morning sun pouring over them emphasising their shabbiness and the thin white face of the child.

The woman moved, shifting her position so that the sun shone full on the black *çarşaf* covering her face and the child moved aimlessly after her, his hands clinging to her skirts.

'I'm hungry,' he said.

'So am I,' said the woman and twisted herself from his grasp. 'But we've no money for food – not yet anyway.'

She started to pace up and down the jetty, for despite the sun it was cold with a sharp wind blowing from the Golden Horn. At such an hour of the day spring was an illusion.

'We came too early,' she said aloud.

'Hungry,' said the child in answer.

'Yes, but you'll be better presently when we're on the boat.' The smell of freshly baked *simit* came from a baker's shop nearby. She could see through the low doorway to the blackness at the far end of the little shop and now and then she saw flames leaping when a man opened one of the ovens to take out a tray of *simit* or put in a tray of dough. The warm smell made her ache with hunger and she moved away from the shop and wished the boat would come. But the cracked notes of a clock striking in the distance told her there was still another half hour to wait.

'Can't we sit down?' the child asked and peered up at her trying to read her face through her veil.

Without replying his mother put down a parcel she had been carrying and sat down herself. She made a space for the boy.

He huddled against her for comfort, a careless little animal wanting nothing more at this moment save food and warmth. He was thin to the point of emaciation and the old felt slippers on his feet were an apology for shoes. His dark eyes stared outwards to the Golden Horn slightly myopipcally. He looked drugged, only half conscious of where he was and now and then he shivered when the fresh sea breeze blew too strongly. Kamelya, his mother, leaned against him, her mind going back to yesterday and the days preceding yesterday; further back than that too, skimming fleetingly over the times when sorrow had seemed remote – a thing to talk about over a winter's fire, an emotion to affect other people but never oneself. It was difficult now, from this harsh place, to look back down the years and see herself a child again playing in the fields about Tırnava, the Bulgarian village where she had been born. It was difficult but not impossible. Names and places once well known now only floated nebulously on the air. Her mother's smile was no longer distinct. Strangely, only her father's great white beard seemed substantial and belonging to the here and now even though he had been dead for many years.

With the screeching seagulls wheeling about her and the waves lapping the edge of the pier, she remembered how she had cried after her marriage. The tall man who became her husband was at best a stranger – the boy she had played with long ago had receded leaving this unknown man of property in his place. He took her to Istanbul, the mythical city of gold with its tall crown of minarets. Tırnava would soon be no more, for the Bulgarians were persecuting the Ottomans and they told Kamelya that if she stayed she would be killed. She seemed to have spent her youth in tears. She cried when she left her village and the white house where she'd been born when her father was in his prime and had been the Ottoman Governor of the province. Istanbul had seemed another world and she was glad that Kati, her mother's maid, accompanied her. Kati's presence seemed to take the craziness from this hurried flight into the unknown.

They had found a house in Eyüp Sultan and her husband, through influence, was admitted to the civil service and looked even more unlike himself in his severe black coat and tight trousers. From a boisterous merry youth he had developed into a melancholy man who regaled his wife with long passages from the Koran, with special emphasis on the chapter 'Women'. Kamelya found it all very boring and chafed under his restrictions. But at other times the guise of the devout man was abandoned and he would emerge amorously, with jolly quips and a passion for kissing her hands. There had always been the two personalities within him; perhaps if he had lived long enough one would have had time to develop properly. As it was, her picture of him remained unfinished and she could never remember anything about him that was not mere incident; the main features by which he should have been remembered were missing, endowing him with an elusiveness he had never in reality had.

After the birth of Murat, her son, memories of Tırnava became less urgent. She might have lived in Eyüp Sultan all her life. She guessed her parents were dead and Kati never spoke of them nor of the white house where she too had been born when her mother was in bondage there. Kati appeared indifferent to everything – dour, morose and uncommunicative. To Kamelya she floated on the outside edge of existence, more her mother's property than her own maid, and never to be regarded as anything more than an impermanence.

Those days had passed quickly. The dependent, dark-eyed baby had enchanted Kamelya and she had busied herself with him only. Her uncertain husband could alarm her no more.

In 1912 came the Balkan War, and the house in Eyüp Sultan was strangely quiet when the master was called to fight the Bulgars. Kamelya did not miss him at all; she was too occupied with the infant Murat.

Time hurried more than ever it seemed, and presently it was the year 1914 and Turkey was at war again and Kamelya knew that the stranger from Tırnava would never come back to Eyüp Sultan. She was distressed thinking of money and who would look after them now. Kati was sent away. She could no longer afford to keep her and she had never liked her in any case.

On that last day, Kati remarked, 'It would have been better to have left me in Tırnava. What am I to do in this strange place *hanım*?'

'You'll find work easily enough.'

'You should have left me if you knew you'd have to send me away one day.'

'Don't be foolish Kati! How could I know?'

After Kati there was nobody but Murat. The women of the street began to gossip. They said it was wrong for a young woman like Kamelya to be alone in the house when there was no husband to protect her. A change came over the owner of the house too. She was no longer so cordial and for a start asked for more rent. She said times were hard and looked astonished when Kamelya said she had no money. Month by month the situation worsened. Kamelya's furniture was mortgaged for arrears of rent and for the first time in her life she knew what it was to go to bed hungry. She could think of nothing to do to save herself. A miracle was needed.

Day after day she visited the holy grave of Eyüp Sultan himself, opening her hands to the sky to pray, taking with her pieces of old material to bind to the already overcrowded railings of the grave. When she was a child she had been told that this was the right thing to do. The saintly ones would grant her requests if she had enough belief. She fed the fat greedy pigeons that fluttered in the mosque garden – she knew they were the messengers of Allah and that whoever fed them would never die destitute. She did everything she could think of to make Allah aware of her – surely the miracle would happen soon?

Bekçi Baba, the nightwatchman, had to be called to the house in the end. He was begged to find a buyer for the bits of furniture not already mortgaged to the landlady and whilst he pawed and examined everything with half-blind clarity, the landlady herself was very much in evidence making it quite clear what belonged to her. All the neighbours came to see as well, commiserating with Kamelya, eyeing one another with guilty pleasure and shoving the tearful Murat out of the way so that they could see better. Whilst Bekçi Baba mumbled under his breath, Kamelya leaned against the dusty window indifferent now that her home was broken. The resentment which had flowered in her all day was dead. She even felt a sort of perverted relief that after this there was nothing else to do.

Needing movement, she had gone over to the mirror to look at herself. Behind her the women talked and Bekçi mumbled and for the moment they were unaware of her. She looked at the face of the girl in the tarnished old mirror: with petulance she surveyed the rounded contours of chin and throat, the dark eyes set far apart, the full-lipped passionate mouth and the curling black strands of hair escaping from the tightly bound *çarşaf*. She ached to be away from poverty. She fancied a stranger stood by her side and she made play with her eyes in the mirror, her expressive hands emphasising a point she hoped to make, charming him with her curving smile, animation lighting the whole of her. Murat wailed and fancy dissolved. She turned back to the chattering women and saw Bekçi's dirty hands going over her linen tablecloth. Her mother had made it for a wedding present.

'It will be useful when you entertain,' she had said.

To entertain without a patterned linen tablecloth was unthinkable. Kamelya's mouth turned downwards at the memory.

'Have you finished now?' she asked the Bekçi and went across to him. He was her best friend. He was old and gentle and Kamelya's plight affected him. He walked miles in her defence. He even went to the big *konaks* in the district to see if they wanted an extra maid, but Murat was the obstacle. Nobody wanted to employ a mother with a young child, and those who were willing interviewed her disdainfully, then sent her away when they saw her face unveiled. She went to the Haseki Hospital, desperation making her brave, but when she saw the rows and rows of sick lying on the ground outside the main gates, all waiting for some attention, her courage failed her and she went away again.

When she arrived home the Bekçi was waiting for her. He had news. A woman he had known in his village was willing to give Kamelya work to do.

'What about Murat? Will she take him too?'

'I explained. She is quite willing to take him.'

'How kind you are Bekçi Baba!'

It was arranged that with whatever money he obtained from selling her bed he would buy the boat tickets.

'You are to take the first boat. It will leave for Galata soon after you hear the muezzin calling the people to the mosque. I shall come with the tickets and to see that you get on safely. Now go home and get yourself ready.'

There wasn't much to prepare. Nothing but an eiderdown remained of her home, a pretty red silk eiderdown that had only been used for feast days. She told herself she would never part with it. It was all that was left of respectability and being the governor's daughter.

Sitting on it now on the cold landing-stage, she felt panic start up in her. Where was she going? To what sort of future? She closed her eyes in fear and found a picture of Tırnava. It flashed clear as lightning for an instant, encapsulating the whole of her life there, but she could not hold it. Tırnava was further away than dreams and she would never go there again.

'The Bekçi's here,' shouted Murat, excitedly driving the past from her, 'and the boat's coming in – oh, mama just look at the big boat!'

He danced away from her, cold and hunger forgotten for the moment, and Kamelya stood up stiffly.

Hoisting the eiderdown under her arm she walked towards Bekçi Baba.

Chapter 2

A T GALATA BRIDGE in the heart of the city, Kamelya and Murat were last to leave the boat.

They climbed the steps leading to the street and then stood for a moment or two on the bridge itself, Kamelya undecided what to do next and Murat looking about him with an air of expectancy.

The air was very clear even though thick grey smoke belched from some of the boats and Kamelya drew a deep breath. There was a fluttery feeling at the pit of her stomach and she wished she could run away somewhere and be free.

'Why are we standing here?' Murat asked. 'Can't we go? I want to see the big boats better.'

Kamelya looked about her. The early morning bustle of the city alarmed and exhilarated her, but she despaired of ever finding the house of the woman who was to employ her – in spite of the clear instructions Bekçi Baba had given her.

'Oh, come along,' said Murat and tugged at her arm with impatience.

'Wait!' said Kamelya and closed her eyes to remember the road she was to take. After a moment or so she said, 'Let's go. There's nothing for us here.'

They started off across the bridge, Murat dancing ahead excitedly. The smell and the sound of the boats, the white seagulls flying and the dark shapes of the looming mosques stimulated him into forgetting hunger. At the end of the bridge were the fish stalls, the wooden stands decorated with shining silvery fish laid out in exotic patterns on beds of fresh green leaves. The sellers were in early morning mood and dressed in an assortment of vivid colours, bright red or yellow aprons tied about their middles. Their moustaches curled like crescents along their upper lips and they made bold black eyes at Kamelya.

Dark Journey

'Come my beauty!' they begged her jovially. 'Come and buy fresh fish caught this morning.'

They twisted the ends of their moustaches but Kamelya hurried past them with a haughty toss of her head. How dared they talk to her! She turned into the Mısır Çarşısı, the Egyptian Bazaar, but the noise and the clamour were a thousand times worse. Gripping Murat tightly by the hand and clutching the eiderdown which was inclined to slip from her hold, she edged her way through the crowds. The stalls sold a variety of objects and touts ran forward to waylay Kamelya, not averse tout juggling with her veil so that they might glimpse the face beneath it. Murat started to wail as he heard a man coaxing his mother to sell her eiderdown.

'Go away,' he shouted with trembling lips, his fists beating a useless tattoo on the strong man's hairy chest.

Kamelya began to feel faint. There was a rancid, unpleasant smell from the second-hand suits on display and from the lumpy, soiled mattresses. She could feel the salty taste of perspiration as it trickled down her face and on to her lips. Tears of rage and self-pity burned in her eyes; she hadn't known such a place as this existed. Pushing and struggling, she found herself at last at the end of the market, in a quiet place of cobblestones, and she stood close to the wall to raise her veil and wipe the perspiration from her face.

'Are we there?' Murat asked.

'Not yet, but I don't think it's much further.' Looking around her she added, 'But I don't know.'

They walked on and at the end of the broken street they turned into Tahtakale, a narrow place full of carpenters' workshops and the smell of sawdust. There was the customary coffee house at one end where bearded old men played with their blue beads and sipped coffee. A few lean, hungry-looking children circulated about the tables and turned to regard Murat with hostility, even though he was scarcely more presentable than themselves.

'I can't ask the way from the men,' Kamelya muttered. She saw a woman selling fish. She had set up a brazier on a makeshift table and was frying and selling them to passers-by. The smell of the fish tantalised Kamelya and she did not realise that she had stopped walking and was staring at the woman until she heard her shout angrily, 'What are you looking at? D'you think I'm up for sale as well as the fish?'

14

There was a guffaw of laughter from the coffee drinkers and Kamelya felt herself reddening. She moved forward hurriedly. 'Forgive me sister,' she said, 'I didn't mean to look at you. It was the smell of the fish that overcame me.' She paused then continued nervously, 'I'm looking for the house of Fatma the washerwoman. Do you know where she lives?'

'A bit up the road,' said the woman still staring at her with hostility. 'And what is your business with her, sister?'

'I'm going to work for her,' said Kamelya.

'Well have a bit of fish before you go,' said the woman in a friendlier voice. 'You won't get much there.'

'But I – I haven't any money to pay you.'

'Eat sister! Pay me when you're rich.'

She took up a handful of fish and thrust it at Kamelya and then gave some to Murat. 'Where d'you come from?'

'Eyüp Sultan. I'm very glad to be going to Fatma to work.'

'Well, tell me *that* when you pass this way again.' And she started to laugh, holding her sides. 'Ask anyone when you get to the top of the hill,' she said once the paroxysm was over. 'We all know Fatma *hanım*.'

Climbing the hill, Kamelya was uneasy to find that in this part there were no houses at all, only the bleak skeletons of houses which had been burned. She saw that hundreds of down-at-heel families had made their homes in the ruins, with sacking for roofs and fly-covered garbage strewn everywhere. There was the sound of babies crying and lines of washing were strung right across the width of the street. She hurried past them and only stopped to draw breath when she reached the top of the hill where an old man sold *simits*.

'Go and ask him where Fatma *hanım* lives,' she bade Murat, and presently the child returned and said that it was only round the corner.

When they reached their destination Kamelya despaired, for Fatma's house was a hastily erected shack of rotten wood with sacking for a door. She approached uncertainly.

'Is Fatma *hanım* within?' she called through the sacking. A cross voice replied asking who wanted her. Not quite knowing how to reply Kamelya remained silent and presently she heard a shuffling step approaching and the sacking parted to reveal a large white-faced woman.

'I'm Fatma. What do you want?'

'I'm Kamelya from Eyüp Sultan. The Bekçi sent me here. He said you would have work for me to do.'

'Yes?' queried Fatma and looked at Murat doubtfully. 'But I didn't know there was a child too.'

Kamelya was about to protest that Bekçi Baba must have told her, but something about Fatma intimidated her.

'Well, you'd better come in anyway,' said Fatma, and Kamelya followed her through the sacking. The little dark room she found herself in was filled with wood smoke and smelled strongly of soap and wet linen. 'Sit down,' said Fatma and pushed forward a chair with a broken back.

Kamelya was grateful to sit down and open her veil. She threw the eiderdown on the floor and it lolled at her feet, making a splurge of colour in the drab room. Murat, trying to make himself inconspicuous, sat down beside it. He was afraid of the strange woman who had spoken so sharply to his mother.

Fatma turned away and stooped to add fresh wood to the fire. Her skirt strained across her large buttocks and she looked grotesque and unbelievably unreal. The wood was green and hissed and sizzled on the fire, throwing out an acrid smoke that made Kamelya cough.

'It's very bad wood,' commented Fatma. 'Everything's bad, what with the war, the men all away and nowhere for people to live. These are bad times altogether.' Fatma finished putting wood on the fire and straightened herself. 'I'll make a cup of coffee,' she said. 'It's scarce and it's dear, but in your honour I'll make a cup.'

'That is kind of you.'

Fatma laughed momentarily, wiping her hands on her apron.

Everywhere in the room were piles of clothing, some of them half washed, some waiting to be washed. The washtub was a long wooden zinc-lined bath, which stood on a wide bench under a glassless window. It was filled with soaking clothes and steam rose from it in little spirals. Kamelya felt depressed. The dampness, the dirt and the sulky hissing fire, the coarse sacking at the door and the hard-eyed old woman preparing coffee made something crack inside her. Resentment flowed through her, although she had not yet had time to give it a name. Drinking the unsweetened coffee, and sharing a slice of black bread with Murat and their ravenous appetites, she bent her sleek head and listened to the husky voice of Fatma complaining.

Presently Fatma said thoughtfully, 'You don't look very strong.'

'I'm strong enough,' said Kamelya bitterly.

'You're good looking as well. I can see I'll likely have trouble with you here. One of these days you'll be running off and marrying one of the porters.'

Kamelya stretched her lips in a smile that was almost painful and asked, 'Where shall we sleep *hanım*?'

'Sleep? So you don't want to talk about marriage eh? Well, we'll see my girl after you've been here awhile.' She broke off to cut more bread for herself. 'There's a room inside,' she said. 'I lie down there when I have the time. You and the boy can have half of it but you won't find much time for sleeping in this job *hanım*. There's too much to be done but you'll be all right if you don't go and get married.'

'Yes,' said Kamelya.

'And that boy of yours is too big to be doing nothing *hanım*. There's no room here for idle hands and big bottoms – he can guard the washing on the lines and then he'll earn his bread for himself. It's never too young to start.'

'Whatever you wish, Fatma *hanım*.'

'That's the spirit!'

'I shall go and spread my eiderdown now *hanım* and then I'll come back and help you. Come Murat, up!'

In the bare room where she was to sleep Kamelya spread the eiderdown on the floor and then, seeing the white face of the child watching her, said to him, 'I know it's daytime son but come and lie down here and sleep. Perhaps later on there won't be enough sleep.'

He ran to her and buried his face in her shoulder but he didn't cry.

'Let me undress you,' said Kamelya gently.

'Mama, are we going to stay here for a long time?'

'Ssh!' said Kamelya. 'Don't let the old woman hear you! We'll stay as long as we have to, but then we'll find some place better and go there instead. Now that's a secret between you and me. You mustn't tell Fatma *hanım*!'

Her eyes looked past him into a mythical life of ease and security, warm rooms and enough food for both of them. Freedom!

The power to do as she pleased! She looked down at Murat tenderly.

'Sleep now,' she said, 'I shall always be with you.'

She watched him curl into a ball on the eiderdown and as she covered him with half of it his dark lashes quivered trustingly. She remained quite still listening to the changing rhythm of his breathing and when he at last dropped into sleep she stood up.

She remembered that outside in the other room, Fatma was waiting for her. She shuddered and drew a deep breath.

'I shall get away,' she thought passionately. 'No matter what it costs me I shall get away from this life.'

Chapter 3

KAMELYA WORKED HARD because she had to. Fatma had no time for laziness in herself or anyone else. Fifteen, sixteen or seventeen hours work in a day were all one to her. She was as strong as two men and accustomed to hard work.

Murat was set to guard the washing lines. All day and far into the night he would sit on a stone with a big stick in his hands ready to shout for help should a neighbour cast so much as a glance at the garments. Kamelya learned not to look at his white, listless face too often and to ignore his cries when Fatma beat his legs because he had wandered away from his stone to look for the other children on the street. He would grow stiff and weary sitting in one position for hours on end but he rarely complained. He was growing into a good, quiet child who was learning the habit of effacing himself too soon. He clung to his mother passionately, anxious as a lover if she had to queue too long at the water pump with the other women. They were so loud-voiced he was afraid they might pick a quarrel with her and beat her. The Kurdish porters in the marketplace alarmed him too. They would leer into Kamelya's veiled face when she called to collect their bundles of dirty washing, attempting to fondle her breasts, cajoling her to enter their rooms. Defying Fatma, Murat would leave his stone and follow his mother on these errands.

'You come back here!' Fatma would shout after him.

'Go back now and do as Fatma *hanım* tells you,' Kamelya would say.

'No, I'm coming with you.'

Clutching his big stick he would trot after her.

'Wait here mama. I will collect the washing,' he'd say when they arrived at the house.

And he would run up the narrow flights of dirty stairs, the stick still in his hands and Kamelya following.

She hated the life but could think of no way of escape. Most of the day she worked mechanically, only part of her mind listening when Fatma became loquacious. Fatma was old and ugly and it came as a fresh shock each time she referred to that far-off time when she had been a 'girl'.

'Sweet coffee for sweet talk!' Fatma the washerwoman would declare gaily, bidding Kamelya take down the large *cezve* and make coffee for them. Although coffee was a luxury, she loved its stimulating effect and after weeks of silence she would suddenly break out in a rash of talkativeness.

'It'll help to keep you awake,' she would titter, holding her hand across her mouth to screen her broken teeth.

Kamelya looked forward to these rare spasms of Fatma's, for it meant a rest from the drudgery of washing. Once Fatma lost herself in talk she didn't notice how little work was being done and after a while Kamelya realised that it was not necessary to bother to listen to her. Fatma only talked to relieve herself and was annoyed at the beginning when Kamelya used to interrupt the flow of her narrative with foolish questions.

So, after making the coffee, Kamelya would seat herself on the floor – Fatma always took the broken-backed chair on such occasions. Leaning her aching body against the wall, Kamelya would indulge in her own dreams. She would examine her hands furtively for signs of roughness, dismayed and saddened by their redness and the furrows of tender flesh at the tips of the fingers.

'Life's hard,' Fatma would begin in a flat voice. 'I've always had to work hard anyway.'

Here she would pause for a moment or two and then the words would come smoothly, repeated for perhaps the thousandth time, each fitting into its own little groove, so that sentence after sentence were linked in a continuous narrative. After the first time there was no need for Kamelya to listen, for nothing new would emerge. Fatma's mind moved slowly along its track, finding the right words with difficulty. Yet though the story never altered, she had a trick of presenting it with freshness, with wonderment that it could be herself talking and that the things she related had not happened to some far-off stranger.

Kamelya saw neither freshness nor Fatma's astonished wonder. For her, these times offered a mental escape.

'I'll get out,' she'd think passionately. Her whole existence revolved around the thought of simply getting out. The pattern repeated itself endlessly.

Summer warmed the air and somewhere the trees were cool and green, but in the little wooden shack wood smoke still smarted the eyes and coarse soap took the beauty from delicate hands.

'This life!' Kamelya would sigh, raising her broken back from the bath of dirty clothes.

'This life!' she'd say as she waited by the pump for the water cans to be filled. She generally fetched the water at night when people were sleeping, for only then did she feel safe from the other women. Sitting on a stone beside the pump, feeling the night breeze on her forehead, she would weep for her ruined chances. She even wasted the precious hours when she should be asleep with her dreaming. Like a child away from home, she would dream of the day when she would be released from hardship. Whilst Fatma disturbed the quietness with her noisy snoring, Kamelya would lean against the window frame staring into the darkness, sniffing the clean air with curiosity, trying to read the star patterns in the sky.

'Come to bed,' Murat would mutter sleepily. He always knew when she was not beside him.

'Yes, yes, presently. Go to sleep.'

'Mama… come now… mama…'

She would lie down beside him, but not to sleep. Staring at the dark ceiling, she remembered the lights of the world she had heard about but never seen, straining to hear the music that played somewhere nearby. Ignorant of the war, uncaring for the dying, she would exhaust herself planning ways of escape.

One night she heard the shrill, terrified screams of a woman running past the window. Her heart beat wildly and she went to look out on to the street. She saw a woman running up the road in bare feet and the sound of her terrified sobbing floated behind her.

'Police!' the woman screamed. 'Police! Police!'

A child cried and a man's voice bade it shut up. The sound of a violent slap was followed by silence – and in the distance the voice of the woman still crying for the police.

Kamelya pressed her hand against her mouth as a man ran under the window. Was he the husband? Would he beat the woman when he caught up with her? What had she done to be running screaming through the night?

'I can't bear it,' said Kamelya, wanting to scream herself so taut were her nerves. Her teeth chattered as though she were dying of cold and long trembles swept savagely through her body.

'Men!' she said.

'What is it mama?'

'Ssh! You'll wake Fatma. It's nothing, go to sleep.'

'You come too...'

She knelt down beside Murat and put her hand to his tousled hair. 'We'll go away together,' she said rapidly, unaware that she was crying. 'We'll have a garden where you can play as much as you want and I'll buy you lovely toys and a pair of shoes with silver buckles like my father used to wear when he was rich.'

The tears fell across her hand.

'Why do you cry mama?'

'Ah, I'm foolish! Go to sleep!'

He moved closer under her hand in contentment.

'I know what I'll do,' said Kamelya into the darkness. 'Yes, that's it – that's the solution.'

She drew her hand away from the child and stood up.

'Perhaps Fatma would know...'

She felt reckless and excited suddenly, until she remembered the crying woman who had run past her window.

'But it needn't be like that,' she said into the darkness. 'My marriage wasn't like that.'

She wouldn't think about it now. Tomorrow was time enough, tomorrow she'd ask Fatma to help her.

Tomorrow anything might happen.

Chapter 4

THE SUMMER OF 1915 passed in a blaze of torrid heat. Mosquitos hummed about the stagnant pools near the ruined houses, young children sickened and died without attention, and Kamelya washed and ironed and carried endless cans of water to the shack.

One day, a short time after the episode of the crying woman in the street, she paused in her washing and said to Fatma, 'If you were my age would you think of marrying again?'

'Marrying?' asked Fatma with wide eyes. 'You don't mean to say you're looking for another husband my girl?'

'No, not me.'

'Then why did you ask me?'

'I don't know. I just thought of it.'

'No one'd marry you,' said Fatma grimly. 'Not while you've got a child with you.'

Kamelya looked down at her wet hands.

'Anyway,' her bitterness rising, 'even without Murat nobody would marry me – just look at my red hands!'

'The sort of man who'd marry you wouldn't want to look at your hands my girl!'

'But he would. I don't want to marry just anyone, I want a gentleman.'

'You set a high value on yourself don't you? Looking for a gentleman indeed! As if they grow on trees. What's wrong with one of the porters in the bazaar?'

'I don't want a porter. I had a gentleman-husband before.'

'Look what it brought you too,' observed Fatma acidly. 'Besides where d'you think you'll find a gentleman around here?'

'I don't know. Anyway, it was just an idea. I never see any men, only the porters.'

'And you're not too good for one of them either,' remarked Fatma contemptuously. 'They're good honest men.'

'Honest! They try to touch every woman they see and, besides, they smell.'

'D'you think a rich gentleman would want to look at *you*?'

'There was one who did. It was in Eyüp Sultan, only he didn't want to marry me. I didn't want him either. He was old and fat – he made me sick.'

'You can't be as fussy as all that my girl when you're desperate. You were a fool. Why didn't you get him to protect you?'

'Why should I? I've always been respectable.'

Fatma looked at her. 'So what?' she said.

'But I don't want to live like a bad woman. I want a nice, kind husband...'

'All husbands are kind if they have a good wife.'

'I mean I don't want a husband who'd beat me.'

'Why should he beat you if you don't deserve it?'

'Well, he might.' She remembered the crying woman.

'You've got some funny ideas Kamelya *hanım*. If you want a good husband, you must be prepared to obey him and wash his feet at the end of the day when he comes home tired from the market, and close your eyes if he goes out at night.'

'Why should I wash his feet? Let a servant do it.'

'There you go again with your nonsense! Who do you think you are?'

'Whatever happens, I'm not going to marry just anybody.'

Fatma's next sentence took the wistful Kamelya by surprise.

'I do know a marriage broker who might be able to help you.'

'You do? Is she good?'

'She's the best in Istanbul. She's famous I tell you and she's rich too – why when she makes a marriage she gets presents and money and is invited to all the weddings. She knows everyone. Imagine! She dresses in silks and has a woman to do her washing for her.'

Kamelya's eyes sparkled.

'Where does she live Fatma?'

'Oh, you can't go to her house. She's very particular. She only sees you at the *hamam*.'

'But we can't go there can we?'

'It'll be difficult to leave the work. Still...' Fatma's eyes narrowed shrewdly. 'I know you'll give me a fine present when you're married Kamelya *hanım*. Perhaps we could manage to go.'

'Of course I'll give you a present Fatma! I'll buy you a silk dress for Sundays and a fur stole for winter!'

'I don't want any finery. I'll do as I am.'

'And when can we go to the *hamam*?'

'Tomorrow, why not? We'll leave a message if Fitnet *hanım*'s not there. Maybe she'll call here.'

Kamelya clasped her hands together excitedly.

'Do you think she'll be able to help me?'

'Well, we'll see. Trouble is though you've got the boy and nobody wants a child to look after as well.'

'Oh that's nonsense Fatma.'

The rest of the day passed in a haze. Kamelya was so full of dreams she didn't know she was doing Fatma's share of the work as well as her own.

***

It was a simple matter finding Fitnet *hanım* in the *hamam*. Fatma pointed her out from a distance and Kamelya was very impressed by her magnificent bathrobe, her flashing gold teeth and the masses of hennaed hair hanging over her ample shoulders.

'Good gracious me Fatma, fancy *you* knowing a person like that!'

'What do you mean? Do you think I'm not good enough to know the likes of her?'

'Of course not, but... well, she *is* rather different from our neighbours isn't she?'

'She's one of us just the same, but she's had luck on her side. She's clever she is.'

She broke off as Fitnet caught sight of her and waved. Fitnet pushed her way through the women.

'Well! Fatma *hanım*!' she declared in disbelief. 'And what brings you here so early in the day?'

She turned to look at Kamelya.

'And who is *this*?'

'She's my helper,' said Fatma in a dour voice.

'She's a great beauty,' said Fitnet graciously and turned back to Kamelya. 'And where do you come from?' she asked.

'From Eyüp Sultan.'

The stares of the other women embarrassed Kamelya and she longed to hide herself behind Fatma's ample figure.

'So? And what brought you to Istanbul?'

'My husband was killed in the war. It wasn't easy to live.'

'No, of course not.' Fitnet surveyed her shrewdly. 'You are quite wasted with Fatma. You're too pretty to be washing your days away like this.'

'She's a waste to me,' muttered Fatma, who was trying to wash her back and finding it very difficult. 'She's not much of a worker Fitnet *hanım.*'

'But of course not! What do you expect? So young and pretty and alone. How can she keep her mind on your washing?'

'She's paid to at least.'

'But ask yourself Fatma! Could *you* keep your mind on washing?' Fitnet smiled sunnily. 'I'm sure I could find a husband for you if you ever think of marrying again *hanım.*'

She'd turned back to face Kamelya and winked suggestively. 'If I could find a good, kind man,' agreed Kamelya, dropping her eyes modestly.

'But she's not alone,' said Fatma, 'she has a boy of five... I dunno... six. D'you think you'd find a stupid man to take *him* on as well?'

Looking displeased, Fitnet said acidly, 'That's up to me, Fatma *hanım.*' From her brusque manner it was obvious that she was disappointed to find the young beauty had a child. She bent forward to examine Kamelya's skin.

'Still,' she said as she straightened up, 'you can't tell you've had a child. There's nothing to show.'

'He was small,' said Kamelya complacently.

'That's all to the good. It spoils a woman when the skin sags across the stomach. A man doesn't want to look at another man's handiwork. In your case there's no need to say you ever had a child.'

'Oh, but I don't intend to part with him.'

'Couldn't you arrange to board him out? There's no need to be foolish and spoil all your chances. You haven't many anyway as you've been married before.'

'No. I want him with me. I've never left him and I'm not going to leave him now.'

'You never had to leave him before,' said Fatma.

'Well, I haven't got to now either.'

'Come, don't let's quarrel,' said Fitnet tetchily. 'But you'll spoil your chances by keeping him with you.'

'Then I won't marry.'

'So why are you wasting our time here?' demanded Fatma crossly.

'Oh now, she doesn't mean that,' said Fitnet quickly. 'She's just pretending, aren't you Kamelya *hanım*? But I'll see what can be done – perhaps a widower with a family of his own needing mothering?'

'I don't think I want a widower.'

'You've a child needing to eat bread,' said Fitnet with a tight little smile. 'You have to think of that too.'

'Still I don't want a widower with children – a widower perhaps, but not with children.'

'Well, leave it now,' begged Fatma, who thought that Fitnet would wash her hands of the whole affair if they weren't careful. 'I'm sure Fitnet *hanım*'ll do her best for you Kamelya.'

'Yes, yes. Naturally,' agreed Fitnet, smiling widely this time. 'I always do my best for my clients.' Times were too uncertain to quarrel with this difficult young woman. She tapped Kamelya playfully on the cheek.

'We'll all eat bread from your lovely shoulders yet,' she said and showed most of her gold teeth.

'That we will,' said Fatma.

'I'll call and see you when I have news,' promised Fitnet. 'It might not be for a while, but I shan't forget you.'

'Well remember, not a widower with children.'

'Of course not. The idea!'

'You'll ruin everything with your high and mighty ideas,' grumbled Fatma as Fitnet took her leave of them. 'Not wanting this, not wanting that!'

'But I *don't* want a widower,' said Kamelya sulkily.

'You should think yourself lucky if she finds anyone for you, my girl!'

'Oh, she'll find someone all right. That's what she's paid for isn't it?'

'Still, you've no right to talk like that. Your Murat'll be the trouble you mark my words!'

'Nonsense!'

***

But as the days passed and there was no news from Fitnet, Kamelya began to wonder if Fatma was right.

She had almost given up the thought of remarriage when one afternoon a gay voice hailed them through the sacking. When Fatma shuffled across to see who it was, there stood Fitnet – a large, capable, efficient Fitnet who was causing a lot of speculation amongst the neighbourhood children who had never seen such a magnificent creature in their lives before.

'Come in, come in *hanım!*' begged Fatma hastily and wiped her hands on her sacking apron.

'Bring the chair, Kamelya,' she called over her shoulder. Kamelya was very ashamed to be caught in her old working dress which had once belonged to Fatma and was so large for her it had to be secured about the middle with a piece of string.

'Well, Kamelya *hanım!*' Fitnet greeted her with great cordiality and sat down in the chair. 'I've good news for you at last!' She flung aside her black silk veil with a theatrical gesture.

'You've not found a husband for her have you?' Fatma demanded in astonishment.

'And why not?' demanded Fitnet coldly. 'Are you suggesting it might be impossible for me, Fatma *hanım?*'

'No, no. But so soon? I am surprised – yes. You astonish me *hanım!* You must be a clever one to find a husband in these days. Let me make some coffee at once – sweet coffee for sweet talk – ha, ha!'

'Ha, ha!' said Fitnet stolidly. She was still affronted.

'And haven't *you* anything to say?' she demanded, turning to the silent Kamelya. Kamelya touched her hair nervously and advanced into the centre of the room.

'Is it true?' she asked. 'Have you really found someone who wants to marry me?'

'But why else am I here if not?'

'I see.'

'You are very cool I must say,' said Fitnet with a shrug. 'Are you not curious at all?'

'Oh yes, but I am quite content to wait until you tell me.'

Fatma tittered and Fitnet looked down her nose at the two women.

'He is not a widower,' she said acidly.

'No?'

'No. Come here girl, let me look at your hands!' Kamelya held out her hands patiently.

'They are very red,' commented Fitnet. 'You must not do any more washing until he has met you. Those hands would spoil everything!'

'And who's going to help me?' demanded Fatma coming forward with the coffee. 'I can't afford to feed an idle...'

'Oh shut up!' said Kamelya contemptuously. 'It won't be for long and I'll see you're all right if he marries me.'

'And supposing he doesn't?'

'Of course he will,' said Fitnet. 'He has only to look at her and he won't be able to resist!'

'But my hands?'

'They'll be all right in a day or two if you don't do any more washing. There's nothing a gentleman likes better than pretty white hands.'

'Is he a gentleman?'

'Of course!'

'Yes, but who is he?' asked Fatma disbelievingly. 'Is he rich *hanım*?'

'Very. He's a farmer and lives in Gemlik. He spends most of his time in Istanbul or Bursa. He's a good catch and I think Kamelya'll be lucky if he marries her... but of course he will,' she added hastily, as the calm eye of Kamelya swivelled towards her mockingly.

'Did you tell him about the boy?' Fatma asked.

'I mentioned him. He doesn't seem to care one way or the other. It's the mother he wants!' She laughed merrily. 'But of course the farm is so big he won't have to see much of the boy,' she added. 'I tell you Fatma *hanım* everything's fine! He's the best catch I've had for a long time... but naturally he wants to see her first. Could he come here, do you think?'

'What! And have all the neighbours break into the poor little house and stone us all as prostitutes? Have you lost your senses *hanım*?'

'But what can we do then?'

'Couldn't I meet him in your house, *hanım*?' asked Kamelya eagerly.

'Impossible! My house isn't a brothel!'

'But how would anyone find out. It'd only be a short meeting. Nobody could talk about that surely!'

'I tell you it's impossible. The neighbours would kill me if I arranged a rendezvous in my house.'

'But can't you think of anything?'

Fitnet bit her lip perplexedly. 'It's very difficult when a girl hasn't got a family,' she said. 'What can I do with a young widow?' she mused, almost to herself.

'Please, Fitnet *hanım*! Let me come to your house, just for a few minutes. We can be careful.'

'Well, perhaps it could be arranged. It's risky – but still…' She was thinking it would be a pity to miss this opportunity. Times had been lean lately owing to the war and the shortage of men. In the end, she agreed. 'It had better be at night. Fatma will bring you as far as the corner of the street and I will meet you there.' She broke off looking worried. 'But we'll have to take great care – if anyone were to see you it would ruin everything.' She turned to Fatma. 'Wednesday night,' she said to her, 'when the people have gone to pray. There's less chance of being seen then.'

'Whatever you say,' said Fatma. 'It's your house, not mine.'

'Oh Fatma, stop it! You know there's not all that much risk!'

'Remains to be seen,' said Fatma woodenly. 'Anyway, I'll be there.'

'I think it'll be all right,' said Fitnet uncertainly. She bit her lip and then looked at the glowing face of Kamelya.

'I hope you're going to bring me luck *hanım*,' she said.

After she had gone Kamelya said to Fatma, 'When I am rich I shall wear only silk against my skin and I shall smell like a flower!'

'Well, whatever next I wonder! You get married first my girl and then we'll see!'

Kamelya glared at her. 'The trouble with you,' she observed, 'is that you've no imagination.'

'I got plenty,' rejoined Fatma. 'But I don't let it run away with me, see?'

'It's not long 'til Wednesday, Fatma. Then we'll see if I've let it run away with me,' her eyes ablaze with hope.

'Yes, and in the meantime I've got all the washing to do. I want a good return for all this my girl!'

Chapter 5

STANDING UNEASILY ON THE CORNER of the strange street, Fatma and Kamelya waited for Fitnet.

Faint starlight softened the ugly outlines of the houses and Kamelya said wistfully, 'My house in Eyüp Sultan was like this, with a shiny door and *kafes* on the windows. I used to peep through the *kafes* every night waiting for my husband to come home. And I had nothing to do all day, for my mother's maid came with me from Tırnava.'

'You've no right to be thinking of your husband when you're going to meet another man,' said Fatma, who found Kamelya's habit of snobbery boring.

'But I can't help remembering him when I see these houses.'

'Humph! *These* are cowsheds compared with what you'll have when you're in Gemlik!'

'Yes... *Oh* Fatma, I hope he likes me!' she said, in a voice undermined by doubt. 'It'll be lovely to be rich and respected, with Murat able to play in the fields all day.'

'You'd better keep your mind off your child for the moment my girl. You'll gain nothing by that nonsense.'

Fitnet hurried to meet them, spoke a few words of greeting to Fatma and then, taking Kamelya by the arm, hurried her away. She was nervous and did not talk much.

Walking down the street beside her, Kamelya noticed that the houses were very close together, so close that they appeared to be supporting one another. She began to understand Fitnet's nervousness. The place was so narrow and restricted that not much could escape the eye of a neighbour. A coffee house and a mosque stood at one end to serve the male members of the community at their varying times.

Kamelya walked primly, but her heart was beating fast with nerves. She hoped Murat would be asleep when she returned home,

31

for he had been tearful when she was leaving with Fatma. He had fingered her dress suspiciously.

'I like you best in your old dress,' he had muttered and clung to her tightly.

'Well!' said Kamelya half angrily. 'That's an old dress of Fatma's!'

'I don't care. You look like my mama when you wear it.'

Kamelya sighed and looked at Fitnet. Better not say anything, she thought forlornly. People never understand when you talk about your child.

Fitnet didn't talk because she was worried. She hoped no inquisitive neighbour would see her with Kamelya. It would cause gossip if a woman was seen entering her house so late at night. She had been born in the district and when respectable widowhood and a knowledge of everybody's business made her a marriage-broker, she had gained her first successes among the sons and daughters of her childhood friends. The street tolerated her, but they did not like her. Although she had been born among them, they didn't think she was much to be proud of and resented her knowing so much about them. However, they found her useful when it came to arranging a marriage for a difficult offspring.

Reaching her own door she pushed Kamelya in before her, then left the latch up because she had told Cemal *bey*, the man from Gemlik, that the door would be open for him.

'There's a room at the back,' she whispered. She led the way and lit the gas jet with a little popping sound and Kamelya stood in the doorway, uncertain.

'Sit down, sit down,' said Fitnet irritably, drawing thick curtains across the tiny windows.

Kamelya sat on the extreme edge of a divan and looked about her. She had never seen such a room before. It was filled with cushions – such gay ones that they hurt her eyes with their unexpected brilliance.

'How elegant!' she gasped.

'Let me look at you,' said Fitnet in reply, 'especially let me see your hands. Now you're here it's up to you to make a good impression.'

Feeling snubbed, Kamelya held out her hands which still looked faintly pink.

'Passable,' said Fitnet abruptly. 'Now take off your *çarşaf.*'

'But...'

'Why "but"? Cemal *bey* will be here soon. Did you think he would want to see only your hands *hanım*?'

Kamelya still hesitated.

'Don't be silly,' said Fitnet. 'In Pera no one wears the *çarşaf.*'

Kamelya unwound the thick black band and shook her hair free.

'That's better,' said Fitnet.

'I feel so... so undressed.'

'That feeling'll wear off. Listen to me my girl. If you want to be rich and successful you'll do as I tell you.'

'Yes *hanım*.'

'Now, keep still while I put some of this on your face.'

'But that's powder *hanım*! Like the prostitutes use in Pera!'

'Nonsense! It's the key to a man's pocket. Keep still!' After a while she said in a pleased voice, 'Take a look at yourself in the mirror.'

At first she had difficulty recognising the face staring back at her from the glass. 'I look beautiful!' she said in awe.

'Of course you do. That's the way you were meant to look. Nobody'd look at you with a shiny red face except one of old Fatma's porters. Now, sit down on those cushions and I'll go and put the coffee on.'

Kamelya's nervousness returned. 'Will he be here soon?'

'I've told you already!' On her way to the kitchen, Fitnet congratulated herself on the plan so far, and hoped that Cemal *bey*'s arrival would be similarly invisible.

***

But Fitnet had reckoned without Zehra *hanım* who lived opposite her. Zehra's pleasures were few nowadays, for she was very old and unable to move from her room and she liked to watch the comings and goings of her neighbours. Her view of life was restricted, for her window was covered with *kafes* like every other window in the street, but on the whole she saw enough to keep her amused.

She was sitting at her window when Fitnet arrived with Kamelya. At first Zehra thought Kamelya must be a local woman trying to arrange a marriage for one of her children, until she remembered that local women never called on Fitnet but arranged their business in the *hamam*. Old Zehra shook with excitement and ached to know what was going on, but when she noticed that the door had been left ajar her excitement subsided.

Nothing intriguing could be going on if Fitnet left her door open! Zehra relaxed and thought it must be time for her to call her daughter-in-law to assist her to bed. She remembered that the muezzin had called the people to the last prayers of the day and that the men had already left their homes for the mosque. Just as she turned to find her stick, she saw the dark shape of a man slip through Fitnet's door. Her heart leapt and she peered intently through the *kafes*. The door was now firmly shut! She knew this, for the knocker was visible.

'Allah!' gasped old Zehra. What was the world coming to! A strange woman and a man in Fitnet's house together!

She reached for her stick with a frail hand. She must summon her daughter-in-law at once. Why, it was enough to give one a heart attack!

***

Cemal *bey* was glad to slip into Fitnet's quiet hall and hear the reassuring click of the lock behind him. It was very trying for a man of his years to be admitted like a thief to a squalid marriage-broker's house in a poor quarter of the city. He was ruffled and slightly out of temper. The day had been irksome and his other affairs coloured by the decision to keep this rendezvous, for it worried him that he knew nothing about Fitnet.

Cemal *bey* liked young women, but had had little success for there were so few who were prepared to take advantage of his generosity without a firm offer of marriage. Usually, marriage-brokers were far too respectable for his purposes, and wanted to pin him down, but Fitnet had seemed different. When she had spoken of a young, unattached widow he had sensed possibilities.

The day had been very long. He had tried to kill time by having his boots polished twice, had visited a barber who made his face so smooth even a fly would have slipped on it, had drunk *rakı* in a bar in the fish market but even so there were still several hours to get through. He remembered that ladies liked sweets, so he went to

Hacı Bekir's and bought two boxes of wartime bonbons which were very expensive but looked pretty tied up with pink ribbon. The *rakı* warming him inside and the festive boxes under his arm gave him hope – so he went and bought another bottle of *rakı* and decided to ask Fitnet to give him *meze*. Perhaps the widow could be persuaded to drink with him…

Fitnet came out to greet him and led him to the room where Kamelya waited apprehensively. She was so shy she was quite ready to faint. No man, other than her father and her husband, had ever seen her unveiled before.

She forced herself to look at Cemal *bey* and saw a well-preserved, oldish man in a smart new suit, stocky and well-fed, with downcast eyes. 'This old man?' she thought, bewildered. She had imagined someone quite different – younger, with vital eyes and an erect body, not this shambling antique who advanced towards her with precise, womanish steps. But as he leaned over her hand to kiss it, she remembered that she was Kamelya, the homeless one. She gave him a dazzling smile and he turned away from her, reluctantly, to speak to Fitnet. He put the boxes of bonbons on the table and withdrew the bottle of *rakı* from his pocket.

'*Rakı*, Cemal *bey*?'

'A little, *hanım*, why not? To make the meeting a success, eh?'

Fitnet pursed her lips in annoyance.

'It is impossible,' she said with finality. 'I cannot have any drinking here. You will have to go soon.' She leaned towards him, noticing the smell of *rakı* on his breath, and her voice grew sharper. 'There wasn't anyone in the street was there?'

'Not a soul,' smirked Cemal *bey*. 'I was very discreet.'

'You waited long enough after the muezzin called?'

'But of course *hanım*. I tell you no one saw me come.'

Chapter 6

Tak-tak-tak went old Zehra's stick on the floor as she thumped furiously and screeched for her daughter-in-law to come immediately. Tak-tak-tak! She pounded until the whole house resounded with the noise.

'Perihan! Perihan!'

Footsteps ran up the stairs and Perihan pushed open the door. Her face wore a startled expression and an oil lamp hung uncertainly from her shaking hand.

'What is it mother-in-law? Oh, how you frightened me!'

'I could die here for all the notice anyone takes of me,' said Zehra querulously. 'Banging away with the stick I was and not one of you answering me!'

Perihan advanced into the room.

'I had to get another lamp,' she said. 'Ahmet didn't go to pray tonight so he's saying his prayers in the kitchen. I couldn't leave him in the dark could I? What's wrong with you? When I heard you thumping like that I said to myself you must be ill.'

'I am,' snapped Zehra, cutting her short. 'I doubt if I'll live to see daylight. I never thought to see such terrible goings on here – what terrible, terrible days these are!'

'What d'you mean?' Perihan held the lamp higher so that she could look into Zehra's face. 'Why! You're trembling!' she said.

'It's a wonder I'm not dying! Tell Ahmet to come straight away. Such wicked days! It's a wonder Allah doesn't open the heavens and pour down his wrath on all of us!'

'What *are* you talking about?'

'That woman! She must be run out of the street before she corrupts us all. One bad apple in a basket makes the rest bad too!'

'What woman are you talking about? *Annem*, have you lost your mind?'

'It's a wonder I haven't with what I've seen tonight – that Fitnet's the one I'm talking about. She brought a woman to her house tonight and when all the men had gone to pray and I was just thinking of going to sleep I saw a man go into her house too. Now! What d'you think of that?'

'No!' breathed Perihan, her eyes as round as marbles. 'A man, mother-in-law?'

'Yes.'

Perihan looked all round her. 'But how could you see all that from here?' she asked in a disappointed voice. 'You're teasing me!'

'Look for yourself. You can see the whole of her door from here. No, go and get Ahmet for me. He'll know what to do. I'm so upset I don't know what I'm saying!'

Perihan put the lamp on a chair.

'I'll tell Ahmet at once,' she said and clattered noisily downstairs.

Ahmet was waiting for her in the hall.

'What's wrong?' he asked.

'A terrible thing!' said Perihan gleefully, and went close to him to whisper in his ear.

'She's making a mistake,' said Ahmet uncertainly. 'Nothing like that's ever happened here!'

'Well, go up to her anyway. She wants to tell you herself.'

After Ahmet had gone upstairs Perihan ran into the kitchen and rapped three times on the wall which adjoined the house next door. This was the signal for the woman next door to open her back door and hear what Perihan had to say. The fact that she knocked at night made it all the more exciting.

Receiving a faint answer to her rapping Perihan ran out on to the porch and told her neighbour what Zehra had seen. The neighbour looked shocked, bade Perihan a hasty good-night, and ran to her own kitchen to rap up *her* neighbour. In this way all the women of the street heard the news. The women in the end houses dared male displeasure by running across to one another's doors and passing on the terrible tidings. Only Fitnet's house was by-passed.

Upstairs in old Zehra's room, Ahmet confronted her and asked if it was true that there was a man in Fitnet's house. Or had Zehra been dreaming? She denied she had been asleep.

'Do I ever go to sleep at the window unless it's summer and hot?'

Without answering her Ahmet went over to the window and applied his eye to a small square in the latticework. He could not deny that Fitnet's door was plainly visible.

'Of course it is,' said Zehra angrily. 'Why would I make it up? Am I likely to tell lies at my age when I'm getting ready to meet my God?'

Ahmet said cautiously, 'But are you sure it was a man? Could it have been one of the women?'

'With trousers on? Hah! Am I a fool?'

'How could you see all that if he went in as quickly as you say?'

'Because I'd seen him before. I thought he was going to the mosque and I knew he'd be late. You'll have to do something about it son. Fitnet must be stopped, one bad apple –'

'I know,' interrupted Ahmet. He was disturbed and indignant.

'Well? What are you going to do, what are you waiting for?'

'I'll see the imam.'

In a bad temper he set off for the coffee house. Inside he found all the men who had been in the mosque. A little Arab boy was running backwards and forwards with brass trays full of coffee. He grinned incessantly but his rolling eyes looked anxious as orders were flung at him from left and right.

'*Peki efendim! Peki! Geliyorum!*' he gasped. 'All right *efendim*! All right! I'm coming!'

The imam was sitting near the unlit stove and Ahmet went across to him.

'Well, Ahmet *bey*!' greeted the imam unctuously. 'You weren't at prayers tonight. Was there anything wrong at home?'

'No, sir,' said Ahmet constrainedly, 'I was too late.'

'As long as you prayed at all it is acceptable in the eyes of Allah,' said the imam and made room for Ahmet to sit beside him.

'Yes, sir.' Ahmet wished he could shake off the feeling of constriction which assailed him in the presence of the imam. He leaned forward and whispered.

'What's that?' shouted the imam and looked pious.

'It's true!' muttered Ahmet sulkily. He did not like anyone shouting at him.

'Well, if it is it must not go unpunished. What a scandal in our very midst, as well as being an offence against Allah!'

'What is?' asked a man at a nearby table.

The imam repeated Ahmet's story – with considerable embellishments.

Ahmet was certain he had not said the half of these things.

'The *pezevenk*!' growled someone threateningly.

The imam looked pained and said, 'Swearing is not necessary. We all know how you feel sir.'

'Still, he's right,' said another man. 'That woman can't keep a rendezvous house here. What about our wives and children?'

'And I've a daughter looking for marriage,' put in someone else. 'Already her mother's spoken to Fitnet about her.'

'And to think that that poor, innocent, old woman witnessed such dirt from her window,' mourned the imam with real tears in his eyes. 'Mercy my sons! The wickedness of the world we live in!'

A man called across the room, 'Hey Bekçi, is this the way you protect us at night?'

'What's that? What's that?' demanded the Bekçi, bridling at the implied slur on his character. 'Have I no right to come and drink a cup of coffee when I'm tired out after the heat of the day?'

'Well, while you're sitting on your backside here, Fitnet's running a rendezvous house under your nose.'

'Rendezvous house? Here? Impossible! I'd know immediately.'

'Well, you didn't know this one.'

'Who's running a rendezvous house?' asked someone else.

Soon all the men were talking together and in the midst of the babble and angry threats the little Arab boy ran to and fro with his trays of coffee, his eyes wide with surprise and delight. Once he so far forgot himself as to remain open mouthed by the side of the imam, now and then wiping the tip of his nose with his apron, but the imam became annoyed with so much sniffing and sent him away with a smart cuff on the ear.

'Are we all *pezevenks* as well?' demanded a man. 'Why's the Bekçi not doing his duty? What's he doing in here when there's a woman to be arrested?'

'Who says it's a rendezvous house?'

'I do,' said Ahmet and looked round him pugnaciously. 'My old mother saw a man going in.'

'By Allah!' said someone else with passion. 'I'll go and break down her door myself.'

'She ought to be run out of the street!'

'Break down her door!'

'Stone the prostitute!'

'Bekçi, it's your duty to arrest them all!'

'It's the *pezevenk* Fitnet – she's the one!'

In a wild stampede, the coffee house emptied and the men were off down the street heading for Fitnet's. The imam led them, for it was felt that as the representative of Allah in their midst he should be the one to open fire on the wrongdoers. Bekçi Baba, representing the law and man's affairs, walked in the rear. His time would come.

In the coffee house the boy waiter drank five cups of coffee straight off and rolled his eyes excitedly. They had all been paid for and it seemed a pity to waste them, especially as the owner had gone with the men and wouldn't know anything about it.

The Arab boy strutted importantly. 'Dirty *pezevenk*!' he said in imitation of the men. 'What next I wonder?'

Chapter 7

FITNET WAS ANXIOUS for her visitors to be gone.
The evening had depressed her from the start, for Cemal *bey* behaved as though he hoped to make a night of it.

'Could we not have a little cheese and bread for the *rakı*?' he had asked wistfully and Fitnet had pursed her lips and looked intimidating.

'Only a little, eh?' he had pleaded.

'Very well then, but after that you must go. Kamelya go and get the cheese for Cemal *bey*.'

After Kamelya left the room Fitnet turned to Cemal *bey* and said sharply, 'And what is your opinion of Kamelya *hanım*?'

'Lovely, Fitnet *hanım*! Lovely! Like a peach waiting to be eaten!'

'Did you notice her figure when she walked?'

'I noticed everything, but everything! She is an angel! Has she the disposition of an angel do you think?'

'But certainly. What do you expect?'

'No temperament? You are a genius *hanım*!'

'And you intend to take her to – to *marry* her I mean?'

Cemal *bey* closed one eye. 'What do you think? Such a lovely young girl! A pity to waste her, yes? You may tell her if you wish that she is very marriageable.'

'The child?'

'Must we talk about the child at this stage?' he wheedled. 'We know, you and I, that these things can be arranged, but first there is the mother to consider.'

'Of course.'

Fitnet looked suddenly prim. 'I'm glad you're satisfied,' she said. 'She's very clean and honest of course.'

'Yes, yes,' said Cemal *bey* hastily. He looked at her with a pained expression. 'I'm sure she is,' he added, as Fitnet's features did not relax.

Fitnet went in search of Kamelya who was cutting cheese in the kitchen.

'He wants to marry you,' she said without preamble.

'Yes?' Kamelya changed colours with such rapidity that Fitnet thought she was going to faint.

'Look out, you'll cut your fingers, you goose!'

Fitnet rescued the knife in time and Kamelya leaned against the table.

'So everything's all right?' she said in amazement. 'And Murat'll be all right too. We'll both have a place to live.' Her eyes shone like stars.

'Well,' said Fitnet uncomfortably and took up the plate of cheese. 'Come on.'

When the *rakı* was opened, Kamelya was persuaded to take a sip and did so with a great deal of expostulation.

'Oh drink it!' snapped Fitnet angrily. She couldn't shake off a feeling of impending doom. Was it to do with deceiving Kamelya?

Kamelya coughed as the *rakı* fumes went down her throat. 'Like Fatma's green wood,' she giggled irrepressibly and Fitnet looked down her nose with disapproval.

'Who is Fatma?' asked Cemal *bey*.

'A washerwoman,' said Kamelya unthinkingly and then she remembered. 'Oh, she's not important – just a washerwoman,' she said lamely.

'Ah yes! I remember Fitnet *hanım* telling me about her.'

'I didn't,' said Fitnet, 'I told you about Kamelya *hanım*. She's a washerwoman too...'

'Indeed!' said Cemal *bey*, looking foolish.

'But I wasn't always,' said Kamelya quickly. 'Once my father was Governor of Tırnava and we used to ride everywhere in a coach with four cream-coloured horses.' She broke off uncomfortably and did not know how to continue.

'Well, you don't look like a washerwoman anyway,' said Cemal *bey* consolingly.

'No. And when we came to Istanbul my mother's maid came with us.'

'Of course.'

'Stop boasting,' said Fitnet. 'We don't care who your father was!' She stopped suddenly. Was that an unusual noise out in the street? 'Wait!' she said and went out of the room.

In the hall she stood in silence. There wasn't anything, she'd been imagining things… and yet there seemed to be *something* different. She went into her bedroom at the front of the house and peered through the *kafes*. Somebody was outside her door. She felt her legs go weak as she saw a lamp flash and heard the mutter of voices.

'Break it down!' said someone wearily.

Her door? Surely not!

'Patience!' said a voice. Was it the imam?

She hurried back to the other room.

'Quick! Quick!' she said urgently, 'You must get out Cemal *bey*, we're being raided. Kamelya help me put the drinks away!'

'Raided?' asked Kamelya disbelievingly.

'But where can I go *hanım*?' demanded Cemal *bey* agitatedly.

'Wherever you like,' flared Fitnet, 'but get out before the men break in.'

He stood undecided in the middle of the room.

'Up the back stairs, Cemal *bey*! They lead to the roof.'

She took him by the shoulders. '*Get out!*' she screamed.

'But if they catch me? They'll be sure to search the roof!'

'Oh, you can jump can't you? Kamelya *hanım*, don't stand there looking foolish, do something! Help me.'

'But what can I do if they catch me on the roof?' insisted Cemal *bey* crossly.

'Do what you like!'

She caught him by the shoulders and propelled him out of the room. 'Those are the stairs,' she said in an angry whisper and ran back to the room to help Kamelya. Kamelya, however, without having moved so much as a plate, had fainted. Fitnet stood and looked down at her.

'Useless bitch!' she said helplessly.

There was a knocking on the street door.

'Open up!' someone shouted. 'We know you're in there *hanım*.'

'I don't believe this!' said Fitnet and sat down in a chair. She stood up again immediately to push glasses and dirty dishes into a cupboard.

'It's no use,' she thought, 'Cemal's *bey*'s cigarettes smell… and the *rakı* too.'

'Open up!'

'Fitnet my daughter, open the door to us!'

Fitnet shivered but did not move. She looked back to Kamelya and thought that if Cemal *bey* could escape from the roof she might be able to brazen it out. Whatever she said would be unsatisfactory, but if they couldn't find Cemal *bey* they couldn't disprove it. She heard heavy fists pounding on her door and then the flimsy *kafes* creaked and gave way. It looked as if they meant business. There followed the tinkle of breaking glass.

'Come out prostitutes!' someone shouted and more glass smashed. When Fitnet heard the front door burst open she let her hands fall to her sides in a gesture of resignation. There was nothing more she could do. She heard the rattling of their sticks in her hall as they approached the lit room. Faces crowded the doorway: white ones, angry ones, wild ones, threatening ones. She wished she could solve her problem as easily as the faint-hearted Kamelya.

'There's Fitnet!' one of the faces said.

'They've been drinking *rakı* – smell it?' another one said. They swooped on the inert figure of Kamelya.

'Look! Here's the one the rendezvous was made for. Look at the paint on her face and that dress!'

They bent over her greedily. Even the imam was heard to suck in his breath noisily at the sight of an exposed white shoulder and the shadow of a rounded breast.

'Where's the man?'

'Speak up Fitnet *hanım*! Where's the man you were seen admitting to your house?'

Fitnet opened her mouth but no words came. She had never been so terrified in her life.

'You – you *pezevenk*!' said a man coming close to her and grasping her arm. 'Carrying on your love-making right under our noses!'

'Look at that one there on the floor. She's ready for anything. Where's the boyfriend gone Fitnet?'

'Perhaps he's in the bed waiting for her,' leered a voice from the crowd.

'Enough! Enough! Hold your tongues my sons!'

'But we want to find the man!'

'Fitnet my daughter, you *must* tell us where the man is!'

Fitnet did not answer and Cemal *bey*, who could hear every word, trembled on the edge of the roof like a sick cat. He was hoping that Fitnet would keep her mouth shut. Perhaps he could escape discovery after all. If the men came searching for him he would jump into the alleyway. The trouble was he was afraid to jump. It looked a terribly long way to him – perhaps he'd even break a leg. But the fear of capture was greater than the fear of personal injury, so he peered over the edge once more. He closed his eyes in terror.

When he heard men fumbling at the inside door he knew that unless he moved fast all was lost. Yet the most he could do was to clamber awkwardly over the edge and cling on with his fingers whilst his legs dangled into nothingness. Only when he felt a man grab at his aching fingers did Cemal *bey* let go. He swung through the black air for what seemed an eternity of terror and then landed like a sack of potatoes at the feet of the Bekçi.

'Here's the scoundrel!' shouted the Bekçi to the men still on the roof. 'I've got him here.'

He attacked Cemal *bey* with his stick until the voice of the imam called sternly from above him, 'Leave it Bekçi Baba! Let the law deal in the proper way with this dishonest man!'

The imam sprang down from the roof. It looked very easy when he did it and Cemal *bey*, in all his misery, could not resist the thought that perhaps it was not the first time the imam had lowered himself from a narrow roof.

'Go and get the women Bekçi Baba. We'll hold this man.' He hauled Cemal *bey* to his feet and shone a Nightingale Lamp on his face.

'It's an old *pezevenk*!' said a man in disgust. 'And nearly bald at that! He ought to be preparing himself for his grave!'

'Wicked man!' said the imam in a deep voice. 'Looking for a rendezvous house in our respectable midst, tempting frail women to carry out your evil designs!'

He wagged a dirty finger in Cemal *bey*'s perspiring face.

'Are you not ashamed of yourself?' he asked.

Cemal *bey* was furious at being treated like a criminal, but realised he was hardly in a position to make the reply he thought suitable.

'I wouldn't take you to the police station,' said one of the men passionately. 'I'd string you to the nearest tree and horsewhip you!'

Cemal *bey* shuddered. Every man in the neighbourhood seemed to have gathered round him. There wasn't a woman to be seen. Yet there wasn't a woman in the street who didn't know.

Fitnet and Kamelya were led round the corner. Fitnet cried incessantly and after a while her snifflings began to annoy Cemal *bey*.

'*Dur be* – shut up!' he said after one especially heart-rending sniff.

Fitnet raised her head to show tearless eyes. 'Well!' she said, 'I've never been *so* insulted in all my life, Cemal *bey*!'

Chapter 8

IT WAS ALMOST MIDNIGHT when they reached the police station and the officers on duty were in no mood to listen to the tearful beseechings of Fitnet or the voluble protests of Cemal *bey*.

'Be quiet!' they shouted and went back to their desks. 'And keep a civil tongue on your head!' they advised the affronted Cemal *bey*.

Kamelya pressed her spine against the dirty wall of the corridor and was aware of a feeling of nausea at the pit of her stomach. Perhaps she was about to faint again? This was the most terrible moment of her sheltered life and she was so dazed by sickness that she was uncertain if she were really living through this nightmare or dreaming it. It seemed inconceivable she would not presently awake in Fatma's airless back room with the warm body of Murat pressed close against her and a day's washing ahead of her.

She was staring at Fitnet's bright red hair, but her gaze became unfocussed as she remembered Murat. For the first time she felt tears sting her eyes. She said to Fitnet, 'What will they do with us?'

'How should I know *hanım*? I've never been in such a place in my life!'

'Why do you cry?'

'If I don't I shall go mad! I have lost everything. I am heartbroken!'

'And what about me?' demanded Cemal *bey* unexpectedly. 'Arrested like a common thief and brought here in the middle of the night!'

'What've *you* to lose?' asked Fitnet with a derisive sniff.

The commissioner came in – a seedy, hungry-looking man with a scar across his right eye. There was a good deal of jumping to attention on the part of the weary police and a lot of saluting the commissioner did not even notice. He stared at the trio propped up against the wall.

'What's this?' he asked with bored loathing.

'A raid *efendim*,' replied one of the police nervously.

'Well, put them in the cells. I'll see them later.'

'Come on,' said the policeman thankfully. He took Kamelya's arm but she shook him off impatiently.

'Leave me,' she said. 'What's it to you?'

They put her in a cell with Fitnet. The place was dark and she thought she heard the scuffling of rats. Her flesh crawled with terror. There was no floor – nothing but a grid of iron slats above running water. She stayed near the door so that she could see the faint glow of the lights from the corridor.

Towards morning the door was unlocked and she was taken away for questioning.

'And what about me?' Fitnet asked crossly.

'Afterwards for you,' said the policeman locking the door carefully. 'And shut up. Stop making so much noise.'

He led Kamelya into a room where a harsh white light burned above a stained deal desk.

'One of the prisoners from the raid,' said the policeman to the commissioner who was seated at the desk writing.

'All right, leave her!' replied the commissioner curtly and went on writing.

Kamelya stood just inside the door. After a time he raised his head and looked at her.

'Your name?' he asked, drawing forward a sheet of paper.

'Kamelya.' She barely whispered.

The questions flowed ceaselessly. Was she married or single? Her parents' names? Where was she born? Her present address? 'Now they know everything,' she thought. She watched him writing down her answers. Murat was at the back of her mind somewhere. It was necessary to get him immediately – after tonight Fatma would never employ her again and the children of the district would shout names at the defenceless boy.

'How long have you been in this business and where is your permit?' The commissioner's words dragged her back to the present. She looked at him stupidly.

'Please?' she asked hesitantly.

'Prostitution,' said the commissioner laconically. He leaned back in his hard chair. 'I must see your permit,' he repeated and held out his hand.

'But I'm not a prostitute,' said Kamelya and felt her face reddening. She clasped her hands together in an attitude of supplication.

'Don't waste my time,' said the commissioner impatiently. 'If you're not a prostitute, what was your business in a rendezvous house, and half-clothed according to the Bekçi's report?'

'It wasn't a rendezvous house,' Kamelya said with difficulty. 'I went there to meet a man who... who is going to marry me.'

'Then it was a rendezvous house for that length of time,' insisted the commissioner. 'And is he still going to marry you?'

'Yes.'

'Oh for Allah's sake!' said the commissioner disgustedly. 'I've heard that a thousand times if I've heard it once. Your kind all say the same thing when they come here. Look! If you don't want trouble show me your card and get out.'

'But I haven't got a card,' protested Kamelya almost in tears. 'I'm not a prostitute. I'm a respectable widow with a child.'

'Yes, yes, I know! You were found in a *most* respectable position, too, with half your clothes off and the smell of drink on your breath. What are you trying to do? Fool me?'

Kamelya drew a deep breath. 'Listen,' she said desperately, 'ask the Bekçi of my district – ask Fatma *hanım* the washerwoman – they'll tell you about me!'

'Hasan!' said the commissioner with a sigh. 'Take this woman back to the cell and bring the other one here!'

'Please believe me!' said Kamelya.

'Get out. I'll check your story later and if you haven't a permit I'll see you get one damned quick. As far as we're concerned you were brought in here tonight for prostitution carried on in an unregistered house.'

Kamelya was escorted back to Fitnet who was still shedding tears. 'Oh, the shame of it!' Fitnet moaned ostentatiously as she was led to the commissioner's room. That was the last Kamelya saw of her for a while.

***

Kamelya was released early in the morning. The Bekçi of At Pazarı, the Horse Bazaar, had confirmed most of her statements – but a large red question mark was placed against her name in the record book. Kamelya shivered apprehensively.

'If you're arrested again there won't be a question mark,' said a policeman matter-of-factly, but her face grew scarlet as she listened to him. She went out into the bright street wondering what to do next and how to rescue Murat from Fatma.

Running footsteps behind her and a voice calling her name made her turn her head. Fitnet hurried up to her. 'Well, I'm glad that's all over,' she said breathlessly and took Kamelya's arm.

'Cemal *bey* is waiting for us,' she said.

'Why? Surely he doesn't hope to continue the party?'

'Kamelya *hanım*! What a thing to say!' Fitnet tittered into her hand. 'Wasn't it a terrible night?'

'Yes.'

'But you're the lucky one *hanım*! You've something to look forward to. Why the next hour with Cemal *bey* may change the whole of your life!'

'Like last night when I went to your house respectable and left it a prostitute!'

'What a thing to say *hanım*! I'm surprised at you – you've no gratitude for those who try to help you.' Fitnet shrugged her large shoulders angrily.

'I don't want to meet Cemal *bey* now.'

'Didn't he say last night he was going to marry you?'

'Yes, but I must get back to Fatma now, and to Murat.'

Fitnet looked at her with hard little eyes. 'Don't be foolish,' she said sharply. 'You'll be missing the opportunity of a lifetime if you don't see him. Come along!'

After the barest hesitation Kamelya followed her. Perhaps she *was* being foolish – perhaps Fitnet was right.

They came to a street of little shops and Fitnet turned into the doorway of one of them and led the way up a flight of narrow stairs. 'Cemal *bey* would prefer it upstairs,' she said to Kamelya. 'It's much more discreet.'

Cemal *bey* was alone in the large room. He rose as he saw them and said, 'I was beginning to think you were not coming.' He pulled out chairs. 'They know me here,' he said as they sat down. 'No one will disturb us.' Turning to Kamelya he said softly, 'You may unveil your face if you wish, *hanım*.'

'Thank you,' said Kamelya, but made no attempt to do so.

Cemal *bey* went to the head of the stairs and shouted for three coffees and when he came back to the table he planted his elbows on it and said, 'There's not a great deal of time to spare so I suggest I make myself quite clear. I shall be returning to Gemlik today.'

'Today?' queried Fitnet sharply.

'Yes. There is only one boat a week and I cannot afford to be away from my farm for too long.' He looked at Kamelya. 'Will you come with me, *hanım*?'

'But – but I thought...'

She didn't know how to put it delicately.

'We shall be married there,' said Cemal *bey* urgently. 'I would have wished it differently but there is no time.'

'I can't go,' said Kamelya and felt Fitnet's eyes on her.

'But why?'

'There is the child to consider...'

'He'll be fine,' Fitnet said in an annoyed voice.

'But, well, you see I thought Cemal *bey* would marry me in Istanbul.'

'But I shall marry you in Gemlik,' said Cemal *bey* smoothly and Kamelya stared at him uncertainly.

'But Murat?'

'We haven't the time to collect him now, but I am often in Istanbul.'

'Wouldn't Fatma keep him?' asked Fitnet, impatiently.

'You know she won't.'

'But if I leave money with Fitnet *hanım* to give her, wouldn't she keep him for awhile?' suggested Cemal *bey*.

'I – I don't know. She's not very kind,' said Kamelya with sadness.

'Oh Kamelya *hanım*, you are distressing Cemal *bey*! You can see it is impossible for him to remain here.'

'But could I not get Murat now?'

Cemal *bey* pulled out an ornate gold watch.

'Impossible!' he said curtly. 'The boat leaves in an hour.'

Kamelya looked desperate. If she were to let Cemal *bey* go now she might never see him again. She could hardly return to Fatma's house with her reputation in tatters, and how could she get work elsewhere with Murat tying her down? 'I don't know what to do,' she said helplessly.

'Leave it to me,' said Fitnet competently. 'I'll go and explain to Fatma that you are marrying Cemal *bey* and that he will come back for Murat.'

'But...'

'No, no, I won't listen! You'll ruin everything. Murat will be all right for now, I'll see to it, and soon you will have him with you.'

'Fine,' said Cemal *bey* and stood up. 'That's an excellent idea, Fitnet *hanım*. I'll just see you to the door and you can go and explain to the child.' He took her arm and led her out of the room where money changed hands.

'Is this all?'

'You think it isn't enough *hanım*?'

'I lost my home through you,' she spat venomously.

'That has nothing to do with me. Did you not take the risk yourself when you suggested I should come to your home?'

'But I've lost everything!'

'In your profession, *hanım*, it should be easy to recover.'

'You insult me Cemal *bey*! If I'd known I...'

'That was up to you *hanım*. We're wasting time here. I have a boat to catch.' He handed her some coins. 'For the child's keep,' he said.

'But this won't keep him a week!'

'So what's that to me?' he sneered. 'I didn't buy him as well. Let the old washerwoman sell him to a merchant if she's not satisfied.'

'He'll be on the street.'

'That's not my business.' He turned away from her and called over his shoulder, 'If I should ever need your help again I'll call on you. It shouldn't be difficult to find you *hanım*.'

Fitnet descended the stairs uncertainly. 'Anyway, I did what they asked me,' she said to herself. 'Why should I care about the child?' She went out to the street. 'Kamelya should be the one to worry.'

Chapter 9

Kamelya very soon discovered that life with Fatma in At Pazarı was preferable to life with Cemal *bey* in Gemlik. He made it clear from the start that he had no intention of marrying her. He taunted her that he had met her in a rendezvous house and insinuated that this was not the first time she'd allowed a man to protect her. He guarded her like a watchdog and when he was absent for any length of time he instructed his old servant, Lâle, to look after her.

'What does he expect?' Kamelya would mutter angrily to Lâle. 'Can I run away from here?'

'You might try,' said Lâle.

'But how? It's miles from anywhere – there are no gendarmes.'

Old Lâle saw the beginning of a cunning look in her eyes.

'No *hanım*,' she would say, 'no use thinking like that. The gendarmes never come any further than the town.'

'But *if* they did?'

'They don't. They never have and I've been here twenty years. What business would they have this far out?'

'In Istanbul this sort of thing couldn't happen.'

'This is Gemlik. Anything can happen here. Why should the gendarmes worry with us? There are too few of them anyway.'

Cemal *bey* alarmed her. He was either drunk and amorous or sober and insulting. Either way she hated him.

'Why don't you let me go into market with Lâle?' she would sometimes ask.

'What is your business in the town?'

It was impossible to escape. The walls of the farm were too high, the dogs about the place too fierce. It was worse than being in prison.

'I might as well be dead,' Kamelya said to Lâle one day. 'Nobody even knows I'm here.'

'And all the better too,' said Lâle indifferently.

On market days the old woman gossiped with the peasants and the townspeople. She said that Cemal *bey* had a high-spirited piece from Istanbul in the house, a beauty. And one day the gossip reached the mountains.

***

There were vast tracts of uninhabited land around Gemlik where the gendarmes – depleted owing to the war – were afraid to go. Bandits made it impossible to travel the roads. Wealthy men like Cemal *bey* paid men for protection. The bandits hired assassins to liquidate their enemies and, living in isolation, did pretty much as they liked.

Kara Kurt was the most powerful of the bandits. He had operated for years from the rough country east of Gemlik and the gendarmes couldn't seem to do anything about him. He heard of Kamelya from one of his men who'd heard it from a peasant on Cemal *bey*'s estate. The idea of taking her for himself appealed to Kara Kurt and he made plans to capture her. It wasn't the first time he'd stolen a woman from Cemal *bey*.

Accordingly, one late afternoon, he took four of his men with him and they rode through the mountains towards Gemlik. With long beards streaming in the wind, their guns slung across their shoulders and belts of glinting bullets about their waists, they made a fearsome quintet.

The day had been still and clear and now, making a detour around the little town, they slackened their speed and reined the horses in to a trot. Thin wisps of smoke were rising from the mud houses of a village in front of them and a hawk hovered overhead in the green sky of evening. When they reached the village, children and dogs came out to watch them pass. '*Güle! Güle!* – bye-bye!' chorused the children fearlessly.

Down the twisting mountain paths trotted the neat, fast feet of the horses. Near Cemal *bey*'s high walls Kara Kurt slowed them to a walk.

'Not much farther now,' he said in Kurdish.

They came to the iron gate and he blew the lock off with his gun.

'Huzza!' shouted his four men, pounding up the broken avenue with dogs snapping at the feet of the horses.

The noise and confusion, the barking of the dogs, and the sound of the shot made Cemal *bey* hurry to the window of his bedroom to look out.

'What is it?' asked Kamelya behind him.

'Get back!' said Cemal *bey*, thrusting her aside.

He leaned his head out and called sharply: 'Who's there?'

A shot was the only answer.

'Hasan! Hasan!' roared Cemal *bey*, hoping for help and too scared to be frightened.

He brought his head in, went to get his gun – and then he saw a smile on Kamelya's face.

'Why do you smile?' he asked, taking up his gun from a chair, staring at her closely. 'Have you a rendezvous?'

Her smile faded.

'Don't be absurd!' she said contemptuously.

Cemal *bey* continued to stare at her.

'You've been deceiving me,' he said slowly. 'You brought this trouble tonight.'

He moved towards her and she screamed, running to the other side of the bed. He fired but the bullet struck the floor beside her. A second shot lodged itself in the rotten wood of the door jamb. She could hear him panting like an animal and she flung herself through the door and sped, terror-stricken, down the stairs. There was a movement in the dark hall and she saw Lâle's white face silent with fear. She wrenched at the heavy door and went out into the open. The dogs snarling around her legs were less frightening than the sound of Cemal *bey*'s crazy voice echoing inside the house. Running across the open to a clump of sheltering trees, she could hear the repeated crazy firing of his gun.

She was limp with exhaustion and fear. What had happened? What had Cemal *bey* seen to make him think she had an assignation?

A bullet whirred over her head and she saw Cemal *bey* stumbling towards her in bare feet. She screamed, a shot rang out from another part of the garden, a horse neighed – and Cemal *bey* dropped dead, almost at her feet.

She looked down at him not really believing what had happened. Coming out from behind the trees, she bent over him cautiously, feeling for his neck in his nightshirt but thick, warm blood met her fingers and she drew back, trembling.

'What do I do now?' she thought.

She remembered that Lâle was still in the house. Had she fired that shot?

She was almost beyond surprise or fear when she saw five dark silhouettes riding towards her. Who were they? What did they want? She remembered stories she'd heard of the bandits in the mountains. But what had bandits to do with Cemal *bey*?

One of the riders dismounted and walked towards her. She wanted to run but her feet betrayed her. 'What do you want?' she asked in panic.

He faced her squarely, a tall bearded man with powerful shoulders. '*Gel* – come,' he said.

He moved nearer to her and she screamed.

'Go away! Leave me alone. How dare you come near me!'

She cowered against a tree.

Ignoring her, he advanced and without uttering another word gathered her in his arms and carried her to his horse.

She struggled uselessly. He was so strong she might have been no more than a sackful of feathers.

'Put me down!' she said, 'Lâle! Lâle! Help me!' She saw the dark bulk of the house on her right.

'Put me down! Put me down!' she shrieked helplessly.

'Be quiet,' said the strong man, and sat her on his horse.

Somebody else supported her whilst the strong man swung himself up behind her.

'Lâle!' shrieked Kamelya despairingly.

Kara Kurt turned the horse and they trotted out of the quiet tangled garden down the pitted avenue and out to the deserted high road. The four other horsemen followed like an escort.

Soon they met a wider track, where the tall trees were splashed silver by the light of the moon and the grim mountains stood out clearly, magnified by the moonlight and looking closer to hand than they really were. It was very still, the sky speckled with stardust, and the few huddled villages they passed through fast asleep. From the nearer slopes foxes barked and once a jackal cried, alarming Kamelya who had never heard these country sounds so near before.

There was the sound of a shot followed by a high thin wail of pain and she shivered.

'What was that?' she gasped.

'A peasant shooting a wild pig. They get in the corn at night and eat it all. If they are not shot there is no harvest.'

After several hours they emerged into a clearing and the horses stood still.

'We are here,' said Kara Kurt.

***

Kamelya found life in the mountains rougher and more primitive than anything she had ever known. She was further from Istanbul than she had ever been. Once she had said to Lâle that being in Gemlik she might just as well be dead, but she realised now that Gemlik had been heaven compared with the solitude of Kara Kurt's domain.

The day began early. When dawn barely streaked the sky the men were riding off for the day's hunting and they seldom returned before evening. Sometimes, led by Kara Kurt, they were away for days. These were times of serious raids, when they robbed merchant caravans on lonely roads, killing and fighting and evading the scattered gendarmerie.

There were a few other women in the camp, mostly Kurds. There was, though, a young girl stolen from a village several kilometres to the east. Kamelya shared Kara Kurt's favours with her. He was rough and unpredictable but no worse than Cemal *bey*. He gave her primitive bracelets of twisted Turkish gold and a chain of gold coins to wear about her neck on *bayram* days. She liked it best when he was away, and she could dream of ways to escape. During fine weather she sat in the sun plaiting reed baskets that were sold to the peasants. They were big wide-lipped panniers to sling across a donkey's back and Kamelya worked at them lazily. There was no compulsion to work fast. Gül, the village beauty who shared Kara Kurt, would have two completed before Kamelya properly got started on one.

During winter the skin tents were abandoned and they lived in caves. She missed the noisy, confused life of the open camp, for the caves were scattered and the sense of isolation greater. When the snows came it was as if nothing existed beyond the great white mountains, yet Kamelya knew that behind those barriers lay freedom.

Every day was a frozen waste to be got through until night came, when a fire was kindled in a sheltered spot and the smell rising from the cooking pots promised transient relief. The men would gather about the fire, bearded and unkempt, slinking out of the bluish shadows looking like strange animals in their half-cured bearskins. Winter was an eternity. The repetitive heavy grey skies, snow so painfully white that it hurt the eyes to look at, and giant icicles adorning the caves made Kamelya long for warmth and bright lights.

Kara Kurt was not unkind – but she longed for change. The far-off fields still held more charm for her than this frightening mountain wildness. When she thought of home it was to Istanbul that her thoughts turned, in her mind searching its streets for Murat. After a while even Fatma's shack took on a glow of security and ease. She forgot the people in the ruined houses and the Kurdish porters in the marketplace and remembered only the sense of teeming abstract humanity and the lights strung across the narrow streets at night. And she remembered the warmth of Murat, snuggled beside her. She ached through the endless days for one glimpse of her son and of the golden city she had built in her imagination.

Chapter 10

TIME PASSED and spring came at last to the mountains. Melting snow ran down to the green valleys making the bad roads more than ever impassable.

Three years had passed but Kamelya's desire to get back to Istanbul, to find the lost Murat, was stronger than ever. Sometimes in panic she would say to herself, 'But supposing I can never get away – perhaps I shall be here until I die!'

It was useless talking to Gül. She only repeated what she heard to Kara Kurt. Kamelya had tried it at first but repeated beatings and Gül's delighted face afterwards made her more wary.

One summer morning one of the men rode into camp, snatched his woman up beside him on his horse, and shouted to the others to scatter.

'What's happened?' Kamelya cried.

'The gendarmes are coming with the peasants.'

'And Kara Kurt?' called Gül.

But the man galloped off without replying and Kamelya stood blinking in the clearing, the sun hot on her bare head.

'We go now,' said Gül coming up to her.

She could hear the sounds of hurried departure made by the other women. They were going to the valleys to hide until the danger had passed.

Kamelya stood irresolute and Gül plucked at her arm impatiently. 'Come hanım,' she said. 'Very bad here now with the gendarmes coming.'

'Where will you go?'

'To my village. It is only a few kilometres.'

Kamelya stared at her.

'Why did you not go before?' she asked.

Gül shrugged and twisted her pretty mouth in amusement.

'I like it better here,' she said. 'Kara Kurt gives me many bracelets.

If I am in my village who will give me bracelets?'

She stopped smiling.

'You come with me,' she said. 'You stay with me.'

'No. I want to wait.'

'But the gendarmes?'

'They won't harm me. I was brought here by force.'

Gül's voice tinkled with laughter. 'They won't believe *that*,' she said. 'They see you and they shoot – bang! Afterwards, perhaps, they'll ask, "Who is this?"'

'Even so I want to stay.'

'Come,' said Gül persuasively.

'No.'

'Very well. I go to my village. If you like you come afterwards.'

'Yes, yes. I know where it is. You go now.'

Presently she was alone. The camp was very silent and only a pot of meat bubbled over the fire.

'I hope they come,' Kamelya thought.

She stood there looking out over the mountains and down to the twisting, half-concealed path below. She seemed to have waited a long time when she finally saw Kara Kurt riding up towards her. Her heart beat with terror and she dropped down on her haunches hoping she had not been seen. Bent half-double, she ran away from the camp in the direction of the caves.

'This is the wrong way,' she kept sobbing to herself.

But if she had gone in the opposite direction she would have met him on the path. She ran to the farthest of the caves. It was dark inside with the fusty smell of a place where bats live. For a long time she stood in the blackness, too afraid to move.

'Did he see me?' she kept asking herself.

She was only reminded of the passage of time by the ache of hunger in her stomach and she moved eventually into the light. She closed her eyes for a moment or two. When she opened them again she noticed that the sun had passed from overhead and that the afternoon was well advanced.

'Have I been in there so long?' she wondered.

Her little gun jabbed against her knees and she took it out of her pocket and looked at it. Kara Kurt had taught her to shoot and then he had given it to her.

'For what?' she had asked.

'To protect yourself when I am away. All the women have a gun – even Gül.'

She had never had to use it. But she thought that if she were to see Kara Kurt coming towards her she would use it now.

'I am free,' she said.

It was still very hot. The sun beat down on the dusty earth and the grass was brown in places where it had been scorched. Great cracks of dryness furrowed the ground.

'A desert,' said Kamelya and put her gun back in her pocket. As long as she had her gun she was moderately safe.

'I shall go to Gül's house,' she thought. 'Perhaps she will tell me where I can get a horse to take me to Gemlik.' But she remembered she had to pass the camp to get to Gül's home.

She looked about to see if anything moved on the opposite slopes and then she turned and made her way back along the pitted track leading to the camp.

'I shall pass it swiftly,' she thought.

Supposing Kara Kurt was lurking there, waiting? She shivered.

'That is ridiculous. The gendarmes will have been there too.' She rounded the bend and had her first sight of the deserted camp. The silence was unnerving.

She moved cautiously into the clearing – and then saw Kara Kurt lying face downwards on the baked earth. Her legs trembled but she forced herself to go over to him. Standing above him she felt her heart leap. He was dead at last and she was safe from him forever. She turned his face so that she could be really sure. There was a bullet wound in his forehead and she leaned closer to examine the neat hole. There were no powder burns, no blackening from the flash.

'The gendarmes must have killed him,' she thought.

She looked at him as attentively as if she had never seen him before – the smooth brown cheeks with stubble sprouting along the jaw, the shaggy eyebrows, and the line of teeth just showing through his parted lips. It was hard to recognise him. Death had chiselled his features, sharpening the proudly jutting nose and giving him a refinement he had never known in life.

'So I'm really free!' said Kamelya aloud.

There was a faint noise behind her and she spun round quickly, the blood draining from her face.

A tall, wild-looking man faced her.

'What do you want here?' she stammered.

He was one of the men who'd ridden with Kara Kurt into Gemlik. She had always feared him.

'You,' said the man. 'You'll be needing someone to protect you now.'

He grinned, revealing a set of blackened teeth.

'Don't come near me!' said Kamelya as he made a soft movement towards her.

The inert body of Kara Kurt lay between them.

'He had money somewhere,' said the man.

'I know nothing,' said Kamelya rapidly.

'You know all right. He gave you those gold coins to wear round your pretty neck.' He advanced still nearer. 'You tell me,' he said, 'And let's get away from here.'

Kamelya pulled out her gun and fired. It was all so swift and unexpected the man had no time even to be surprised.

'Ugh!' gasped Kamelya hysterically.

She looked at the little gun in her hand.

'You've killed him!' she said in awe, then doubled over on the burnt grass and vomited.

The day was almost over and where the sun was not shining the hills looked dark and lowering. Kamelya stood up weakly and left the camp by the familiar path to Gül's home. She was light-headed with hunger and emotion but she plodded on stolidly, not pausing to rest so that she might reach the village before night descended. Mists swirled up from the valleys although the sky was still golden and tender. The way was lonely. She clutched her gun fiercely, ready to use it again should the occasion arise, determined, now that Kara Kurt was dead, to get back to Istanbul.

Night covered the valleys and the light of the rising moon showed the outlines of Gül's village ahead before Kamelya permitted herself to rest.

'I'm so tired,' she said and her voice surprised her. She pressed her back against a dry ditch.

'Soon I'll be in Gemlik.'

More than three years ago she'd come to Gemlik with Cemal *bey*, a foolish young woman with a high opinion of herself and the desire for an easy marriage so that she could gain security for her child.

She suddenly remembered Fitnet and her house. 'Those pretty green shutters…' How long ago it all seemed now, much more than three years.

She blew her nose into the long grasses, as a man might, and dragged herself upright. It was hard to walk now that she had rested. All her joints seemed set.

She stumbled through the village and at last found the brown mud house where Gül lived with her half-blind father. She rapped on the rickety door and heard someone coming to open it.

'Who's there?' asked Gül's frightened voice.

'Kamelya. Let me in.'

The door was opened and Kamelya inhaled the smell of oil from a dim lamp. Silhouetted against the uncertain light, looking larger than lifesize, sinister and unreal, stood Gül.

'Kamelya!' she said.

Realising this stage of her long journey was done, Kamelya's face crumpled. She fell into Gül's arms with a juddering sob.

Chapter 11

1919

AS THE MINARETS OF ISTANBUL broke upon the skyline, Kamelya felt tears burn her eyes.

She leaned over the rail of the boat and lifted her coarse black veil to sniff the air and at Galata she was one of the first to go ashore. On the floating bridge, having paid her toll to the official in white uniform, she stood looking about her in much the same expectant fashion as she had the morning she came from Eyüp Sultan with Murat.

The noise seemed tremendous to her ears, accustomed now to mountain silences, and the energy of the loudly swearing porters amazed her. Against the railings, of best German iron, she cut a drab figure in her old soiled dress, an unremarkable figure but for her eyes, which shone with wonder. People pushed and jostled her, indignant when she did not make way for them quickly enough. A mule with panniers filled with bright lemons passed by on the road, and red trams clanged their perilous course in the centre of the street, their drivers hurling abuse at foolhardy pedestrians. A porter staggered by, half hidden under a large brass bedstead, and two gipsy women hawked flowers. Kamelya clasped her hands with nervous excitement; *how* she had missed the clamour and the splendid, colourful bustle!

A man touched her not quite accidentally and she drew herself up to her full height, contempt shaping the lines of her mouth. How astonished he would be if he knew she carried a gun in the folds of her dress!

The encounter shook her out of her dream and she remembered her mission to go to Fatma's house. She walked briskly, her eyes and ears drinking in every colour and sound of her beloved city. As she came to the street of straggling ruined houses, the families living underground in verminous cellars, the children playing on dusty corners, distaste invaded her. This was a more immediate poverty than any displayed on the bridge.

Kamelya shivered and hurried on. For the first time it occurred to her that she was homeless again, that she would have to work supporting Murat as well as herself.

She looked all about her as she neared Fatma's house, wondering if Murat would be among the children playing on the waste ground, but he was not there.

She called Fatma's name through the open doorway and noticed there were two strange women at the washing tub. Smoke still filtered bluely through the tiny room and the steam rose in familiar spirals. She felt its clamminess enfold her in memory.

One of the women said sharply: 'What do you want? Fatma *hanım*'s not here.'

'Not here? What do you mean?'

The other woman, older, said wearily: 'She's in the back room having her coffee. What do you want with her?'

The two of them stared at Kamelya with hostility.

'There's no work here,' said the young woman sullenly. Kamelya tossed her head.

'I'm not looking for work,' she said haughtily.

She entered the low room feeling uneasy. The women continued to eye her doubtfully.

'There was a child here...' she began, and turned to the older of the women. 'Do you know anything about him?'

'No. There's been no child here for a long time.'

Kamelya's body grew slack.

'What happened to him?'

'How should I know? There was no child here when we came.'

'I want to speak to Fatma *hanım*.'

'Well, I suppose it's all right if you go in to her.'

Feeling as if everything was happening in a dream, Kamelya went into the back room. Here she used to sleep beside Murat on the red silk eiderdown she had thought so elegant. Here old Fatma had snored the night away.

The room was still essentially the same, except that what remained of the eiderdown now supported Fatma's broad buttocks while an old straw mattress, placed under the broken window, obviously belonged to the women in the kitchen.

Fatma stared at her for a moment or two and then, as she recognised her, almost dropped her coffee cup in shock.

'Kamelya!' she whispered and her face changed colour. Kamelya looked at her.

'Well, well! What a thing! What a thing!' tittered Fatma in an attempt at joviality.

'You haven't changed much,' said Kamelya.

She leaned against the jamb of the door, the poverty stricken air and the squalor of the little room depressing her in the old way. She would never come here again. Too many unhappy memories crowded the air.

'What a thing, what a thing!' Fatma kept repeating nervously. 'Fancy seeing you again. We heard you were dead!'

'Did you? Why ever should you think I was dead?'

'We heard it somewhere. I've forgotten now – perhaps Fitnet told me. Yes! That was it! Fitnet told me. She said so a long time ago, that you and the rich man were killed by rebels from the hills.'

'The man was killed. I escaped.'

Fatma eyed her shrewdly.

'And where've you been all this time?' she asked. 'Why didn't any of us ever hear of you?'

'I stayed near Gemlik. I – I...' she broke off and bit her lip. Why should she discuss these things with Fatma?

'Where's Murat?' she asked sharply. 'That's why I came here today, to get him.'

Fatma stretched herself and called to the kitchen for more coffee to be brought.

'I don't want coffee,' said Kamelya. 'Tell me where Murat is.'

Fatma turned to face her, a look of cruel obstinacy tapering her features, her eyes uneasy.

'Eh, my daughter!' she sighed. 'I'm getting old. I must sit and rest a bit in my old age and surely you'll have a cup of good coffee with me? We'll talk afterwards while those lazy cows wash for me.'

'Where's Murat?' Kamelya interrupted.

She looked at Fatma's slack face, the silence alarming her. Was Murat dead?

'Answer me Fatma!' she said angrily, already half hysterical. She shook the old woman's arm.

'Let me go!' shouted Fatma in some alarm. 'Sit down over there and let me alone. Murat's all right, I tell you! I looked after him same as if he was my own child. I did everything for him – even gave him my last slice of bread when he was hungry – but he was bad, Kamelya *hanım*. Bad, I tell you! He stole from me and I had to tell the police and they beat him for me but he stole again after that. And one day he tried to kill me – Allah be my witness! What a way to repay my goodness to him!'

She paused, out of breath, and Kamelya said rapidly, 'You? Kind? You were never kind in your life! I never saw you give the child anything but kicks as long as I was with you. You were always ready to kick him out of your way like a football. Where is he?'

'Let go of my arm!' shouted Fatma, regaining her spirit. 'Leave me alone or I'll call the police again!'

As Kamelya released her hold, Fatma felt her arm cautiously.

'Did you expect me to keep him forever?' she demanded. 'A thief – a danger in my house? After I did everything for him too!' She paused and eyed Kamelya malevolently. 'Anyway he's a gentleman now,' she finished with a sneer.

'What do you mean?'

'A big *konak* took him in. I hope he's repaying them better than he did me.'

'Cemal *bey* sent you money to look after him.'

'Money? Are you dreaming, *hanım*? I never got a penny.'

'You did, you did, you old liar! You got it and spent it on yourself. Why did a *konak* take him?'

'It was better so.'

'But why? Was he on the streets?'

Fatma's eyes slid away from her.

'Would I do such a thing, even after the way he treated me?'

'Then why?'

Fatma said evasively, 'I think he was stealing chickens from a mosque garden one day. He couldn't keep his hands off anything that didn't belong to him. The first thing I knew about it was when a big black servant comes rapping on the window and asks me what I know about the brat. I told him you'd gone away somewhere –

perhaps I said you were dead, I forget now. Then the servant tells me the lady of the *konak*, a general's widow, has taken a fancy to Murat and wants to keep him.' She watched Kamelya carefully. What was she thinking, the white faced bitch? Coming back after three years to look for her child, as if people had nothing better to do than look after him?

'Where's the *konak*?'

'I'll tell you if you really want to know, but my advice is to leave him where he is. What'll *you* be able to give him? What did you give him before but a bad name to carry around with him? You should've heard the children calling after him!'

'I can look after him,' said Kamelya interrupting her.

'Got money, eh? Well, he cost me plenty anyway.'

'I expect he earned his keep *hanım*. It wouldn't have been like you to keep him sitting idle.'

'Well, I lost plenty by him too,' shouted Fatma in a temper, 'while *you* were off enjoying yourself with your rich farmer.' They stared at one another with hate.

'What's the address of the *konak*?' asked Kamelya, recovering first.

Fatma rummaged in a box beside her… then produced a scrap of paper.

'Here,' she said. 'And if I hadn't said you were dead they'd never have taken him in.'

'No?'

'No! I did more for him than you ever did – and you his mother.' Fatma fell silent, staring intently at the despairing woman before her. 'Where'd you get those gold coins round your neck, and them bracelets on your arms?' she asked.

'They're all I have in the world,' said Kamelya. 'They are my payment for having been away so long.'

Fatma looked at her uncertainly.

'You done well for yourself anyway.'

'Yes.'

'What you gonna do about the boy?'

'I don't know. I'll go and see the house.' A thought occurred to her. 'Where's Fitnet?' she asked.

'In Pera, living like a lady.'

'In *Pera*? Does she still marriage broke?'

'No. You're not looking for another husband are you?' Fatma chuckled at the idea.

'No. I just wondered about Fitnet that's all.'

'She's all right. She's richer than ever. All the foreign soldiers here were a lucky opportunity for Fitnet.'

'I see.'

Kamelya looked down at the scrap of paper in her hands, half afraid to read the scribbled address, her mood despondent.

'You're not going are you?'

'Yes. There's nothing here for me.'

'Where are you going?'

'Oh, I'll find a place. It shouldn't be difficult.'

'You can stay here for a bit if you want. I can move those two cows into the kitchen to sleep.'

'No. No, thank you.'

She looked at Fatma warily. Did she think she had money? She was too bitter to tell her she had nothing but the clothes she was wearing and the few gold trinkets Kara Kurt had given all the women in camp from time to time.

'I'll manage,' she said.

It was almost like four years ago. Wherever she went, she couldn't seem to find a resting place.

'Well, goodbye,' she said awkwardly, her anger gone. It wasn't much use blaming Fatma for something that had happened long ago. Perhaps Murat *was* better off…

'If you're looking for Fitnet, you'll find her in Papatya Sokak,' said Fatma. 'No. 26. Don't forget now.'

'I won't.'

She blinked back the welling tears. What was she going to do now?

Chapter 12

AFTER LEAVING FATMA'S HOUSE Kamelya started to walk uphill towards Beyazıt. She was hungry but not brave enough to venture into one of the smaller restaurants. She did not think she had the money either. Gül's father had given her enough for a boat ticket in exchange for a bracelet, but of this there were only a few *kuruş* left.

It was very hot but as she approached Beyazıt the way seemed cooler for there were trees here and glimpses of green gardens. She remembered she was walking this way in search of Murat and that no solution as to his future had yet been reached.

'I'll think about it afterwards,' she told herself firmly and lifted her veil cautiously so that she could wipe the perspiration off her upper lip.

When she came at last to the street she sought, she stood at the corner uncertainly. It was a short, narrow little street facing the courtyard of the Süleymaniye Mosque. The houses were all large and imposing, but the house of the dead general whose widow had taken such a liking to Murat was the largest of them all.

This dismayed her. She did not think she had the courage necessary to face the owner and explain her errand.

She retraced her steps to the end of the street, feeling conspicuous even though her veil covered her closely and the street was deserted. The sun was hot and all the windows of the houses were closely latticed. Kamelya did not know what to do. If she sat down – and there was only the kerb for such a purpose – she feared a servant would be sent to sweep her away.

Facing the houses was the high stone wall of the mosque garden, with iron grilles set in it at intervals. Kamelya decided to find herself a seat in the courtyard of the mosque where she could keep the windows of the house she wanted to observe in view without being too noticeable herself. She found a stone near one of the grilles and sat down without any plan in her mind. Now that she was here, what was it she wished to do? Was she going to claim her son or not?

She folded her hands under her long veil, slackened her rigid back and all the time she watched the windows. But there was no sign of life at all. As she watched, uneasiness pervaded her. When Fatma had mentioned a *konak* she had not expected to find a veritable palace. What had she to offer Murat in return for such rich living? What if he refused to have anything to do with her after so long a time? How would he be able to recognise her – she whom he thought was dead?

'What shall I do?' she said aloud.

She looked back to the still house.

'He must be well looked after there. I know these old *konak*s and the sort of people who rescue homeless children. They've money and security so it isn't necessary for them to be harsh the way I was or Fatma. They've no need to be bad. When you've money it's easy enough to be good.'

She sighed and decided that if she had a long time to wait here in this courtyard she had better buy some food to stay the hunger pangs.

'But what are you waiting for?' she asked herself contemptuously. 'Do you think you're going to take him away with you?' She stood up and hurried to the grocer's shop she had passed on her way to the *konak* and after buying half a loaf of bread and a little sticky *helva* she went back to the stone again. Had anything occurred in her absence?

Under her veil her hands were busy with the bread pulling off bits of fresh warm crust and stuffing them into her mouth with the *helva*. She sat facing the house, her shrewd eyes patrolling it for the least movement.

***

She would have been very surprised had she known what an odd, unexpected sight she was to at least one of the *konak*'s occupants.

Saadet *hanım*, the general's widow, found her most disturbing. Like many old Turkish ladies she took her pleasures from the window of her room, much as old Zehra *hanım* had in another quarter of the city at another time. Saadet *hanım* had never cared for walking – having spent all her life behind *kafes* she had lost the desire long ago. But each afternoon, when her salon became too hot for comfortable relaxation, she went to her bedroom and spent the time peering through the squares of latticework over her windows. Usually there was not a great deal to see – perhaps a neighbour or two hurrying to the mosque for prayers, her protegé Murat walking primly beside the big Arab servant Kasım Ağa, or a married child come to pay her a visit with a sulky grandchild in tow.

She had noted Kamelya's arrival in the street and the odd place she chose to sit, with the sun beating full on her head. At first Saadet *hanım* had been intrigued, but as time wore on and the stranger did not move she became apprehensive. What did she want that she watched the house so incessantly? Was she mad?

She rang her little silver handbell for Rabia her maid to come to her and when Rabia came into the room Saadet *hanım* said irritably, 'Come here Rabia! Look at that woman in the coloured dress sitting on that stone in the mosque yard – she's been there for over an hour and she worries me. Go and ask Kasım Ağa to find out what she wants from us.'

'All right *hanım*,' said Rabia, peering at what she could see of Kamelya. 'And if she's only hungry?'

'Then tell Kasım Ağa she's to be taken to the kitchen and given a meal. Send Murat to me.'

Rabia went in search of Kasım Ağa. He was the black servant who had so intimidated Fatma once upon a time, and when Rabia told him about the stranger in the yard he at once set off to investigate.

Murat, who was his special friend, disobeyed the high-nosed Rabia's instructions to go to Saadet *hanım*'s room and went out after him. He wanted to see the beggar woman for himself. He had a passionate interest in beggars and always wondered what would happen to them.

Kamelya, still stuffing *helva* into her mouth, was taken by surprise when at last the imposing door of the *konak* opened and she saw the fearsome Kasım Ağa advancing towards her. And when she saw the tall child following him, her heart leaped into her throat.

Standing up from her uncomfortable stone she decided to follow them, for she thought perhaps they were going to the mosque.

Stealing a rapid glance at Murat, she was conscious of some of the physical changes in him.

'How tall he is!' she thought proudly and then with dismay, 'But how haughty he looks!'

But Murat was only curious. Perhaps he was a bit nervous too, for poverty distressed him to the point of hysteria. He was a very highly strung child altogether.

He hoped Kasım Ağa would not use his 'best' voice when speaking to the woman, for Kasım Ağa's 'best' voice was every bit as disturbing as his appearance.

'You won't shout at her will you?' he asked the old man urgently.

'Mind your own business boy! I know how to deal with these beggars!'

They drew abreast of Kamelya and stopped. This unnerved her for she had not thought they were coming to her. She stared at them through her veil like one hypnotised.

'My mistress sent me to ask if you are hungry,' commenced Kasım Ağa abruptly. 'She wished to know if you would care to come and rest awhile in the kitchen with the servants...'

'Oh no, no!' stammered Kamelya, interrupting him wildly.

She caught Murat's anxious eye on her. He was looking polite and attentive; his smile begged her not to be afraid of Kasım Ağa even though he had a gruff voice – really he had a heart of gold! Kamelya's eyes looked away from him. There he was in front of her, not quite as she had imagined him for three years. The rubbery indeterminate features of babyhood had moulded themselves into the shape they would wear in adult life. His smile was shy and uncertain. He looked gentler than she had expected.

'Won't you come into the house?' he asked.

'Keep your place boy!' growled Kasım Ağa warningly.

'No, no, please... leave me alone.'

Kamelya stretched out a hand to pick up the paper bag of *helva* from the ground and the sleeve of her dress rolled back as she straightened revealing a slim brown wrist and her collection of shining bracelets.

'You are welcome to eat with us,' said Kasım Ağa uncertainly.

'No!' said Kamelya hysterically and ran off across the yard towards the main gateway. She could hear a sharp tapping on one of the windows of the house, the sound of voices and then swift footsteps pursuing her.

She halted and allowed the runner to catch up with her. It was Murat. Her next action took her by surprise. She turned and clasped the astonished child to her breast, smoothed back the sleek, controlled hair from his forehead then released him abruptly and ran away sobbing. She did not see the horrified face of Murat, nor hear the sharp, acid voice of Saadet *hanım* calling to him to return to the house at once. Murat did not hear Saadet *hanım* at first either. He was shaking, with fear and excitement. The poor thing really was crazy – fancy doing a thing like that!

Kasım Ağa caught up with him.

'What did you do that for?'

'Saadet *hanım* tapped on the windows, didn't you hear her? She told me to go after her. She thought perhaps you'd frightened her.'

'Am I an ogre?'

'Well Saadet *hanım* said to go.'

'Beggars!' said Kasım Ağa in rage. 'Asking for trouble to have anything to do with them. Don't come near me until you've been washed boy!'

Murat laughed.

'All right,' he said, 'But she really was mad you know. She kept staring and staring through her veil, but it was so thick you couldn't see her properly and that made it worse! She was laughing and crying together.'

'Hold your tongue!'

Later Murat said to Saadet *hanım* when they were alone, 'That woman wore gold bracelets like the ones you sometimes wear *hanım*. I don't think she was a beggar you know, I think she was just mad!'

'Perhaps so,' said Saadet *hanım* testily, 'but she was very worrying sitting there on the stone without moving. Perhaps she wanted to steal from us? Perhaps the bracelets she wore were stolen?'

'Oh I shouldn't think so,' said Murat. 'She was just a madwoman *hanım*. Not important.' But, inside himself, he could not dismiss what had happened that afternoon quite so easily.

Chapter 13

SWINGING HIS LEGS over the side of a chair Murat was uneasy. He could not rid his mind of the extraordinary scene in the street earlier in the day. He felt excited and depressed alternately. What had she wanted? Had Kasım Ağa frightened her? Murat was fond of the old man but he quite saw that on first acquaintance he was liable to strike fear into a timid heart. Murat had a timid heart himself. Too many beatings and too little affection had left their mark on him, although under Saadet *hanım's* influence he had managed to acquire a certain superficial self-possession.

Kasım Ağa, who was superintending the cook's labours, noticed Murat's restless legs and said sharply, 'Either get out of my kitchen or make yourself useful boy!'

'Can't I just watch?'

'No. You're disturbing me. Stop swinging your legs in that dangerous way and go to help Zehra clean the rice for the *pilav.*'

'All right,' said Murat sulkily.

While he was cleaning the rice he began to think about Fatma the washerwoman and moved restlessly for he never wanted to think about her again. But the old monster Fatma kept creeping round his mind, appearing when he least expected her as he feared she might one day in real life. He was afraid she would come and take him.

Once he told this to Saadet *hanım* but she did not understand and laughed at him.

'Nobody can take you away from me,' she assured him.

'But supposing she did?' Murat persisted.

'Don't talk nonsense,' snapped Saadet *hanım* who was tired of the whole thing.

Her tone was so decisive that Murat was comforted momentarily, but whenever Kasım Ağa or the other servants were angry with him *they* said something quite different. *They* said he was nobody at all, that he didn't have a father or mother and belonged to nobody properly, not even to Saadet *hanım*, who would probably throw him on to the streets if he wasn't good.

Their assertions sent fear shivering darkly and coldly through Murat and he did not know how to obtain comfort. After a time he was afraid to even discuss the possibility with Saadet *hanım*, for she grew impatient easily and discouraged what she called 'morbid talk'.

He could not remember his mother clearly, although he associated comfort and a sense of familiarity with the word and for three years his mind had held only flickering images of her which grew dimmer as he was absorbed more and more into the life of the *konak*. Feature by feature, her face grew more hazy. He was too young to have said with certainty the colour of her eyes or the shape of her quick, amused smile, but he never forgot the comfort in her which he had found with no one else. He had been brushed with that feeling for a fraction of time this afternoon when he had talked to the woman in the street. It had been stronger when she held him against her and it was this that made him uneasy.

As he sat and cleaned the stones from the rice there was a fluttery, excited feeling in the pit of his stomach, a taut nervousness that made him want to be sick.

'Look what you're doing boy,' growled Kasım Ağa. 'That's a stone you're putting in the bowl.'

'No it isn't.'

'Don't you answer me like that!'

He had made a great effort to fit in to the regularised, artificial life of the *konak* but there were times when he wanted to assert himself to prove he was Murat with a background and not a nameless child off the streets. At such times Saadet *hanım*, with her disapproving air, seemed every bit as fearsome as Fatma who had called his mother a prostitute.

Sometimes at night, even after three years of separation, he awoke in the dark little room they had given him, crying for his mother. The nightmare followed the same pattern always. He would see her very clearly at first, in a way he could never see her when he was awake, but then she would grow smaller and smaller, fading away from him until she disappeared altogether. Sea would appear, a boat would hoot, he would feel the cold of a stony shore beneath his bare feet, permeating the whole of his body, while he cried for his mother to come back. He would hear himself crying in his sleep and struggle to wake but swirling dark seas held him down. Then the dark hull of a boat would shoot out of the darkness, threatening to crush him, and he would wake screaming with fear.

Kasım Ağa was the only one who knew about the nightmares. It was one of the reasons Murat loved him and was rarely disturbed by his violent outbursts of temper.

'Haven't I told you before not to put dirty rice in with the clean. Now it'll have to be cleaned all over again – what a waste!' said Kasım Ağa exasperatedly. 'What do you think you're doing?'

'I'm as good as Zehra anyway,' retorted Murat moodily. 'She can't see properly and she's putting stones in as well.'

'You mind your own business!' said Zehra and leaned across the table to give him a smart cuff on the ear.

'Leave me alone you old devil!'

'I'll give you more than that in a minute my boy!'

'Now, now!' warned Kasım Ağa. 'Enough!'

Murat remembered the day he had first been brought to the house by a *hoca* from the Süleymaniye Mosque. He had been caught stealing chickens in the ruined schools of the mosque and the *hoca* brought him to the Paşa's house so that someone in authority could beat him.

'I'd have done it myself,' he said. 'But I'm not a strong man and you've a fist like iron, brother!'

Kasım Ağa had grunted. He had pushed Murat into the coal house until he was ready to chastise him. He planned to do it at a time when Saadet *hanım* was in her salon on the other side of the house, so that the brat's screams would not disturb her.

Murat, however, had been so terrified of the dark coal hole and the locked door that he had screamed with all his might and Saadet *hanım* had sent Rabia to discover the reason for all the noise and why a child was screaming in her house which had had no child in it for years.

Kasım Ağa explained somewhat testily, for the *hoca*, on hearing that the voice of authority was interested, had slunk away and Kasım Ağa felt he had been left in an unfair position. Saadet *hanım* ordered that the boy be released immediately, be washed and fed, and brought before her for questioning. As for Murat, he screamed more than ever when they dragged him into the house, tore off his clothes and thrust him into a tin bath of hot water. He had heard stories of the tortures that went on in the palace and was inclined to believe that Kasım Ağa, with his fierce black face, was the Sultan himself. Like all insecure people he never quite trusted his luck, and this annoyed Saadet *hanım* who disliked moodiness and had never been insecure in her life.

As he cleaned the rice he listened to the complaining voice of Zehra.

'I've too much to do here,' said Zehra directing a sour look at Kasım Ağa. 'I'd want three pairs of hands to get through what I'm expected to do.'

'It's nothing to what it was in the old days when she was young,' said the cook. 'I remember the parties she used to give then.'

'That was when Major Ahmet was at home,' said Kasım Ağa. 'She hoped to find a wife for him.'

'Well, we had more servants then,' said Zehra. 'Now I have to do it all myself.'

'I help you,' said Murat.

'You? You hinder more than help – look at you now, giving me all this trouble with the rice!'

'I like Major Ahmet,' said Murat wistfully. 'Why doesn't he come home so much?'

'That's not your business,' said Kasım Ağa testily.

'Yes, but why doesn't he?'

''Cause he's got something better to do,' said the cook with a chuckle. 'A fine young man like that doesn't want to spend all his time with the *hanım*.'

'Have you finished?' Zehra asked Murat, who nodded. 'Then go and get the onions for me.'

'I haven't got to chop them have I?'

He remembered the piles of onions he had had to chop when Fatma sold him to the *börek* maker at Galata. He was only seven at the time and he chopped more of his fingers than he did onions. After the onions had been chopped, there had been piles of dough waiting to be kneaded under his bare feet. After a while his thin young legs gave way under him and one of the men kicked him out of the way like a dog and finished the job himself, his huge hairy legs working like pistons.

'I don't like the smell of onions,' he said defiantly.

'Well that's a pity,' said Kasım Ağa, 'because there's no one else to do them.'

'Saadet *hanım* doesn't like me working in the kitchen,' he said defiantly as he took onions out of a sack and put them on the table.

'She doesn't care,' said the cook. 'It isn't as if you're one of her own.'

That was the trouble. He belonged to no one.

'Still...' he demurred.

'That's enough!' said Kasım Ağa. 'Get those onions ready or I'll beat you until I bring blood to your bottom!'

'I'm strong,' said Murat jeeringly.

For over a year after his mother left him he had not known what it was to change his clothes. His feet were bare during the rawest winter and he never had a coat to hide his tattered shirt. He was a ragamuffin like the rest of the homeless children on Galata Bridge.

Once, an army officer kicked him because he wore greasy, torn trousers. He roared at Murat that he was a good for nothing and wasn't he ashamed of being seen in such a condition? Wasn't water free in the mosque gardens?

'No wonder we're a dying nation,' he said.

He wore an immaculate uniform and carried a malacca cane, his stomach pendulous with good feeding.

'You should be exterminated,' he said and he gave Murat a vicious slap on the side of the head, sending a heavy tray of freshly baked *börek* flying in all directions. 'That'll teach you!'

Murat put the last onion on the table.

'Must I really do them?' he asked wistfully.

Kasım Ağa looked at him uncertainly. Finally, he said, 'Oh go away!'

'I wish I could go into the street.'

'Well you can't. The *hanım* said you weren't to.'

'Still, he'd be better off with other children,' said Zehra, taking up a knife for the onions.

Kasım Ağa thought the same thing but whenever he mentioned this to Saadet *hanım* she disagreed.

'He's spent enough time in the streets,' she'd say with a sniff. 'Let him get a taste of security now.' Later, she added, Murat would be sent to school. 'And that'll give him plenty of companionship Kasım Ağa.'

'Yes *hanım*.'

But still he could not agree.

Neither did he agree with her plans for schooling Murat. She wanted her youngest son, Major Ahmet, to have him entered for the military school and Kasım Ağa, like the other servants of his day, thought this was carrying hospitality too far. It was one thing to care for a street brat, but quite another to send him to a school for gentlemen. Kasım Ağa segregated the classes most strictly.

'Couldn't I go into the street, Kasım Ağa?'

'No. Go into the garden and I'll call you when your dinner's ready.' He looked at the flushed, sullen face of the child and added sharply, 'Go on now! Sharp about it my boy!'

'I don't want to.' Murat looked through the window to the clear afternoon light reflected from the beds of glowing flowers he was never allowed to touch.

'What's wrong with you boy?'

'I don't know.' He thought the fault lay with Kasım Ağa, although he could not define it. He looked at him with hostility. He shouldn't have frightened that woman with his gruff voice and his air of authority. 'Didn't her hand look pretty with those gold bracelets?' he said musingly.

'Whose hand?'

'That woman in the street.'

'I didn't see. Why was she wearing gold bracelets if she was begging?'

'She wasn't begging! She was...' But he didn't know what she was trying to do.

'Oh well,' he said resignedly and stuck his finger in the sugar bowl.

'Stop that!' warned Zehra. 'All those dirty habits you have!'

Murat licked his finger with appetite and when she wasn't looking stuck it in again. 'I wish...' he said and then everything started to get confused and he forgot what he was going to say.

His lower lip started to tremble but he bit it fiercely. He did not want to let the others see what a baby he was. He tried to remember how kind Saadet *hanım* had been to him. She had given him a white bed to sleep in and lots of food and yet he felt wary of her, uncertain of her mood. He never felt familiar and safe, even though she had made him tell her all about his mother and had not laughed when he wept in the middle of his tale. At the time, she had seemed as if she understood. She had even coaxed him into telling the story of the officer who had kicked him on the bridge. She had asked about Fatma, and he told how she used to come home drunk sometimes and put him into the street to sleep all night. How she had sold him to the *börek* maker and the *simit* maker, how he had slept in a stable with another boy and a donkey to keep them warm. And how one night the other boy had had his ear bitten through by a rat and Murat had run screaming into the street. Bit by bit he told her everything, even about the policeman who beat him because Fatma said he had stolen a *kuruş* from her.

'And did you take the money?'

'No, *hanım*.'

'But what about the chickens belonging to the mosque?'

So he had told her about that too.

He glared at the lush green lawn outside the kitchen windows and wished to use up some of his energy by picking a fight. His head ached but he didn't know quite how to stop his memories from tormenting him.

The light washed over his thin shoulders but his face was in shadow when he said to Kasım Ağa abruptly: 'Did Fatma tell *you* I stole money?'

'Who? What are you talking about boy?'

'Fatma the washerwoman,' persisted Murat stubbornly. 'You know Kasım Ağa! The one you went to see when Saadet *hanım* said I could stay here.'

Kasım Ağa stared at him woodenly.

'And what makes you think of that old harridan?' he asked slowly.

Murat looked surprised.

'I often think about her,' he said.

'Then it's time you forgot her,' said Zehra with a sniff of disdain.

'But did she tell you Kasım Ağa?'

Kasım Ağa still wanted to hold his nose when he remembered the washerwoman and her abominable house. He had never quite forgiven Saadet *hanım* for sending him to such an unsavoury quarter of the city.

'I can't remember everything boy!'

'But I remember lots of things Kasım Ağa!'

'If you had enough to do with your time you wouldn't remember anything.'

'I told you, he needs boys of his own age to play with,' said the cook. 'It isn't natural keeping him here with us.'

'But Kasım Ağa, I remember! She told everyone I stole money. She said I took the *simits* too!' His eyes slid away from the company in the room. 'It was the day I left the *simits* on a stone to look at the firefighters and someone took them and when I got home Fatma said I'd eaten them myself.'

'What a memory!' jeered Zehra.

Murat looked at her not quite understanding what she meant. She looked cross and forbidding and he felt chilled. It was nicer to remember the exciting firemen. They'd never seemed so exciting to him since that day, even though they still played the bugle as if they were going into battle, their pumps were still as bright and shiny, the men still as brave and brawny in their coloured shirts and leather jackets and funny tight trousers. The horses were as large and fearsome-looking as ever, and the man who carried the district pump still shouted that his pump was the best in the country, a tiger on land and a lion in the sea whatever that might mean – yet the magic of the first impression had gone out of it. The brave firefighters were never again quite so beautiful as the day he'd seen them for the first time.

'I heard nothing,' said Kasım Ağa.

'But you must have!' insisted Murat with a sort of imperious anger. 'Do listen to me Kasım Ağa! I know Fatma told you.'

'Then what are you asking for?' demanded Zehra.

'But the firefighters were wonderful,' said Murat ignoring her and jumping from one subject to the other, following his own interests. His eyes lit up for a brief moment, then he frowned trying to remember what he had been saying before. 'But I took the eggs from the chickens,' he confessed, looking suddenly shy.

He'd wandered away from the *börek* maker as far as the Süleymaniye Mosque, although he had not known its name. When he reached the place where the schools had been, he found them in ruins. Only the tall strong walls remained and the iron grilles which had held windows. It was a wonderful place to discover and he crept inside to rest on the ground where the wild grasses and the citrus-scented feverfew grew thick and rank like a meadow. The wall protected him from the wind but the open roof let the warm sun find him and he had drowsed happily, wishing he might remain there forever. On waking he heard the clucking of hens and the country sound enchanted him although he knew nothing of life outside the city. When he clambered up the broken wall he had seen a few brown hens pecking in the dust on the other side. He climbed over, trying to pick one of them up in his arms but they had run in all directions clucking angrily.

One day a hen laid an egg on the broken down partition and came through the opening to look at him with her bright beady eyes and cackle triumphantly. He ate the egg raw but it made him sick so he did not touch them any more. An idea grew in his mind that if he could catch one of the hens he would take it to Galata Bridge and sell it to a passer-by. The thought of earning money he could hide from Fatma intoxicated him, but the hens were too agile for him and he could not catch them, so he grew bored and thought perhaps it was better to take only their eggs.

He spent a part of every day there, nodding off in the warm sun, watching the hens searching for worms and talking to one another. But one day, as he was pocketing two eggs, his peace was shattered. A large hand descended on his shoulder with such force that he screamed with pain and the voice of the *hoca* demanded to know what he was doing.

From then on Kasım Ağa and the life of the *konak* had enveloped him.

'I've never liked eggs much,' he said suddenly.

'Funny thing, neither do I,' said Zehra, not knowing to what he was alluding.

But Kasım Ağa, in a sudden blaze of intuition, knew.

'Fool! Cucumber!' he said contemptuously. 'Haven't you anything better to think about?'

Chapter 14

WHEN KAMELYA TURNED THE CORNER of the Süleymaniye Mosque and was out of sight of her followers she leaned against a wall gasping for breath.

She had not known what to expect from today's journey, but from the moment she beheld the *konak* she had not thought to hear Murat talking to her, nor feel his rigid, surprised body pressed against her. Had she been mad?

She knew with certainty that whatever she decided now she would never try to claim Murat from his new life. 'There's nothing I can offer him,' she thought.

She felt weak with loss and shock. There was nothing for her in Istanbul after all.

'He's so different,' she said aloud. 'How can I approach him and say I'm his mother? Would he believe me?'

She imagined herself in the presence of the general's wife, stumbling through her story with embarrassment, stumbling through it for who would believe that any good woman could allow herself to be kept in the mountains against her will? She remembered the loneliness of her life with Kara Kurt – the terrible isolation – and her lip curled scornfully. These sheltered city women would not believe such conditions existed. She imagined the cold face of the general's wife, disdaining to believe she could not have escaped had she wished. 'I shall go and see Fitnet,' she thought defiantly, as despairing tears fell down her cheeks. 'If I had kept Murat perhaps he'd have been nothing but a porter, but at least I'd have had him with me.'

After a while she went across to the fountains to wash her face. She flung back her heavy veil and plunged her hot face under the icy coldness of the water, scooping up some with her hand to drink. Arranging her veil in position again she spattered drops of water across the skirt of her dress smoothing it down with her hands in an effort to take away some of the creases.

She took a last look in the direction of the *konak*, for perhaps she would never pass this way again, and set off briskly in the direction of Pera.

***

At Beyazıt Square she stood still for a few minutes to watch the people. She liked the wide old square with the red trams swaying through it, the cries of the street sellers and the shuffling uncertain steps of the older women as they passed her in their funereal black.

'They're what are called good women,' said Kamelya to herself, 'but I'd rather be bad and free than be like them. It's better to be bad and free than good and a slave to someone like Fatma.' Some of the women eyed her with hostility. 'How cruel women are!' She remembered the duty of the mother who throughout the night would wait outside her newly married son's bedchamber so that in the morning she would be the first to examine the sheets for signs that her daughter-in-law had been a virgin on marriage.

'I don't believe I'd care very much,' she thought, remembering Murat and realising that one day he would be a grown man.

She walked over to a mosque garden to watch the pigeons circling in the air. Once, she'd fed them at Eyüp Sultan. Moved by impulse, she went over to the old woman selling packets of seed, handing over her last two *kuruş*.

'Give me two.'

It was a long time since she had fed the pigeons. A good Muslim would think that a terrible thing.

'Oh well,' she said sentimentally, 'I may as well make certain that someone remembers me when I die.'

The pigeons fluttered greedily just above her head and Kamelya threw some of the seed.

'The first bag for Murat's happiness,' she said, 'and the second for my luck. That's important too.'

She stood gazing as the pigeons swooped. Then she turned away to continue her journey to Pera.

***

Pera excited her. It was another world, a far cry from the street sellers and drab old women of Beyazıt.

The women beguiled her and maddened her with pangs of jealousy. The smartly dressed ones did not wear veils and their clothes astonished Kamelya. How short their skirts were! They flaunted their painted faces to the world and smelled like flowers as they rustled past her in brightly coloured silks with jewels at their throat and on their pretty fingers.

Kamelya was outraged. She dismissed them immediately as foreigners or mistresses, yet she longed to look like them. She thought that this was the way a woman ought to look – like a doll or a flower. She felt dowdy in her soiled dress, the metal in the brocade splitting with age and usage. She was doubly conscious of her unwashed body and the rank smell of perspiration. 'Like an animal,' she said contemptuously and someone looked at her in passing. 'I've never known how to live at all.'

She watched resentfully as the women sauntered past her with their escorts. This was a different world. She saw a water seller and she went across to him forgetting she had no money left to buy a drink. But perhaps the pigeons had remembered to bring her luck for the old man gave her a glass of water nevertheless.

'*Teşekkür ederiz* – thank you,' said Kamelya, lowering her veil.

He shuffled his feet and looked embarrassed. It displeased him to see her raise her veil in public.

In Papatya Sokak she found Fitnet's apartment easily enough but when she enquired for her she was told that nobody of that name lived in the flats.

This dismayed her and she was vaguely alarmed when she caught sight of a half-naked young woman leaning through an opposite window and carrying on a spirited conversation with a lemon seller.

The pretty young woman noticed Kamelya's eyes on her and gave her a friendly smile. She had an open, rather childish face and her fair hair was tied back with a knot of blue ribbon.

'Are you looking for someone?' she asked.

'I'm looking for Fitnet *hanım*.'

'I've never heard of her,' said the friendly young woman, 'but if I were you I'd try Bakkal Yani at the corner shop. He knows everyone in the district.'

Bakkal Yani turned out to be a large voluble Greek and after a few minutes conversation with him Kamelya felt as if she'd known him all her life.

Of course he knew the good Fitnet *hanım*! Who didn't? He'd give her the address right away. He gesticulated wildly as he talked and kept showing all his gold teeth. Kamelya was impressed. She left his shop glowing with assurance but when she reached the large house where Fitnet lived her assurance faded and she grew apprehensive. How could Fitnet possibly afford to live in such a place? Would she refuse to see her?

Nerving herself against possible rebuffs, she went into the hall and found a porter sitting at a cheaply impressive desk. She stuttered as she gave her name and the porter looked her up and down with familiarity.

'I'm an old friend of Fitnet *hanım*'s,' she said in a dignified voice.

She stared at the porter haughtily.

'I wish to see her at once,' she said.

'Is that so?' enquired the porter with interest and crossed one leg over the other.

'Yes. I haven't any time to waste.'

'Well, Fitnet *hanım*'s very particular who she sees but I'll tell her you're here. What did you say your name was?'

'Ka… Kamelya.'

He got up leisurely.

'Well, I'll tell her,' he repeated and gestured to a chair. 'Sit down,' he said.

'I prefer to stand, thank you,' said Kamelya, biting her lip in temper.

The porter ambled off to Fitnet but returned quickly.

'She says she doesn't know you,' he said, 'but that as you're here you may as well wait. She'll be down to see you presently.'

He opened a door off the hall. 'In here,' he said.

He ushered her into a long room and Kamelya stood looking about her uncertainly. Was this room, with its ornate furniture and its fanciful gilt mirrors, Fitnet's too? She seated herself nervously on the extreme edge of a spindle-legged chair and looked about her at the floor-length curtains and the crystal chandelier hanging from the centre of the high ceiling and was conscious of a smell of cheap stale perfume.

The porter returned to tell her that Fitnet had changed her mind after all and would see Kamelya upstairs. He watched her with a professional eye as she crossed the room and she felt herself reddening. What a horrible creature he was!

She found Fitnet lying on a wide divan bed with an alert-looking Alsatian dog stretched beside her.

It was difficult to recognise her at once. She was so much more obvious. Even her red hair had become redder and glowed like a light against the plain walls. She wore rouge on her cheeks and several new teeth gleamed in a tight little smile between her reddened lips. One elegant hand played with a rope of pearls about her neck and her ample body was covered by a blue satin dressing robe lavishly trimmed with swansdown. Kamelya felt insignificant before such magnificence.

'Come over here and let me see who you are,' said Fitnet in an artificial voice, and she rolled over on the bed exposing large soft white breasts.

'I can't remember you,' she said languidly.

Kamelya advanced into the room and the dog pointed his ears and growled.

'Quiet Güzel!' said Fitnet lovingly and dropped a hand to fondle his head. 'He's so jealous,' she said to Kamelya.

She stared at Kamelya critically after she had unveiled her face and then she started. 'Why of course I remember you – the little washerwoman from At Pazarı! How very odd – I thought you were dead years ago!'

'Yes?'

'But of course. We all heard it. We...' she stopped.

A cunning look ran across her face. 'What are you doing in Istanbul?' she asked as her eyes took in the state of Kamelya's clothes.

'I came back from Gemlik. I stayed there after Cemal *bey* was killed.'

'So? And how did you know where to find me?'

'Fatma gave me the address. It was the wrong one but the grocer knew.'

'I see. And what do you intend to do now that you are here again?'

'I don't know.'

Fitnet's attitude grew harder.

'Well, I can't help you,' she said and stretched out her hand to select a peach from a dish beside her bed. 'I have my own troubles,' she said.

Kamelya remained silent and after a time Fitnet said, 'Didn't you have a child – a boy wasn't it?'

'Yes. He's with a general's wife now in a big *konak*. He's all right.'

'That's good. You'll be better off without a child tied to your heels.'

'Yes.'

Kamelya's face contracted with a spasm of emotion and she looked down at the carpet, blinking tears from her eyes.

'I thought perhaps you'd let me stay with you for a while,' she said.

Fitnet's eyes narrowed.

'Quite impossible,' she said coldly. 'The last time I helped you I got into trouble with the police. I can't afford the same thing again.'

'Just until I find work to do,' pleaded Kamelya, disliking being under an obligation but unable to think of anything else to do.

Fitnet seemed to reconsider.

'Have you any money?'

'I have these gold bracelets and some gold coins.' She pulled out the necklace of gold liras and Fitnet's eyes grew round with surprise.

'Have you nothing else?'

Kamelya's mouth curled contemptuously.

'Aren't these enough?' she asked.

Fitnet considered her for a moment and then she said rapidly, 'Well, you can stay here for tonight. Tomorrow we'll discuss it again and you'll have to sell those coins anyway. We'll see how long you can afford to pay me.'

'I shall look for work,' said Kamelya.

'What, with a pretty face like yours? Are you still anxious to go to someone like Fatma?'

'I must work.'

'Of course.'

She eyed Kamelya unsmilingly and then rang a little handbell.

'I'll get a woman to show you a room,' she said. 'It'll be a loss to me tonight but no matter. You'll settle up with me when we sell those coins of yours!'

A maid came into the room and Fitnet instructed her. As Kamelya was leaving the room Fitnet said, with her artificial smile, 'I hope my girls won't disturb you later on. We are unused to having guests like you.'

Kamelya felt her face flame again. If she had not known it before, she knew now that Fitnet was running a brothel.

***

Alone in the room the maid had shown her, she closed the door and stood looking about at the tawdry elegance and the vast mirror beside the bed.

After a while she moved over to the dressing table and pulled her shabby dress over her head, revealing tattered underclothes. She threw the dress across the bed and heard the dull sound her gun made as it struck the iron rail. She allowed herself a smile as she thought how incongruous a gun seemed in this amorous room. She turned back to survey herself in the mirror and bright sunlight fell across her curling dark hair.

'I'm so tired!' she thought and searched deeply into the face of the girl in the mirror.

She pulled off the torn underclothing and half-cupped, half-caressed her breasts imagining how she would look in the sort of clothes the women of Pera wore. All the Kamelyas she had ever been looked over her shoulder into the glass, frightening her with their faces of vice and innocence. Had they all been her at some time? Her nakedness repulsed her and she pulled the shapeless dress back over her head. But without a veil, and with no cumbersome underwear to restrict her movement, the lines of her body suddenly took on another dimension.

'You look like a prostitute!' she said to the girl in the mirror, and flung herself across the wide bed in tears. She fell asleep still crying and she was still asleep when evening came and girls chattered in the vast salon downstairs or giggled beside the men who tramped with noisy, careless feet down the corridor to the bedrooms.

She awoke when she heard someone trying her door. It opened a little and her heart stood still but a girl's voice said something and the door closed again.

Kamelya sat up, her heart beginning to function again. After a moment or two she stood up and went across to the window, bright with the light from a street lamp. She stared down the empty *sokak* trying to force her attention away from the sounds of rising, falling lust somewhere above her but there was no escape from it. As long as she remained here, there would never be any escape.

She pressed her forehead against the cool window pane and thought of Murat sleeping in his quiet room in the *konak* and was passionately glad she had not brought him with her to this life. Now and then a solitary person hurried along the street and she could hear the tinny crackle of a gramophone playing somewhere. The house seemed suddenly quiet – save for the creaking of beds and the gasps that came through the walls. Kamelya shivered and wished for dawn to come.

She heard someone at her door. A man stumbled in and switched on the light impatiently.

He looked at Kamelya.

'I thought I'd never find you,' he said drunkenly.

She put her hand to her mouth as he kicked off his shoes.

'*You* thought you'd got away,' he said thickly and she realised he thought she was someone else.

'But *I* knew where to look,' he grinned to himself, taking off his jacket.

Kamelya felt for her gun automatically and the smooth cold feel of the metal gave her confidence.

'Come to bed,' said the man and stared at her uncertainly. She saw him coming towards her and then she screamed and ran past him and along the carpeted corridor. Once, in another life, she had run away from a man in the same way, only then it was he who had the gun.

'Please let me get out!' she prayed frantically.

The hall was deserted, although sounds of laughter still came from the salon. She thought she heard Fitnet's high voice. Opening the front door, Kamelya went out to the dark street and ran in the direction of the main thoroughfare.

She ran blindly and with no object in mind save to reach a place where there were lights and she ran with her head down because although the *çarşaf* still bound her forehead she had forgotten her veil.

She bumped into a tall figure coming out of a side street and gasped as a hand steadied her.

'Oh,' she said and would not look at her rescuer because she wore no veil.

'What's all this?' asked a deep, cross voice. She looked up at the tall stranger who held her arm.

She tried to twist herself away from him but he held her the tighter.

'Let me go!' she panted wildly.

'In a minute. What's the hurry and what are you doing out at this time of the morning alone?'

He peered into her unveiled face, seeing the *çarşaf* around her forehead and recognising her as a Turk.

'What is your business here?' he asked.

'Please, let me go,' said Kamelya.

Her voice sounded exhausted.

'Are you in trouble?' the Stranger asked. 'Why were you running away?'

'A man,,,' she said, as the Stranger released her arm. 'He came into my room – horrible, drunk – and he mistook me for somebody else – he – he...'

She could not finish her story and looked at him limply. For a long moment they stared at one another.

'Come and have a hot drink,' he said at last. 'It's all right. There's a place in the main street that's open all night.'

She was more composed now, less apprehensive.

'It's not a respectable place I'm taking you to,' the Stranger said grimly. 'But then this isn't a very respectable hour of the night for you to be out.'

'No,' said Kamelya humbly.

'Where do you live?'

She did not answer at first until he persisted and then she said defiantly, 'I don't live anywhere. I have no home.'

He glanced at her sideways.

'You wouldn't be telling lies by any chance would you?'

'No. It's true. I've just left a… a brothel.'

'You astonish me! You are the essence of respectability!'

Kamelya smiled. 'Yes,' she said, 'I thought so too.'

They turned into a small café where a few painted women and a handful of men who couldn't seem to make up their minds what they wanted to do next lingered.

'I told you it wasn't respectable,' said the Stranger as he saw the haughty look descend on Kamelya's face. He saw too that she was extravagantly beautiful.

Over coffee she told him what had happened in Fitnet's house and how she had only arrived hours earlier from Gemlik. He listened patiently and after a time he said, 'I didn't ask for your life history, but it's obvious you need a place to stay for the night.'

He paused and Kamelya looked down at the dirty tablecloth and said nothing.

'There's a woman I know. She's Greek and she might be able to help you.'

He stopped uncertainly, 'Would you like to come with me to the Greek woman?' he asked.

'Yes.'

'I think she will help you.'

'You are kind,' said Kamelya, looking at him intently.

She saw that he was handsome and carried himself well. He looked the sort of man who was used to commanding and even though he wore civilian clothing she wondered if he might be an officer. She felt a sense of security with him that was comforting and after a while he said amusedly: 'Well, what have you decided about me *hanım*?'

The respectful title brought her back to the present and she flushed.

'I'm sorry,' she muttered and hung her head.

'Never mind.' He called a waiter over, asked for the bill, and they went out into the street together. He hailed a passing cab and gave the driver an address. 'I'm not running away with you,' he said as he thrust her inside, 'but this is the quickest way to get where I want.'

He settled himself in a corner and Kamelya sat opposite him unwilling to believe she was really here at all. A short time ago she'd been running aimlessly through the Pera backstreets and now here she was riding in a cab with a stranger. They arrived at a shop in the fashionable quarter and the cab stopped.

'Here?' asked Kamelya diffidently.

The Stranger paid off the driver. The woman he wanted, he said, owned the shop and the flat over it.

'This is Madame Toto,' he said later as he introduced Kamelya to a tall elegant woman with prematurely silver hair. He led the way into the flat as if he knew every inch of it and then he and Madame Toto went into another room. When they came back Kamelya was just on the point of flight, since she was convinced there was something sinister in the whole thing.

'I shall be very pleased if you stay here,' said Madame Toto, staring at her critically. 'Tomorrow we shall discuss what is the best thing to be done.'

'Thank you,' said Kamelya faintly, and Madame Toto smiled.

'You are quite safe with me,' she said. 'I even have an old mother who lives with me. You need not fear to stay the night with us.'

'She has a suspicious nature,' half-smiled the Stranger, who looked even more handsome in the subtle lighting.

Madame Toto glanced at him with a brief look of regret. Sometimes when she saw him in this gay mood she was sorry their association was over. It was tedious being nothing more than friends.

'She was lucky it was you who met her,' she said smilingly.

The Stranger looked down at Kamelya.

'You'll be all right here,' he said. 'Toto will not ask any questions.'

'Oh, but it doesn't matter,' said Kamelya eagerly.

'It is better not to know,' said Madame Toto in her soft voice. 'If you stay here perhaps you will wish to work with me in my shop and then you will pay me for your room. In that case your life is your own. I do not wish to know anything.'

Kamelya felt inadequate.

'I must go,' said the Stranger abruptly.

He took Madame Toto's hand and kissed it and then he bowed to Kamelya.

'Goodbye,' he said.

'Goodbye.'

'You will not come again perhaps?' asked Madame Toto resignedly.

'Perhaps!'

He straightened himself and smiled at them.

'This has been an adventure for me too,' he said and Madame Toto smiled at him.

They went out together and Kamelya looked around her at the quietly elegant room and the flowers, arranged on the polished central table.

Where would she go from here?

Chapter 15

KAMELYA REMAINED with Madame Toto.

At first she was only given the odd simple sewing job, but as time passed she grew increasingly proficient and took on more delicate work as well.

One day Madame Toto said to her, 'Well Kamelya *hanım*, you've been here quite a while now and I think it's time you altered your style a bit.'

Kamelya stared at her uncertainly. 'What do you mean Madame?'

'You're pretty. You're wasted in those old clothes. Wouldn't you like to wear pretty new ones?'

'Y… Yes! But I haven't any money.'

'We must sell your gold liras.'

Kamelya looked distressed.

'And the bracelets too?'

'No. It should be enough to sell the liras. You'd be more useful to me if you were dressed more smartly. You could even attend in the shop occasionally.'

Kamelya blushed. Most Turkish women were still hidden behind *kafes*. Few, if any, were to be seen working in shops.

Toto, watching her carefully, said on impulse, 'You have your living to earn. It is as well to face the facts and be sensible about it, and if you wish to remain here with me you must change. It is time you threw away that *çarşaf* altogether.'

Kamelya still hesitated. 'But I should feel so ashamed. People would talk.'

'Who would talk? You know no one here. You are even more of a stranger than I am. Times have changed *hanım*, and I can't afford to keep you as a luxury while I pay another girl to attend to my customers.'

'But I am being useful now Madame. Do I not sew for you and pay you for my keep?'

Madame Toto laughed good-naturedly.

'*Ahmak, ahmak* – what an idiot you are,' she said. 'The few liras you're worth to me through your work aren't sufficient to keep you in food and a room. So… what d'you think?'

'You mean you've been keeping me as a charity?'

'Hardly that *hanım*, but at a loss definitely.'

Kamelya cupped her chin in her hands and thought for a moment or two.

'How odd it was to meet you Madame!' she said. 'I'll never forget how kind you have been to me. You even took me in without knowing anything about me …'

'I took you in because many years ago I had a *tendresse* for the man who brought you here. He was always a discerning creature, and in any case when I saw you myself I realised that his judgement was correct. You looked, as he said, a respectable woman in distress.'

'Do you usually act on impulse Madame?'

'Sometimes it is good. In your case *hanım* it could be very profitable, for you have distinct possibilities.'

'For what?'

'Oh, nothing bad I assure you!' Toto laughed at the scandalised expression on Kamelya's transparent face. 'I run a very legitimate business in the shop,' she continued, 'and I should like to see you more actively engaged in it. You're so young, it is folly to hide yourself behind that ugly *çarşaf*!'

Kamelya longed to ask about the Stranger, but she knew how discreet Madame Toto was. Sometimes at night she remembered him and the amused curl to his mouth when he smiled. She wondered if it was his practice to rescue unknown women from the Pera streets and then smiled to herself at the idea. The fact that he apparently intended to remain a stranger intrigued her, for he had appeared well bred and sophisticated. She would have liked to have known him better.

'You are not good at hiding your thoughts, *hanım*!'

'You mean?'

'I mean you are deluding yourself when you give more than a passing thought to the man who brought you here.'

'He does not come often?'

'He has not been here for a long time. He is unlikely to come again.'

Kamelya smiled roguishly.

'But perhaps he will rescue someone else Madame!'

'In that case he will come, for I am the most likely person he will turn to. When a man wishes to be chivalrous to another woman it is generally to his old mistress he turns for help.'

'You were his mistress once?'

'Yes.'

Madame Toto turned away and gathered some silks into her arms. Her expression was guarded and secret and Kamelya realised she would never discuss him further.

The Stranger had rescued her from despair and had set her on an unforeseeable road to her future. For him it had been nothing more than a passing incident, but to Kamelya it was the turning point of her existence.

***

Time passed. The years flew by like days. It was 1922.

The gold liras had long been sold and Kamelya had changed beyond recognition. Under Madame Toto's influence she had learned to dress well, and entirely of her own accord had dyed her luxuriant hair a soft dark red which became her amazingly well. Perhaps the ghost of Fitnet's magnificence still lingered, for when Kamelya thought of successful women she associated them with red hair. She wore discreet perfumes and black as a sort of uniform with a camelia pinned affectedly to the lapel of her suit. Tottering about on the absurdest high heels, she forgot the shabby creature rescued one dark night in Pera. Madame Toto taught her some French and she dealt with fussy customers with assurance and a determination to get her own way. She grew gay and reckless and now and then dined with rich men who paid her compliments and bought her presents. About her name there lingered in the intimate city of Istanbul a quality of legend yet she remained childish and a little naïve, the face of innocence still breaking through the cosmopolitan beauty.

The Stranger had faded from her thoughts although she still cried in the night for Murat.

Having established a certain intimacy with Madame Toto, she felt secure and sheltered in her room at the top of the tall old house. She was seldom lonely.

'How beautiful you are!' Toto would say wistfully.

'How brazen you are!' Toto's mother would counter with a grumble. 'You use paint and powder with abandon and you will come to a bad end!'

'You know that's not true!'

'Nothing's truer my daughter!'

'But how can I come to a bad end when I am here with you nearly every night?'

'It's the nights when you're *not* here, daughter!'

The old woman was a simple peasant who'd come to Istanbul many years before but had never learned to speak the language properly. She had a lined, homely face and always bound her head with a black silk scarf. She was very proud of Madame Toto's success.

'She could have been married a long time ago,' she told Kamelya wistfully, 'but she preferred it like this. Once, when she was young and beautiful like you, she had a lover, but he was a Turkish officer and could not marry her. Perhaps he didn't want to, perhaps he was only playing with her. Who knows with men?' Forgetful of the eagerly listening Kamelya and thinking of other days, she mumbled something in Greek, gravelled and indistinguishable.

'And then?' Kamelya prompted after a while.

'Eh? Eh? What's that you say daughter? Eh?'

'Afterwards – tell me what happened afterwards.'

'It's years ago now. I forget. She could have been married to someone else, too. She'd have had children now if she'd married him – a fine man he was, a captain of a ship. He'd have treated her well.'

'But she wouldn't be rich like she is now if she'd married him would she?'

'Eh, I don't know. Whatever is to be will be. It wasn't Allah's will that I should see my grandchildren... That Toto, she's an obstinate one,' she sighed heavily. 'She could not marry her lover so she preferred to stay like this. He gave her the shop and looked after her until she did not need him any more and then he forgot her.

Now she has no one at all. She's growing old Kamelya *hanım*, she's growing old and has no one but me!'

'But she's only thirty-seven!'

'It is too old. She will never marry now.'

'Perhaps she doesn't care. She has made her life now.'

For a long time now she had known the secret of Toto's wealth. At first she'd supposed it was from the shop, but as she grew closer to the family she discovered Toto used her elegant salon for other purposes.

Couples would sometimes come to the flat. She would hear their animated voices talking to Toto, there would be a chink of glasses and Toto would emerge to say that the salon was occupied for a little while.

'Discretion!' she ordered Kamelya sharply.

'But of course! Why not?'

'My clients are important. It would not be good for scandal to start.'

'I understand, Madame. Why should I talk?'

These people were nothing to her. She never saw them clearly, although she could recognise their voices after a time.

'My Toto is clever,' the old woman would say. 'She knows how to make money and keep it!'

'Stop talking like that,' Kamelya would say severely. 'You're not supposed to know anything about it!'

'Ah, I'm too old to be deceived now daughter!'

***

Toto prospered. After a time she even talked of giving up the shop altogether and Kamelya grew frightened. She had grown used to earning her living and liked living under Toto's patronage.

'You should take a lover,' said Toto one day.

'There is no one I would choose,' said a composed Kamelya and Toto laughed.

'I was not serious,' she said, 'and it's odd that you should think I was. How you have changed! I remember so well when you first came here. You were so prim!'

'That's a long time ago,' said Kamelya, annoyed that Toto should remind her.

'Only three years. You were so respectable I doubted you would stay a week.'

'I am still respectable.'

'Are you?'

Kamelya stamped her foot angrily. 'You know I am! Why tease me?'

Toto's face sobered. 'You do not know yourself,' she said and dropped the subject.

***

One day Toto asked Kamelya to deliver a box of French gloves to the house of a government minister.

'It will be better for you to go,' she explained, 'because it will be necessary to wait while Madame, the minister's wife, makes up her mind.'

'Will she not think it odd if I go?'

'Why? You are likely to be of far more use to her in the matter of choice than the foolish girl who usually delivers our messages.'

'Of course.'

'She is particular and acid-tongued. She will dislike you on sight.'

'You think so?'

'But of course. Look at yourself in the mirror! She is old and fat and afraid.'

Kamelya laughed. She set off in a taxi with the long white box containing the gloves tucked under her arm. She looked chic and beautiful and the day was so fine that she noticed she felt ripe for adventure. Perhaps now she might meet the charming Stranger of long ago. She was shown into the ornate salon where the minister's wife waited for her.

'I am from Madame Toto,' said Kamelya brightly.

'Oh yes,' said the woman tonelessly and indicated a chair at the farthest end of the room. 'Sit down.'

Kamelya handed over the box of gloves and sat down. Her spirits were somewhat dampened by her reception.

She watched as the woman handled the gloves tossing them all aside with petulance until at last she looked at Kamelya and said defiantly: 'Come and help me choose from these. There are so many it is difficult for me.'

Kamelya went to help her but the woman liked nothing at all. In the end she said in despair, 'Perhaps there are some other gloves I could bring for you *hanım*?'

The minister's wife wetted her lips nervously.

'Yes, that would be better,' she said, eyeing Kamelya suspiciously. 'Do you always deliver for Madame Toto?' she asked.

'Oh no.'

'I see.' She touched a pair of dove grey gloves undecidedly. 'It is very difficult,' she said.

The minister came into the salon but stopped when he saw Kamelya.

'It is only the woman from Madame Toto,' said his wife coldly. 'She is just going.'

The minister hesitated.

'You are choosing something?' he asked his wife.

'Some gloves only. They are not the right ones. Madame Toto will send some others.'

The minister continued to eye Kamelya obliquely. He stepped forward and picked up a pair of gloves from the box.

'These are very pretty,' he said diffidently.

'They are the wrong colour,' snapped his wife and a bitter look passed between them.

'These then, perhaps?' suggested Kamelya as a last hope. She could feel the eager eyes of the minister on her and she slightly turned her back.

'Leave them all here and I shall decide later,' piped the minister's wife querulously. 'Tell Madame Toto I shall return them with my maid tomorrow.'

'Very well,' said Kamelya and bit her lip.

The minister could not keep his eyes off her. He was so pathetic it was difficult to resist smiling.

She went out of the room determined that in future someone else should be sent to the minister's wife.

'Silly woman!' said Kamelya to herself as she hailed a passing taxi. 'Fancy being married to that – it's like dressing old Fatma up in silk clothes and calling her a lady!' The thought of Fatma reminded her of Murat and she was depressed for a moment or two. But it was so long ago now, she could shrug the past away with relative ease.

'The minister would be easy,' she thought carelessly. 'How he stared! *How!*'

Chapter 16

1924

KAMELYA WOKE FROM A DREAM about Murat. The dream lingered through bathing and dressing and through her solitary breakfast. When she was at last ready to go out she looked at herself in the glass and decided she would go to Beyazıt. 'There can be no harm after all this time,' she thought defensively.

She fingered the objects on her dressing table absent-mindedly and thought how lonely her life was.

It was a little over a year since she had left Madame Toto's establishment and taken a small, elegant flat which the minister paid for. He was seldom in Istanbul so she spent a good deal of time by herself. She found it boring, but easy living had made her lazy.

Directly responsible for the upheaval in her life was the minister's wife, having discovered that her husband had got into the habit of visiting Madame Toto's on the flimsiest of pretexts. She formed the opinion that Kamelya was the attraction, for she had seen the way the minister looked at her the afternoon she delivered the gloves. A formidable woman, she went immediately to Madame Toto and said that unless Kamelya was dismissed from her employment she would cease to patronise the shop and would see that her acquaintances did likewise.

Toto, impressed by her strategy, had no option but to obey. She could not afford to lose important customers through quixotry on behalf of Kamelya.

'You will be all right now,' she said when she told Kamelya. 'You will find something else easily enough.'

'The minister has suggested I take a flat,' said Kamelya.

'Well, he didn't lose much time!'

'No.'

'You agree?'

'Why not? He's rich.'

'You will be lonely. You will never be able to be seen in public together. There may be scandal.'

'It doesn't matter.'

'But he is so old!'

'He will pay better.'

'You astonish me Kamelya!'

But she had really been sorry to say goodbye. There had been a homeliness about her life with Toto and her mother she knew she would miss. As the mistress of the minister she was no longer so free.

Fingering the things on her dressing table she called to Rana, the maid Toto had found for her, to telephone and break a luncheon appointment she had.

'Say anything you like,' she added.

She peered earnestly at herself in the mirror, looking for traces of the old Kamelya in the charming face that stared back at her. Would Murat recognise her without a veil? Would it be possible after so long? The sun fell across the glass while she stared at herself, at the rouged face, the short, curling red hair, the delicately pencilled eyebrows above the searching dark eyes. She could find nothing of the old Kamelya. 'Who am I?' she thought wildly. The poised stranger in the mirror stared back at her with frenzied eyes.

'That'll be all right Madame,' said Rana in her best voice, coming away from the telephone. 'Will you telephone when you are free?'

Kamelya turned away from the mirror.

'Thank you, Rana,' she said and pulled on her gloves. They had been bought in Paris and were the last word in elegance. What had they to do with her?

'You look lovely Madame,' said Rana with a sigh. 'What shall I say if anyone rings you?'

'I shall be back at four,' said Kamelya and snapped closed the wrist buttons. She hesitated. 'If the minister rings, tell him I've gone to visit Madame Toto.'

The day was so fine when she descended into the street, the air so crisp, she was exhilarated. She took a tram to Beyazıt, for today she was going in search of herself and a tram was necessary. Alighting at Beyazıt Square she looked about her with pleasure – what had ever given her the impression this was a dowdy place? It was quite perfect, even the old women in their black dresses were just right in this setting.

She went to walk in the gardens of the mosque but soon turned back to the street leading to the *konak*. She began to walk slower, her heart beating nervously. She was being drawn back to the past, to a time around five years ago when she was here, fresh from the mountains, in a shabby dress and with a gun in her pocket. There was a tapping in her ears, someone tapping on a window. The voice of a child entreated her to come into the house and eat, the gruff voice of the black servant stilled the echo of the tapping. It was all so clear it might have been yesterday. It seemed she had forgotten nothing and that her memories had only been sleeping. Her pace faltered, and she wore the blank unseeing expression of a sleepwalker.

'I shouldn't have come back,' she thought in panic.

There was nothing here for her but remembered sorrow. The persistent clicking of her high heels disturbed her. Why had she come?

Feeling faint and foolish she turned into the narrow street but when she looked up at the house all hope died away. What had happened? Had she come to the wrong place after all? The *konak* was empty. It looked as if it had been empty for a long time. The *kafes* swung loosely, the blind eyes of the windows were mostly glassless, and a rusty stove pipe hung drunkenly from an upper floor.

With blanched face she looked at the derelict house. Did the ghost of the general's widow watch her as once before?

What had happened to make this rich, assured family abandon their home in such fashion? And where was Murat?

The street was still, as still as it had been the first time she ever saw it. She looked back to the forsaken house and shivered, deciding that it would be best to ask at the local grocer's for news. Shopkeepers were always the best informants.

But the grocer, a saintly looking man with a white beard, more fitted one would have thought to the religious life than to sustaining the stomachs of the carnal, knew very little. He glanced at her without much interest as she entered his shop. Long ago she had bought fresh bread and a handful of *helva* from him but he would not recognise her now. Looking at him, she felt nostalgic.

She asked if he could tell her anything about the general's family who had lived in the house down the road, the house which was now shut up.

The grocer peered at her short sightedly.

'Old Saadet *hanım* died,' he said after awhile, 'and the servants were distributed among her children. They didn't want the house any more so they just let it go.'

'There was a child there,' said Kamelya. 'Was he also sent to her children do you know?'

'I remember the child well,' said the old man, 'but I don't think he was sent to the children. I'd have heard it I'm sure but I can't remember.'

'Please try. Try to remember what happened to him, please!' She leaned towards him, the fragrance of her expensive perfume rising between them so that he blinked and looked puzzled.

'The woman would know maybe.' He went to the head of the basement stairs and called down to his wife, asking her what she knew of the child Saadet *hanım* had rescued. The woman came up to the shop, a wizened little creature with a black shawl over her shoulders and a *çarşaf* binding her broad forehead.

She gave Kamelya a sharp bitter look and said, 'I think he went off with Kasım Ağa.' She stared at Kamelya. 'Why do you want to know?' she asked.

'I'm interested in the child. Please tell me who was Kasım Ağa – was he the big black servant?'

'Yes. He wanted to go to Mecca to spend his last days looking after Muhammad's grave. He wouldn't go to the old lady's children. He came here to work for the *padişah* when he was young and then the general took him on. He didn't want to have anything to do with the Young Turks.'

She looked at Kamelya again. It was a bitter look for she did not like to see a Turkish woman dressed like a foreigner, and with a painted face and no *çarşaf*.

'He'd have gone with Major Ahmet,' said the grocer.

The old woman snorted. 'Major Ahmet had nowhere to take him.'

'Did Murat – I mean did the child go with him to Mecca?' Kamelya asked weakly. If he was there or in Medina he was lost forever.

'I don't know,' said the woman. 'It's a few years ago now and I forget easily these days.'

'Doesn't anything at all come back to you?' Kamelya asked humbly.

The old woman shook her head. 'I can't remember,' she said irritably. 'You'd best go and see one of the children. There's Major

Ahmet in the military school – he'd know perhaps. There was a time when they all said the child was going there.'

'And you don't know whether it happened or not?'

'I couldn't say. There were some who said a military school was too much for a charity boy. He was only a child off the streets you know. He couldn't ever be anybody.'

'I see.' Kamelya felt her heart hammering nervously. 'So you think he may have gone to Mecca or Medina?' she said in despair.

'*I* don't know,' said the woman sharply. 'I can't remember everything!'

'I remember him well,' said the shopkeeper unexpectedly. 'He used to buy sweets here.'

'I see.'

Kamelya turned to leave.

'You'd better go and ask the *hoca* in the mosque,' said the woman, relenting a little. 'He'd know maybe.'

'Oh, thank you. That's a good idea. I will.'

She found the *hoca* sitting in the sunlight in a corner of the mosque gardens, but he seemed to know even less than the grocer and his wife.

'Go and see the nightwatchman at the police station,' he advised and turned his back on her.

At the station Bekçi Baba remembered hearing the boy had been put into a school.

'The military school?' Kamelya asked eagerly. The old man looked shocked.

'He was a charity boy,' he said severely. 'They wouldn't take a charity boy in the military school *hanım*!'

'Then which school could it have been?'

'I can't remember *hanım*. It's a long time ago. Why should I remember?'

'But this is an unusual case surely,' said Kamelya wearily. 'Please try to help me.'

The watchman scratched his head.

'You'd better go and see Major Ahmet,' he suggested at last. 'After the old *hanım* died, he'd have arranged everything.'

Kamelya went out into the street again. There was nothing to do but return to Beyazıt.

As she walked along she looked into the face of every child she met searching for the face of Murat.

It rankled that memories were so long. Even the grooming he must have received from Saadet *hanım* had not been enough to wipe away the unsavoury fact that he was a child rescued from the streets. A charity child they had all called him. She had left him to bear *that* alone.

'It's not much better than being called the son of a prostitute,' she reflected bitterly.

She would search Istanbul until she found him again. She would not rest until she knew he was safe. But what would she do then? Would she step forward and claim him after all these years? Would she take him to the quiet flat in Pera? Maybe he was uncouth now, no longer the charming child of five years ago. Could she bear his adolescent exuberance, his knowing eyes watching her, aware of everything she did? She took a taxi from Beyazıt. She was no longer in the mood to travel in a noisy, clattering tram. A sense of disaster hung over her. She should never have come at all when she had not had the courage to claim him before.

Faces trooped through her mind's eye. The man from Tırnava who had been a little mad – his eyes slid past her, surprised. He would not recognise her now. The grey face of Cemal *bey* floated a little outside remembrance. Kara Kurt looked at her with desire while Gül the jealous wraith peered over his broad shoulder. Last of all came Murat with his lost eyes looking past her. The car was full of their uneasy ghosts.

She stared through the window at the streets full of sunshine and hurrying people. There was no need for her to hurry. Nothing waited for her. It wouldn't really matter if she never went home.

'You're nothing,' she said bitterly. 'You never were. You only thought you were.'

The taxi drew up outside her flat.

Chapter 17

KAMELYA WALKED THROUGH the flag decorated streets of Pera on a *bayram* day.

The pavements were crowded and there was the sound of a band playing in the distance. She looked an elegant figure clad in black, with her red hair gleaming in the autumn sun where it had escaped from her hat. A Borzoi trotted docilely at her heels. He'd been a present from the minister and was so well bred Kamelya called him Le Roi.

As the sound of the band grew nearer she stood still and Le Roi squatted in a bored fashion beside her. Several people jostled his rump and he looked offended and stood up again. He started to bark and Kamelya said impatiently, 'Stop it!'

The band came into sight and Kamelya craned her neck with the rest of the sightseers.

It was the military band from Kuleli and the entire school of cadets marched behind it. Their officers rode proudly on high-stepping horses and the crowd began to cheer. Kamelya moved forward to the edge of the pavement and scanned as many passing faces as she could. She had never given up the quest for Murat. Crossing to the Asiatic side on Saturday afternoons she'd even gone to the school's local boat station at Çengelköy in search of him. Instinct told her he must be there for Saadet *hanım*'s children would never have thrown him on to the streets. It would be against tradition and the old grocer and the watchman had both said there was talk of Saadet *hanım* wished him schooled for the army.

The marching boys looked hopelessly alike in their dark blue uniforms, their brown faces set in expressions of extreme self-consciousness. When Kamelya at last saw Murat she didn't recognise him immediately. It was instinct that made her look again at the tall boy – and then she felt her heart begin to pound. He passed so quickly she did not know what to do and she jerked Le Roi's lead, pushing her way through the watching crowds.

She had an appointment with her hairdresser but this she forgot in her new excitement.

She teetered along on her high heels all the way through Pera, trying to keep up with the marching lines, trying to keep the back of Murat's cropped head in view. Down the long hill to Galata she plodded, her feet hurting her with every step, tired with emotion and dragging Le Roi who objected to so much speed.

'Come *along*!' she said impatiently and shortened the lead. At Galata Bridge the lines of marching boys broke up and some of them rushed to buy chocolate or *simit* to eat on their journey up the Bosphorus. Kamelya edged nearer to Murat.

She was so filled with emotion she wanted to touch him or feel his rough sleeve under her hand. She looked at him fondly as a boy called his name and he turned his head in a quick, bird-like gesture.

'Murat!' called the boy. 'Save a seat for me will you?' She saw Murat smile in the direction of the boy who had called him – the smile of the boy in the *konak*! Kamelya caught her breath in delight. How good looking he was! She could not see that the cast of his features was her own. The sudden turn of the head – that was her too – the smile that flashed for an instant animating his dark eyes. He was all Kamelya, but she could not see.

She watched as an officer marshalled them on to the boat. She wondered what Murat did for pocket money and fought a crazy impulse to get closer to him so that she could slip some coins, even a note, into his pocket.

She did not know what to do to establish contact with him, and all the way back to Pera and her belated hair appointment plans hatched in her fertile mind. There must be *some* way of getting money to him, she thought.

For several Saturdays afterwards she haunted Galata Bridge, once even taking the ferry back to Çengelköy. Here she was lucky for he came down to the boat station in the first batch of students. She watched them as they hung around, trying to make herself inconspicuous in the little knot of adults who were also waiting.

Smoke on the wind, gulls on the wing, *çay* from the Black Sea coast. Once aboard, it was easy to keep close to Murat and at Galata she stayed behind him as the crowd surged to disembark. There was money in her glove. She thought it would be easy to rid herself of it unnoticed for there were so many people milling about. Everyone hit against one another and as she thrust the note into Murat's pocket he didn't even turn his head. Breathless with relief that at last she had succeeded, Kamelya moved away from him and as the boat docked she alighted quickly, disappearing into the crowds.

She was so pleased with her success that she decided she would repeat the operation on another occasion.

***

Murat, separating from his comrades on the bridge, decided he would start his afternoon by going to a *muhallebi* shop to eat his way through at least half the pocket money Major Ahmet had given him for the weekend. He was always hungry and sweet, milky puddings were a particular favourite. What bliss to eat his way through most of this day of freedom!

When he discovered the fifty-lira note Kamelya had put into his pocket he was already sitting down, waiting to be served. He looked at it in surprise before his ruddy colour faded and he hurriedly pushed the note back into his pocket. He had no idea how it came to be there.

Eating the *muhallebi*, he thought about it with panic. What could he do with so much money? He was afraid to report it to the school authorities lest they think he had stolen it. Whichever way he looked at it his day was ruined! He returned to Kuleli on an early boat having spent little of his pocket money.

On the boat he took the precaution of stuffing the note down his jacket sleeve where part of the lining was torn. He was still uncertain what he was going to do but he hadn't the heart to throw such a large sum of money away. As the ferry neared Çengelköy he grew sticky with perspiration, imagining his dilemma if his deception was discovered. Students were forbidden to carry unauthorised money. He was not sure what the punishment might be, but he thought it would be severe.

Turning in through Kuleli's gates he was as nervous as if he had actually been caught stealing and the note seemed to be making an awful lot of noise in his sleeve.

It was unfortunate for him that on the very same day one of the students had reported the loss of five liras. The loss had come to light after the first batch of students had left the school, so when Murat returned he was unaware of what was in store for him.

His sergeant stopped him as he walked across the wide hall.

'Report to your captain immediately,' said the sergeant and Murat blanched.

'What's wrong?' he asked.

'You'll soon find out,' replied the sergeant and looked mysterious.

Murat, feeling weak at the knees, turned towards the captain's office.

The captain, who had already questioned the students who had returned on earlier boats, looked at Murat with weary loathing. He was already sick of the whole thing and it was his private opinion that whoever had stolen the money had already spent it in the city.

He came straight to the point and told Murat what had happened.

'Do you know anything?' the captain asked.

'No, sir,' said Murat.

His face was so white however that the captain decided he was keeping something back, so he ordered the sergeant to search him.

The fifty-lira note was discovered almost at once for the sergeant was an experienced man and knew all the places to look. He withdrew the note carefully and laid it on the captain's desk.

'There you are sir,' he said cheerfully.

The captain stared at the money with annoyance, for it now appeared he had two problems on his hands. Five liras was bad enough but *fifty* was as much as he got in a month.

'Where did you get this money?'

Murat tried to explain but the longer he talked the thinner his story sounded. Even he found it difficult to believe.

'Tell me the truth, damn you!' shouted the captain. He was in need of his dinner and in no mood to listen to fabrications.

He looked at Murat with dislike.

'Tell me the truth,' he repeated, 'or I'll break your wooden head!'

'It is the truth, sir!'

Murat was almost in tears at such indignity.

'Do you know anybody in Istanbul who would be likely to give you this money?'

'No, sir.'

The captain looked at him keenly.

'Your father and mother are dead aren't they?'

'Yes, sir.'

'Did Major Ahmet give you this money?'

'No, sir.'

'Does he give you pocket money?'

'Every two weeks, sir.'

'But never as much as fifty liras?'

'Oh no, sir!'

'Tell me how you got this money!' He pushed the note on his desk with the tip of a finger and Murat watched him desperately.

'I don't know sir. It was just in my pocket. It's the truth sir.'

'Do you know any man who could have given it to you?'

Murat blushed deeply. 'No, sir.'

'Or a woman?'

Murat became even redder. 'No, sir,' he said, and hung his head in shame.

The captain grew exasperated, tapping his pencil angrily.

'Tell me something definite damn you!' he said. 'A boy here lost money today and now you're discovered with this large amount in your possession and with no explanation as to how you came by it.' He shot Murat a sour glance. 'Were you going to report it to me?' he asked.

'Y – yes, sir.'

'You damned little liar! If you were going to report it why did you hide it?'

Murat looked down at his feet.

'Answer me!'

'I'm sorry sir.'

'Sorry! Why did you hide it?'

'I – I was afraid to report it sir. I don't know where it came from – I...'

'Stand to attention when you talk to me. Hold your head up and your hands by your side!'

Murat straightened himself.

'What do you do when you go to Istanbul?'

'Nothing sir. I don't go often.'

'And you know no man there?'

'No sir.'

The captain jumped to his feet and roared for the sergeant to come in and bring the duty book with him.

'Dishonest fool!' he sneered at Murat.

The sergeant brought the book and the captain thumbed through it angrily, but he could find no faults reported against Murat so he decided to pass the whole affair over to Major Ahmet.

'And you'd better tell him the truth,' he warned threateningly, 'or you'll find yourself in the streets where you belong!'

Murat bit his lip angrily. Wherever he went, however hard he tried, someone always reminded him that he was a nobody.

'If the commanding officer hears about this you'll be in trouble my lad!'

But Major Ahmet fared little better than the captain. Murat repeated the same story over and over again.

'You're like a damned parrot!' flared Major Ahmet, who was responsible for him now that Saadet *hanım* was dead. 'Can't you say anything else?'

'I'm telling the truth, sir,' muttered Murat sulkily.

He was more at ease with Major Ahmet.

'Well, I don't know what the hell to do with you,' said the major and thrust his hands into his pockets.

He was fond of Murat and proud of him too. Nothing had ever happened to spoil his record at the military school.

'But why didn't you report it?' he asked exasperatedly.

'I was afraid to, sir.'

'Afraid! Why were you afraid if you didn't steal it?' A memory stirred of Saadet *hanım* reporting that Murat once stole chickens from a mosque garden.

'Why didn't you come to me?' he asked.

'You weren't here sir. At least you may have been but I didn't know and the sergeant took me to the captain's room straight away because of the missing five liras. I know nothing of the five liras' he said earnestly.

'They are not my affair,' snapped Major Ahmet. He looked at Murat and the boy stared back at him unafraid. He worshipped Major Ahmet and wished to be exactly like him one day.

'I didn't steal the money sir.'

'I suppose you're aware you can be dismissed from the school for this Murat?'

Murat blanched.

'I did nothing wrong, sir.'

'You broke the rules by carrying unauthorised money and you didn't report that you had it. The commanding officer would take a very serious view of it.'

'Will it be reported, sir?'

The major ignored his question.

'You may go back to your captain,' he said, 'and don't let me hear any more bad reports about you!'

'No sir. Thank you, sir.'

'You needn't thank me my boy. You don't know what's in store for you yet!'

Murat paled again. 'You wouldn't let them discharge me would you sir?' Such faith was both touching and flattering and the major patted his shoulder.

'The trouble with you is you're too damned secretive,' he said. 'Now get out of here!'

The matter was dropped discreetly. The five liras was never discovered but neither did anybody report the loss of fifty.

Murat was reprimanded by his captain and sentenced to fifteen days in the school prison, which battered his pride and made him an object of some interest to his companions. He grew ice cold with apprehension when he thought of being discharged and made a resolution that if ever he went to the city again he would not separate from his friends.

***

Kamelya meanwhile sat in her warm flat and purred with contentment because her child had enough pocket money to last him quite a time.

The major could not make head or tail of it, but judged Murat compassionately as young and foolish. But there were doubts in his mind. 'I suppose he *did* tell me the truth?'

He gazed into space remembering Saadet *hanım* and her concern for the boy. Even when she was dying she had begged Ahmet to look after him.

'He may come of bad stock,' she had said. 'Maybe he'll need watching Ahmet. But we must do what we can for him now that he is our concern.'

'Pity we know nothing at all about him,' Ahmet thought with brief annoyance. 'Maybe fifteen days confinement'll knock some sense into him.'

Chapter 18

'I HAVEN'T FELT so gay for years,' said Toto and peered earnestly at herself in the long mirror.

'Well, it's a gay occasion,' said Kamelya staring at her with admiration. 'I think it was very daring of you to think of such a thing at all! It'll be the talk of Istanbul for days!'

'For longer than that I hope!' said Toto grimly. 'I haven't spent all this money for a few days gossip!'

'Come on Toto, you know you can afford it! Business is good.'

'Business must be better. Tonight's reception might be one way of achieving that.'

'Fancy the shop being ten years old today!' said Kamelya animatedly. 'Isn't it thrilling when you look back Toto and see what you've done with your life in ten years?'

Toto looked away from the glass.

'In a way it makes me feel sad,' she said. 'That was such a happy time in my life and somehow or other now that I've got most of the things I wanted I'm not as happy as I thought I would be.' Her mouth twisted wryly. 'Besides being ten years older,' she added.

'Ah, you were pretty then,' said her mother with a sigh.

She sat hunched up in a chair with a black shawl thrown round her spare shoulders. 'You could have been anything you liked then,' she said fiercely, 'but you'd set your mind on the shop and he encouraged you. You wouldn't listen to anyone else in those days!'

'I don't know where we'd have been today *mana* if he hadn't encouraged me!'

'You'd have been married well my daughter and I'd have had my grandchildren around me instead of sitting here lonely all day long!'

'Don't talk like that,' said Toto irritably. 'You know I couldn't have married!'

Dark Journey

Kamelya trailed her fingers along the back of the settee where she was sitting and listened to their soft complaining voices speaking in Turkish because she was present, their tongues slurring the vowels in an unfamiliar rhythm.

'Perhaps she wouldn't have been as happy,' she suggested and smiled at the cross old woman.

'Happy!' said the old woman. 'She didn't know what she wanted, that was the trouble *hanım!*'

'Nonsense!' insisted Toto passionately, emotion making her young again. 'But I couldn't have what I wanted so I preferred to do this. What would I have gained if I'd married that old sea captain you had in mind?' Her expressive eyes swept the elegant room. 'I'd never have known this,' she said angrily, 'and you wouldn't have had so much comfort either *mana!*'

The old woman eyed her shrewdly.

'And you think he'll be at your fine party tonight?' she asked bitterly. 'Do you think he's likely to come after all these years?'

'Why not? If he's free he'll come. He started the shop after all – if he hadn't put money in, I'd never have had it.'

'Who was he?' Kamelya asked, affected by the tension in the room, feeling old hostilities creeping all about her. 'Was he an old lover, Toto?'

'Don't you remember? He brought you here to me that first night when you had nowhere else to go. He was always doing odd things like that – it was the same spirit which made him finance the shop for me. He couldn't bear not to be generous in return for all he had himself. He came from a very rich family. He had never known trouble or poverty but they always affected him.'

'You still think about him!' accused her mother. 'He ruined you!'

'Oh, be quiet! What do you know about it?'

She fluffed powder across her cheeks recklessly. 'He was the handsomest man I ever met,' she said.

'I wish I could remember him,' said Kamelya. 'It seems such a long time ago. I was too frightened to look at him properly.'

She broke off, trying to remember what she knew of him. Toto's mother had talked a lot at one time. He was an army officer and wouldn't marry Toto, or couldn't. Which was it now? He would be about Toto's age.

'You see I never thought I'd meet him again,' she said, continuing her thoughts aloud.

'He won't come,' said the old woman positively.

'You can't know,' said Toto and patted her shining silver hair. 'He'll come if he can.'

She turned to Kamelya.

'We must go,' she said. 'The taxi has been waiting long enough.'

'Extravagance!' grumbled the old woman.

Kamelya leaned across and took her hand.

'You should be proud,' she said. 'Toto has achieved so much! Why will you not come with us tonight and see how gay she is with all the famous people of Istanbul?'

'I am too old child. I tire easily and I would never understand what they were all saying.' She patted Kamelya's hand wistfully. 'I remember you when you came here,' she said, 'and perhaps you're right too about my Toto. She's a lady of fashion now, she can even speak French!'

For the first time she looked at the sleek, elegant, Grecian figure of her daughter.

'Run along and enjoy yourselves!' she grumbled and wrapped the shawl closer about her shoulders. 'I'm cold,' she said. 'You'll catch your death in those silk things you're wearing.'

They laughed at her and Toto kissed her cheek.

'Be sure to wait up for me,' she said.

***

The reception was held at the Tokatlian Hotel in Pera. Toto had booked a room and, for what was probably the first time in the history of the old city, was giving a business party. Kamelya was full of admiration for her daring especially as the Republic and emancipation were still so new.

'There'll be only a few people there,' Toto said, 'mostly importers who sell me things and a few rich Turkish women who are my clients.'

'The New Turkish Woman,' said Kamelya, and smiled.

'The New Turkish Woman is very important,' said Toto. 'She will lead all those who are slower to embrace their freedom. There will be one or two foreign women, too, with their husbands. You know, they say that in Europe these kinds of receptions are becoming quite common.'

'Fancy!' said Kamelya.

She looked at Toto fondly.

'You have wonderful business instincts,' she said.

'All the Greeks have. We are not afraid of change, perhaps that is the reason.' She sighed a little. 'But I think I'd have let them all go if I could have had other things.'

In the private room of the hotel, exotically embellished in its post-war restoration, she received her guests. Kamelya stood beside her and was presented to each person in turn but she was very bored, for the men were mostly old and fat and obviously more interested in selling things to Toto than looking at Kamelya with anything more than fleeting interest. She came to life when Toto suddenly said urgently, 'He has come! I knew he would not disappoint me!'

Kamelya started to say something then stopped as the Stranger made his way over to them. She watched as he bowed over Toto's hand and then saw his eyes brighten with interest as he straightened up and looked in her direction.

'You don't remember Kamelya *hanim*?' Toto asked, after she had greeted him.

He looked puzzled.

'No,' he said.

'But I think I would have remembered you,' said Kamelya and smiled at him. 'But then you have not changed as much as I!'

He continued to look puzzled.

'You brought her to my house some years ago,' explained Toto with an indulgent smile. 'You met her in Pera when she was in need of help. Really Ahmet, do you not remember?'

He still looked blank.

'You are not complimentary!' gurgled Toto with delight in her voice. 'Surely you must recollect the occasion!'

'I was running away,' said Kamelya. 'I bumped into you in the dark and you took me to a café and we drank coffee there.'

She smiled brilliantly and he blinked and looked away. After a time he said slowly, 'But you are not that person *hanim*!'

'Yes.'

A waiter came up to them with a tray of sherry and Kamelya felt better with a drink in her hand.

'What is this?' asked the Stranger suspiciously.

'It is sherry,' said Toto. 'It is very fashionable in Paris.'

He smiled at her warmly.

'We poor Turks are too uncouth to properly appreciate your grand party,' he said. 'Have you forgotten Toto that we are *rakı* drinkers?'

'But it would have been so out of place here Ahmet! All these foreigners would have viewed it with as much distrust as you do our sherry!'

He laughed good humouredly.

'Your health!' he said jovially and looked at Kamelya. Toto did not see the look for she was watching her guests circulating.

'I must leave you for a few moments,' she said. 'There is someone I must speak to over there. He is very important and can bring me much business if I am nice to him!'

She hurried across the room and they saw her smiling up at a tall, swarthy man.

'She has such a wonderful instinct for business,' sighed Kamelya, feeling artificial. Small talk was not her strength.

She felt the Stranger's amused eyes on her low-cut dress and the nestling shadows within.

'I would not have known you,' he said. 'You are no longer the same person.'

'Times change,' said Kamelya idly and sipped her sherry, 'and besides it's a good many years since we last met.'

'I remember you wore a *çarşaf.*'

'Yes.'

'And your hair was dark. Why did you change it?'

Her eyes took on a faraway expression.

'Red hair is a symbol of success,' she said and laughed at his look of enquiry. 'I once knew a woman with red hair. She was a marriage broker and very successful. When I was very young I used to envy her. Perhaps it is because of her that my hair is red today.' She touched the shining curls admiringly.

'You're not by any chance a marriage broker yourself, *hanım*?'

She laughed.

'No.'

'You were so young and frightened that night I met you. It's astonishing! But now I remember it quite clearly. I think red hair suits you,' he added irrelevantly.

'Yes. I have another personality with it,' her face momentarily taking on a pinched, withdrawn look. She remembered Fitnet and the drunken man who had burst into her room and the couples making love above her. 'I'm glad I changed,' she said fiercely and drank some more sherry.

'You are the New Woman of Turkey?'

They both laughed at the idea. Then the Stranger said urgently, 'We have never really been introduced. How like Toto that is, to take for granted that because we have spoken we must know all about one another!'

'You know my name is Kamelya. Is that not enough?'

'I am Major Ahmet of Kuleli. At your service!'

He bowed exaggeratedly and so did not see her eyes dilate as she stared down at his sleek black head.

'Of Kuleli?' she asked, recovering herself so that he would not see anything was the matter. 'That's the military school along the Bosphor is it not, the long white building?'

'Yes.'

She suddenly felt ice cold and the skin prickled uncomfortably along the nape of her neck.

'Is anything wrong *hanım*?'

'Oh no. No, no!'

She felt her mouth stretching in a travesty of a smile. Perhaps it was stupid to be disturbed – there must be more than one Major Ahmet in Kuleli. The name was not uncommon. But could it be possible that this was the son of Saadet *hanım*?

'There is nothing wrong. I am all right,' she said rapidly and twirled the glass in her hands.

'You must have many students,' she remarked nervously and looked away from him down the long room to where Toto was the centre of an animated little group.

She heard his cheerful, unaware voice.

'Thousands,' he said, 'of all shapes and sizes.'

'Of course there would be. It is such a big place.'

She ran the fine tip of her tongue across her lips.

'Are – are there many officers of your name there Major?' He looked uncomprehending.

'My name?'

'Yes. The name "Ahmet" I mean.'

She was so nervous she thought she would suffocate.

'Oh, I see!' he laughed at her earnest face. 'Well I'm the only one in my rank,' he said as though he were speaking to a child. 'But there are older officers of similar name. Why?'

'No reason,' said Kamelya, 'no reason,' and smiled her brilliant smile. 'I only asked,' she said and stared at him over the rim of her empty glass. 'Perhaps I was just making conversation,' she added.

'It would be more interesting to talk about you,' he ventured boldly. 'I know nothing of what happened to you after that night.'

'You never came back to find out,' she said reproachfully and spread her hands in a gesture of excitement. 'I worked in Toto's shop,' she explained proudly.

'Ah, the famous shop! Of course! And it is ten years old today and that is the reason we are here. How long ago it seems!'

'It is better than ever,' she assured him, excitement making her large eyes shine. 'Only the famous and the very rich patronise her now and when foreigners come here they are always recommended to Madame Toto's salon. And her prices!' she raised her hands in mock horror.

'You are still with her?'

All at once she looked withdrawn, as though he had touched upon a secret.

'No,' she said primly, looking away.

It was plain she did not wish to discuss the subject any more and he looked at her with interest. He thought he knew the reason for her silence.

Toto rejoined them.

'It is all going very well,' she assured them in a happy whisper. 'You cannot believe how well Ahmet! It was money well spent after all.'

She bubbled into laughter. 'I was so afraid I was being extravagant,' she confided. 'It was so new to do such a thing here!'

'I knew you would carry it off,' said Kamelya merrily. 'We watched you when you were talking to all those people. You looked so sure of yourself!'

'They are old friends,' said Toto carelessly. 'But of course they are always useful to me!'

She turned to look at Ahmet.

'And do you think I did the right thing after all?' she asked him.

'By starting the shop? But of course I do! You are magnificent. In no other way could you have achieved so much fame!'

He smiled at her teasingly.

'Your energy makes me envious,' he said.

Kamelya watched them as they tossed their meaningless words to and fro. She had never seen Toto so happy and guessed that the youthful tie which had bound her to the happy-go-lucky Ahmet was as strong as ever. She stole a sideways glance at his strong, handsome face and remembered that this man knew Murat. If she wished she could find out whatever she liked from him, but she knew with certainty that she would never have the courage to admit her identity. It would be wiser never to see him again.

'More sherry?' said Toto's gay voice. 'Ahmet you must drink one more glass to toast my success!'

'To continued success!' he toasted, tossing off the sherry in one gulp. 'I betray my savage ways,' he said as he replaced the empty glass on the tray. 'It must be obvious to these sophisticated foreigners that I am a barbarous fellow who cannot do justice to their favourite drink!'

Toto patted his sleeve possessively.

'It does not matter,' she said. 'You have added distinction to the evening.'

She eyed him lovingly.

'You are better looking than ever,' she said.

'Ah, you flatter me Toto! I am almost middle-aged and soon I shall have a paunch and all the young girls will run away from me. Already I hear my students refer to me as "the old man" whereas a year or two ago they were jealous of my looks!' He smiled mockingly, and his eyes drifted off to rest on Kamelya.

'You see?' he said, turning back to Toto.

'I see you are conceited,' she said severely, her eyes narrowed by jealousy.

Later on, just before her reception broke up, she whispered to Kamelya privately, 'You must not take him too seriously my dear Kamelya.'

'I won't.'

'He can be very fascinating when he likes, you know, but he tires fatally easily I assure you!'

Kamelya laughed merrily.

'*I* don't want him,' she said.

She did not think it necessary to add that on the morrow she would be dining with him.

Chapter 19

THE FRIENDSHIP BETWEEN Kamelya and Ahmet grew rapidly. It wasn't long before she began inviting him occasionally to her flat for dinner.

'Playing with *ateş* – fire!' Rana would mutter as she was given some elaborate menu to prepare.

'Don't be silly Rana!'

'What'll happen if His Excellency comes here one night when you're least expecting it?'

'You know he always tells me when he is coming!'

'Maybe one day he wont!' Rana sniffed her disapproval and stamped off to the kitchen, leaving a disgruntled Kamelya to reflect on her words.

'She's nothing but a silly old woman,' she would whisper to Le Roi, patting his head gently while he stared up at her with devotion. 'You and I know how to manage the minister, don't we?'

***

One night Ahmet took her to dine at the Pera Palas Hotel. Their table was in a corner, sufficiently remote from the rest of the diners to give them an illusion of privacy.

'You grow more beautiful every time I see you,' Ahmet said as he ordered drinks for them.

She smiled mistily. She was so much in love with him she thought she could not help but glow with beauty.

'It's a long time since we dined out,' she said and looked about her at the other diners. They looked much less interesting to her than herself and Ahmet.

'It isn't good to be seen together too often,' said Ahmet humorously and raised an eyebrow at her. 'You stand out too much,' he explained to her wide-eyed look of enquiry. 'We'd soon be the talk of the town!'

'I suppose it is astonishing really that we've escaped attention for so long.'

A waiter brought soup and Kamelya reached out to take a roll from the bread basket.

'I am not hungry,' she said with happy directness. 'I shall merely be going through the motions of eating!'

'I hate to disappoint your romantic notions,' he said, 'but I am extremely hungry, and if you dined off the food we are given in Mess you would appreciate dinner in a place like this!'

'Perhaps.' She looked at him with eyes brilliant with love and crumbled her roll thoughtlessly.

'And, I ought to add, with a companion like you,' he said, answering the message of her eyes with tenderness curving his passionate mouth. 'You must not look at me like that,' he said.

'It is quite respectable.'

'It gives me anything but respectable thoughts.'

She closed her lips primly.

'We are in public,' she said.

He remarked thoughtfully, 'I know so little about you.'

'You know enough. I am really nothing more than I appear to be.'

'Toto knows you better than I do.'

'No. She only knows what she sees on the surface. There is nothing more to know anyway.'

'There must be. *I* know for instance that you were once married and that you came to Istanbul when you were very young.'

'Isn't that enough?' she interrupted with the colour high in her cheeks like a flag. 'I haven't asked anything about you.'

'I have already told you everything of importance.'

'Let us say then that I have told you the same. *Must* we know all the little things too?'

'It would help. They're just as responsible for shaping you.'

She shrugged, pettishly anxious to keep away from the subject of herself. 'I don't think so. Only the big events stand out in my mind and I think *they're* the things that shaped me.'

'Why won't you ever come closer?'

'I can't.'

'Is it because you don't want to?'

'Oh, Ahmet! Must we talk about these things now? You look so serious. How you have changed! There was a time when you never concerned yourself with such things.' She smiled at him, trying to coax him back to lightness. 'They're past,' she said urgently. 'They're nothing to do with *us*.'

'I'm not so sure,' he said with a rough edge to his voice. The truth was, he thought, he was jealous of her. He knew so little about her – but her flat, her maid and her pedigree dog had not come from hard work.

He'd heard rumours that a certain minister supported her and that it was the same minister's wife who'd been responsible for having her discharged from Toto's employment.

He eyed her flowing white dress, the emerald glowing wickedly on her left hand, and the gleam of precious stones in her ears.

'You look at me as if you had never seen me before.'

'I was admiring your jewels,' he said and saw her bite her lip as though his words had touched an exposed nerve.

'I'm sorry,' he said penitently. He ached to possess her for himself alone. The thought that he shared her with someone else drove him to a frenzy.

'How fierce you look!' said Kamelya, mocking him.

'You do not know your own power,' he said.

'Oh, come on, let us enjoy ourselves Ahmet! I do not care for you at all in this mood!'

She swayed in her seat to the rhythm of a Balkan tango. 'Isn't the music lovely?' she said. She turned a radiant face to the rest of the decorous room. Her eyes locked with Toto's.

'Toto's here!' she whispered, mesmerised.

'There is no need to look so stricken! Has she not the same right as us to dine here?'

'But she looks so different – so cross somehow.'

'You are imagining things and I will not gratify you by turning to look at her.'

He attacked his fish with appetite. 'She is probably as embarrassed at being caught out as you are.'

'No, no, I don't think so. She is dining with a fat old man. He must be a business acquaintance and this is a business dinner they are having.'

He laughed at her curiosity.

'Well, perhaps she might even think ours was a business meeting too!' he suggested.

Toto was astonished to see them. It had never occurred to her that they might be meeting without her knowledge, though she had several times commented to her mother upon Kamelya's absence from the flat. Her escort chatted to her pompously about Paris and perfumes and flowers for the hair and she sat smiling at him mechanically, jealousy shooting through her like a flame. How *could* she concentrate on business when Kamelya and Ahmet sat at a nearby table. I am old now, she thought regretfully, although I am barely forty. They are in love. I hope he breaks her heart. She patted her hair nervously and fingered the ruby cross at her throat and all the time went through the motions of eating and drinking with drilled precision. She was tortured, *too* aware of those lovers smiling into each other's eyes. She thought it must be obvious to anyone who saw them together. She had never seen such radiance before.

'Toto's going,' said Kamelya feverishly. 'She's not even coming over to speak to us!'

'Stop concerning yourself with Toto.'

'But you didn't see the way she was looking at us Ahmet. Oh, I shall never be able to face her again!'

***

Later that week, a large black saloon carrying the corpulent, pin-striped form of the minister drove through Pera at a funereal pace and stopped outside Madame Toto's shop. The chauffeur slipped from behind the wheel and opened the door so that the minister could emerge. This he did with many gruntings and grumblings.

Toto greeted him smilingly and with a touch of pride to her manner. It was not the first time the minister had honoured her shop by calling personally and she knew by this time what his purchases would be.

'Well Madame Toto,' he greeted her jovially and rubbed his hands together. 'You are looking very well as usual! I hope that business is good too?'

'Very good Your Excellency,' said Toto modestly.

The minister leaned towards her and said in a conspiratorial whisper, 'I wish to choose a little something for my wife Madame. She is unwell and had to remain in Ankara and I should like to take something back with me to cheer her.'

'Some perfume perhaps Your Excellency?'

'Oh, no, no! Perhaps some flowers for a dress – you will know the sort of thing Madame – and a little eau de toilette.'

'But of course. Maybe some *Jardin de France*.'

Toto made the selections herself and when he was leaving she said hesitantly, 'Might I have a word with you in private, Your Excellency?'

'Certainly,' said the minister, indulgently thinking it was some matter of promotion she wished to discuss.

He followed her into the room she used for herself and splayed his feet outwards on the thick carpet.

'Well Madame? What is it you wish to discuss with me?'

'It is a delicate matter Your Excellency. Perhaps you will even think I have no right to interfere.' She hesitated a fraction of a second. 'It concerns Kamelya *hanım*,' she said and looked away from him.

'She is all right?'

'Oh, yes! It is not that at all.'

'Then what is it Madame? You are keeping me in suspense!'

'I hardly like to tell you Your Excellency. Perhaps you will be very angry with me?'

Her voice ended on an uplifted note and the minister stared at her frenziedly.

'Tell me at once!' he said in a high squeaky voice and felt himself perspiring with apprehension.

'She has been seen dining with another man Your Excellency.' Toto hung her head in sorrow, her heart beating very fast.

'*Another* man?' the minister repeated in a shocked whisper.

'It is true. I myself saw them on several occasions.'

'You know who he is?'

'Yes Excellency. He is an officer at Kuleli.'

'You know his name also?'

'But yes! It is Major Ahmet, Excellency.'

The minister frowned at her and after a moment he said stiffly, 'Thank you for telling me Madame.'

'I thought it was my duty, Your Excellency.'

'You did quite right. It was recently you saw them together Madame?'

'Yes. At the Pera Palas Hotel. There were many other people dining there also.'

He gave her a long bitter look and felt wounded. 'Thank you Madame,' he repeated and made a movement to go. 'I shall know how to deal with this,' he said softly.

'I would not wish to cause trouble,' Toto murmured gently.

'It is all right.' He looked distraught. 'Did I leave my parcels somewhere?' he asked.

'They have been given to your chauffeur, Excellency.' Toto moved in front of him so that he was forced to look at her. 'I hope, Excellency, that this will not make any difference to your patronage of my poor little shop?'

'No, no, of course not. You have undoubtedly done me a great service, Madame.' He patted her shoulder absently. 'I hope you continue to prosper,' he said.

After he had driven off Toto sat down and smiled to herself. 'You only did your duty,' she kept telling herself, but self-hatred mingled with the sweet satisfaction of revenge.

***

Kamelya waited impatiently for Ahmet to arrive.

It was over two weeks since she had seen him, for the minister had been longer than usual in Istanbul and without the chilling influence of his wife to restrict him had spent all his free time in her flat. He had bored her unendurably and there had been moments when she had wanted to scream that their association must end but prudence, and fear for her future, had restrained her.

He had not mentioned anything to her of his talk with Toto. Never once did he question her as to what she did when he was in Ankara. She was serenely unaware that he knew anything about herself or Ahmet.

She heard a ring at the door and Rana shuffling to open it and then Ahmet came into the room, tossed his cap into a chair, and took her in his arms.

'I thought you'd never come!' she said with a catch in her voice.

He released her and stared hungrily into her eyes.

'Must we dine out tonight?' he asked at last.

'But of course not. I prefer it here and I have already warned Rana we would probably be dining at home.'

He kissed the tip of her nose.

'Sometimes you are very thoughtful,' he sighed.

'Has anything happened Ahmet? You look strange.'

He turned away from her.

'I am leaving Istanbul,' he said, his voice trembling.

'Leaving? But it is impossible! After all these years!'

'I have been transferred to the east of Turkey – the very furthest, most desolate point they could find for me, the sort of place they send unruly officers to cool off. I have no idea why or how this happened or even what I have done! The CO gave me the order this morning.'

She stared at him foolishly, her mouth half open with shock.

'But why?' she asked stupidly.

'I don't know. It was completely unexpected. We can't understand it at all. At first the CO thought there was some mistake and phoned Ankara, but they said there was no mistake. The order was meant for me all right.'

'I hope it won't be for long,' she said.

'I don't know.'

He sat down resting his elbows on his knees and said bewilderedly, 'It's so odd. I wish I could understand it.'

She poured two glasses of cognac and sat down beside him.

'Has there been any trouble lately?'

'No. The odd thing is that they haven't anyone to replace me yet either but I have to leave tomorrow morning.' He stopped talking and drank the cognac. 'I thought I was in Kuleli for the rest of my life,' he said.

Rana appeared for instructions and Kamelya told her they would be remaining at home. Le Roi slipped in through the half-open door and put his head on Ahmet's knee.

'You look as if you understand,' Ahmet said to him and fondled his soft head. Le Roi licked his hand and then went on staring at him in his sad way.

'He is very fond of you,' said Kamelya. 'Perhaps he knows you are going away.' Le Roi settled his chin firmly on Ahmet's hand and closed his eyes and Kamelya said half laughingly, 'He is simply swooning with love for you Ahmet!' But the effort of laughter was too much and she rested her cheek against Ahmet's sleeve. 'I shall so miss you,' she whispered with passion. Life had been lonely before she had met him. Now, without him, it would be desolate.

During dinner Ahmet said abruptly, 'There is another reason why I'm reluctant to go so far away Kamelya.'

He hesitated and she said encouragingly, 'Go on. You know you may tell me whatever you wish.'

'There's a boy in Kuleli...'

'Yes?' Her heart seemed to miss several beats.

'He is, in a way, like my own son. When my mother died she asked me to see he was admitted to the military school and to keep an eye on him.' He stared at Kamelya searchingly. 'She rescued him years ago when he was quite a small child and somehow we grew fond of him.'

He poured *rakı* into their glasses and lifted his in silent salute.

'He's a good boy,' he said and wiped his mouth on his napkin, 'but there's always been an element of uncertainty about him. We never were able to find out who his parents were so that makes us all the more cautious.'

He smiled at Kamelya charmingly. 'You're not bored?'

'Of course not.'

'I'd hoped to stay in Kuleli 'til he qualified for Harbiye, the military college. It is my dearest ambition to see him become an officer. It would help establish him.'

'Why?'

'Well, I think he has always had the feeling he's a nobody, has no claim on anything. He's secretive but sometimes he talks to me a little. I always have the feeling he's lonely.'

'I see.'

'I feel a certain responsibility for him you know.'

'Why? Haven't you done your duty towards him?'

She could not keep the coldness out of her voice. It was quite ridiculous, she knew, but she was jealous. Ahmet's whole expression altered when he spoke of the boy.

He looked at her with concern.

'I thought you would understand,' he said.

'I do, but surely he is able to look after himself now!'

'It's not that. Try to understand! He is a boy without a home, he suffered most hideously when he was a child, and is still inclined to believe that all the world is after him to rob him of his good luck.'

Hurt stabbed through her. She loved and hated Murat at once. Pride shrieked denial that he was a homeless boy without a name, but she could not bring herself to utter the words to Ahmet.

'I am certain you have done your best,' she said stiffly. She would not look at his worried face. Was this the time to think of Murat when it was their last night together for perhaps a very long time?

He took her hand across the table. 'He means a great deal to me,' he said.

'You are sorrier to part from him than you are from me!'

'Now you're being ridiculous! It is a different feeling altogether. You would not understand it perhaps, but...' He paused to look into her cold white face. 'I love you no less because I love him too,' he said gently.

The thought that he loved her brought tears to her eyes.

'I wish you were not going,' she said pathetically and traced a pattern on the palm of his hand with her fingernails.

'I shall come back,' he said.

'It might not be for years.'

'It will make no difference. I shall still love you.'

'You will have forgotten. You will meet someone else.'

He laughed. 'Where I am going there's no one but Kurds and peasants. I am unlikely to be attracted by either!'

'Some peasants are beautiful...'

She remembered Gül.

'You amuse yourself.'

'You will write to me sometimes?'

'Where shall I write? Are you going to stay in this flat for a long time?'

She flushed rosily and withdrew her hand.

'I do not know,' she said awkwardly.

'It would be wiser to send your letters *poste restante*. Don't you think?'

They stared at one another silently and Kamelya's defiant eyes were the first to drop.

In his mind there loomed the figure of a possessive man – it might be the minister, he did not know, or it might be somebody new by now. The immediacy of their situation, their separation, rose like an obstacle between them.

'I shall never know you entirely,' he said despairingly.

Chapter 20

1930

AHMET'S ABSENCE STRETCHED UNFATHOMABLY. For a long time after he left Istanbul, Kamelya found it difficult to settle down. Existence seemed to have no point. It did not greatly matter what she did.

She began to visit Toto again but Toto was distant, her mother boldly inquisitive, and the savour had gone out of their friendship. It required effort to extract entertainment out of the long, dull evenings.

'Has your lover deserted you?' the old woman would ask sharply, her beady black eyes travelling over Kamelya's white face with malice.

'What lover?' Kamelya would ask, wide-eyed with pretend surprise.

'It was not a lover who kept you away from us?'

'Of course not!'

'The minister was with you more often perhaps?'

'Yes.'

She would see Toto's thoughtful eyes looking at her and would feel guilty remembering Ahmet.

Sometimes she thought Toto hated her and wondered if it had anything to do with the night she had seen her and Ahmet dining at the Pera Palas. She wished she could stop going to see her, but there was nothing else to do and she was terrified of being alone.

Once Toto said, 'Do you still see Ahmet?'

'No. He was not amusing.'

'So? You prefer the minister?'

'Why not? He looks after me.'

'Is he not curious what you do when you are alone here?'

'He doesn't ask me questions.'

Toto knew then that the minister had not spoken of Ahmet. She watched Kamelya dispassionately and wondered what he had done to end the relationship.

'You must be lonely,' she said without warmth. 'You are losing your looks.'

***

Ahmet wrote long, spasmodic letters giving her word pictures of the isolation of his life, chilling her with the certainty that separation would be for a long time. She wrote to him less frequently, being inarticulate and never quite knowing what to say. How ever hard she tried, her letters were dull, cold affairs. She was shy of writing her love. It would be different, she felt, if she could see him and talk with him, and feel the nuances of speech. The spoken word was soon dissolved. No matter what happened one could not be confronted with it in the same manner as the written word. Besides, there was always the danger the letter might fall into other hands.

She never saw Murat either. In vain she would stand on Galata Bridge watching the crowds of eager students coming in on the boats from Çengelköy but Murat was never among them. Before Ahmet had left Kuleli he'd already warned him that 'it would be better for you not to see Istanbul again until you pass into Harbiye. If anybody else finds money in the way we found it before it might be very unpleasant.'

'I know,' the boy had replied.

After a time Kamelya grew bored and stopped going to Galata. She wrote less frequently to Ahmet and was perpetually aggrieved.

The minister started to come to Istanbul more often, never warning her of his intentions, always seeking to catch her with a lover, unable to forget the story Madame Toto had told him.

'Why didn't you let me know you were coming?' she would flare irritably.

Their association was old now. She would talk to him how she liked.

'Does it matter?'

'Of course it matters! I never know when to expect you. It's irritating never knowing what's going to happen next!'

She craved security yet seemed suddenly delirious for gaiety and doubtful company. She was tired of living on the fringe of respectability in a half world of mistresses and expensive prostitutes. She emerged only at night to dine in smart hotels with men who bored her, sleeping most of the day and never belonging to anyone. Yet she could not break away.

She began to make use of Toto's discreet salon and Toto grew expansive and friendly again, although it was never quite the friendship of earlier days. She introduced Kamelya to rich men and shielded her from the minister's curiosity. She never mentioned Ahmet.

'Oh Toto!' Kamelya would giggle, 'You must say I am visiting your mother who is sick and that I shall be leaving soon.' Toto would do anything for her so long as Ahmet was not in the picture.

***

It was during Kamelya's occasional visits to Toto's salon that she met the schoolgirl, Neriman by name.

'She's an amusing little thing, pretty,' she said to Toto afterwards.

'She's just a tango, why should I care.'

'But she's so young!'

'She's fifteen,' said Toto's mother with a chuckle. 'When I was her age I was married and Toto was on the way.'

'You don't mean she comes here to meet men?' Kamelya asked, feeling shocked.

'Of course she does,' said Toto scornfully.

'But not often,' added the old woman. 'She's still at school, see? She couldn't come too often.'

'She looks so innocent,' said Kamelya.

'Yes. That's what attracts the men.'

Kamelya felt disgusted.

'It's a pity you met her here today. I'm normally more careful. She has a sharp tongue.'

'But she's too young to be believed. Honestly, Toto, nobody would guess she even knew of such things at her age!'

***

Istanbul is a small city. If one waits long enough one sees everybody at some time or another.

Kamelya was lunching alone in Hacı Abdullah's one Sunday when she saw Murat passing by the window. She was bored and lonely. Sunday was a horrible day. There was nothing to do and all the shops were closed. She called impatiently for the bill and her heart leaped with pleasure when she at last stood outside. Murat and his companion were returning slowly along the pavement. She moved as they came abreast of her, her eyes seeking Murat who did not notice her, but she felt the interested glance the other boy gave her. She stared after them, undecided what to do, and then saw them enter a cinema in time for the two o'clock matinée. Excited and full of plans, boredom forgotten, she returned to her flat. She was bubbling over with happiness. She wished there was someone with whom she could discuss Murat.

The following Sunday she was in Pera again at the same time. She watched as they strolled towards her, followed them a little way, and then saw them go into the same cinema. This was their weekly routine. Sunday after Sunday Kamelya waited for them to come. Sunday after Sunday her eyes sought Murat.

'There's that woman again,' Murat's friend said. 'She looks at you as if she's ready to eat you.'

'Oh shut up!' Murat whispered savagely, furious because he knew he was blushing.

'I've never seen a woman so barefaced.'

'It's you she looks at.'

'Nonsense! I've tried smiling at her half a dozen times or more but she doesn't even see me!'

Sunday afternoon became the highlight of the week. Murat was excited by the encounters, but would have died rather than admit this to his friend Celal.

One Sunday Celal stood directly in front of her, barring her way and smiling invitingly. Kamelya gave him a haughty, horrified look and brushed him aside impatiently, leaving a delicious perfume in her wake.

'No luck!' said Celal ruefully. 'It definitely isn't me she wants!'

Murat looked sulky.

'You utter cucumber!' said Celal dispassionately. 'Why, she's simply begging to be picked up!'

'I don't believe it.'

'I tell you Murat, all these women in Pera are the same. They like a young man now and then. It helps them to feel young.'

'She doesn't look the sort,' Murat muttered. He was still sulky, and insanely jealous of Celal's aplomb.

'If I had your opportunities I wouldn't be so slow I tell you! These women know everything, they train you like the women do in France. I shouldn't be surprised if your girlfriend isn't French. She looks it in a way. Do you suppose her hair is dyed?'

'How should I know?'

Murat turned on his heel showing indifference.

'She's too old,' he said.

'What's it matter? They're all the same in the dark.'

Murat couldn't resist laughing. Celal knew everything.

Kamelya, her eyes ablaze with maternal pride and joy, would have been very surprised if she'd known how they discussed her. It never occurred to her that her behaviour might appear odd to a pair of twenty-year-old cadets. To her they were just children.

One Sunday she followed them into the cinema.

Murat, looking back over his shoulder, was astonished to see her behind him. It made him go hot and cold together – so, assuming a very fierce expression, he hurried after Celal, Kamelya alongside. When they were shown into their seats the lights were still on. The matinée was due to start in a moment or two. Boldly, without the slightest trace of embarrassment, Kamelya sat down beside her son. This alarmed him for wasn't it was a well-known fact that, once it was dark, simply anything could happen in a picture palace? He wanted to change places with Celal immediately.

'Don't be a fool!' said Celal witheringly. 'If I sit there she'll go!'

Kamelya lit a cigarette and loosened the sable fur at her throat. There was an awkward moment when an officious attendant appeared and asked for the cigarette to be put out. She'd forgotten that smoking wasn't permitted. With nervous impatience she stubbed it out, and caught a smothered laugh from beside her. She wished the lights would dim.

As soon as they did and the film had started she peered at Murat's stern young profile, her heart weak with emotion. She was unconscious of quite how lonely she was. What it would be to have this tall young man visit her for the weekend, telling her friends with contrived regret, 'I'm so sorry – no, I can't go. My son is coming from Harbiye to visit me. Oh, didn't you know? But yes, he'll be an officer soon. We see one another so seldom I have to devote my weekend to him when he comes. Yes, some other time perhaps...' She stared at the screen with blind eyes, endeavouring to master her bitter emotion. After a while she was able to look back again at Murat and saw that his overcoat lay across his knees. It should be easy to slip money into the pocket nearest her. Murat, aware of her intense interest, was nearly suffocating with the tension. He longed to turn and look at her.

For weeks now her face had haunted him. He had held so many imaginary conversations with her she was no longer a stranger in the street but an enchanting companion. He moved through his days of study in a romantic blaze of first love – tender, protective, aching – never to be quite the same again. He only lived for Sunday afternoons – to see her perfect face, to feel the exquisite tenderness of her eyes upon him.

She was as fragile and precious as a fleeting dream, and it was divinest torture to be teased about her by Celal. It did not matter who she was or where she came from, or indeed what exactly she wanted with him.

'I'm sorry I didn't change places with you after all,' hissed Celal's voice, interrupting his romantic thoughts. 'The poor woman will sit there forever if she waits for you to make a move!'

'Stop it!' Murat spat back.

'*Eşek* – son of a donkey!' whispered Celal with equal heat. 'You don't know what you're missing! I bet she'll feel for your hand soon.'

'Leave it!' muttered Murat in sweaty despair. He was so acutely miserable. He ached to be away from her yet at the same time ached to be pressed close to her breast.

'Is *nothing* happening?'

Murat ignored the urgent whisper.

'Listen you cucumber son of a fool! Press your leg against hers, that'll wake her up all right, and show her you're not so bloody green!'

'*Quiet*, she'll hear you!'

Kamelya, however, was busy trying to put money into his coat pocket. With infinite caution she stretched out her hand. Murat, out of the corner of his eye, thought the scrap of paper between her fingers was for a rendezvous. He was almost hypnotised with terror. Of it's own volition it seemed his hand shot out and clutched hers. A little frisson ran through his whole body and his hold tightened involuntarily.

Kamelya, no longer blind, snatched her hand away and fled from her seat. She was white to the lips and her legs trembled so much she was forced to support herself against the wall of the foyer for a few moments.

The cashier and the commissionaire were talking animatedly. Music from the film came faintly through the closed doors behind her. Her brain felt near to exploding.

'*He thought I was trying to pick him up!*' she said, in shock, and the bright painted face of the cashier looked at her curiously.

Outside, in the bright wintry street, she hailed a taxi.

'*He thought I was a woman looking for a lover!*'

When at last she let herself into her flat, she stood for a moment or two in the quiet hall trying to collect herself. Rana came out from the kitchen.

'What's wrong *hanım*? Has there been an accident?' she asked, catching sight of Kamelya's distraught air.

'No, no, it's nothing. I had a shock. It's nothing Rana. Don't look like that!'

She laughed hysterically.

'The minister rang from Ankara *hanım*. I said you were visiting Madame Toto.'

'Thank you. That was good of you.'

'He's ringing again tonight.'

'Yes, I see. Thank you Rana.'

Rana stared at her, fascinated. She had never seen her look like this before.

'Oh and *bayan* Neriman called.'

'I see.'

She could not concentrate on Rana's messages. Her cheeks flamed as she remembered Murat. Rana asked sharply, 'Are you well *hanım*?'

'I'm all right,' said Kamelya, pushing past her into her bedroom.

She pulled off her close fitting hat and stared at herself in the oval mirror of her dressing table.

'*He thought you wanted a lover!*'

She would never be able to forget that as long as she lived.

She went across to the hand basin and splashed cold water over her wrist, feeling again the fierce clasp of Murat's strong fingers. Then she lifted it to her lips and kissed it.

She sat down in a chair and, for the first time, knew the full force of her loss.

***

Murat, looking down at his hand which still seemed to burn with the impress of Kamelya's long white fingers, noticed the paper that lay crumpled on his overcoat and picked it up eagerly. He remembered now the scrap of paper she'd held in her hands. At last he would know her name, perhaps her address!

With his heart hammering he undid the crumpled folds and peered at it in the flickering light from the screen.

Money? His heart ceased its hammering. What was she giving him money for? What did she want?

'What happened?' Celal was asking anxiously.

Murat did not answer immediately and Celal repeated his question, louder. People in the row in front of them turned to glare.

'Eh, Murat?'

Murat said at last, 'I don't know. She put out her hand to me and I took it, then she snatched hers away and ran out of the cinema!'

'That's just a trick,' said Celal confidently. 'That's to keep your interest.'

He saw the note in Murat's hand.

'What's that?' he asked eagerly.

'Money.'

'*Money*? How much?'

One hundred liras, Murat told him unhappily.

'My God, she's trying to buy you.'

'But I shan't keep this. I don't understand it. I'll give it back to her next week.'

'That's what she wants – to establish contact...'

Murat hardly heard him. He looked again at the money, tenderness curving his young lips into a smile. She'd held it! It was still warm from her hand!

Nurtured in loneliness, his heart cried out for her. Who was she? Memories stirred faintly. A face flickered but was gone before he could recognise it. A crash of music from the screen brought him back to the present and the past, already nebulous, dissolved. The memories were not strong enough to claim him.

'You're a lucky *pezevenk*,' said Celal enviously. 'She must be very rich!'

'But I shall give it back to her,' said Murat and smiled brilliantly in the darkness as he unbuttoned the top pocket of his tunic and inserted the note carefully. When he pressed his hand against it he felt it crackle just above his heart.

'Spend it!' said Celal impatiently. 'What d'you think she gave it to you for?'

'I don't know but I don't want it. I'd like to give it back.'

But when he went to Pera the following week there was no sign of Kamelya. He walked Celal up and down, down and up, in desperation. They even missed the matinée. But Kamelya did not come. Murat was in despair. Now it was his turn to look for her in the face of every woman who passed. But never again was she to haunt his Sundays.

Chapter 21

1933

AHMET RETURNED TO ISTANBUL a few weeks before Murat was due to pass out of Harbiye. He was back for good, promoted to colonel during his long sojourn in the wilds of eastern Anatolia.

Murat was delighted to see him back. The void within him narrowed.

'Well, you'll soon be independent of us all,' said Ahmet. Murat kissed his hands with joy.

'It's all thanks to you,' he said. 'If I hadn't had your help I should have been nothing at all.'

'Nonsense!' said Ahmet, clearing his throat. 'Whatever you are, Murat, is all due to yourself.'

He looked at the tall, handsome young man.

'My mother should have been alive to see you,' he said.

Murat's face creased into a smile. 'She would have found fault with everything I did. She would have said I have no presence!'

'That would have been because she was proud of you.'

'Yes. When I was a child it took me a long time to realise that she did not give praise easily.'

They were silent for a moment, remembering Saadet *hanım*.

'She was very good to me,' said Murat at last.

'She adored you, but she was always afraid of giving herself away. That was why she pretended to be harsh.'

'She was my father and my mother.'

'It was her dearest wish to see you settled.'

'And now you are my father and my mother,' said Murat and flashed his brilliant troubled smile.

'I should like you to dine with me the night you become an officer, unless you have other plans of course?' said Ahmet.

'I should like nothing better, but I have half-promised Celal that we would celebrate together.'

'Let Celal come as well then. I shall not restrict your gaiety I promise. After dinner I expect we shall all have something better to do than remain together.'

He laughed at the look of relief in Murat's eyes.

'You didn't think I'd wish to keep you by my side for the whole of the night?' he asked.

'It would not have mattered, sir,' said Murat sheepishly, fearing he had given himself away.

Ahmet patted his shoulder.

'We'll dine in a smart restaurant,' he said, 'and I shall take a back seat while all the women admire you and Celal, the new young officers. Perhaps I shall have a companion,' he said hesitantly, 'a charming woman who will make you feel at ease and who will help to temper your shyness.'

'That would be very pleasant, sir.'

***

Kamelya felt more ambivalent at Ahmet's return. She had managed her agony at his sudden exile years before by building a carapace around her heart, and though she knew she still loved him, and although they had never completely lost touch, she knew it would take a while for her to accept him back.

They'd agreed to rekindle their friendship by degrees, but when he asked her to be his hostess at a dinner in honour of his protegé Murat her mind froze. There and then she realised how much had changed while Ahmet had been away. She felt caged by secrets. A desperate sadness gripped her as she realised that there was nothing she would have enjoyed more, and yet she heard herself refuse him with great force.

'It is out of the question!' she said curtly.

'But why, my dearest? You will add interest to our party.'

'You know I cannot do it,' she said.

'You do not wish to dine in public?'

She felt the blood leave her face and bit her lip nervously.

'You cannot go on leading a double life forever,' said Ahmet impatiently. 'At some point you'll have to make up your mind and choose between us!'

It was the first mention he'd ever made that another man supported her. Kamelya raised her head sharply.

'It has nothing to do with you,' she said. 'You were too long away,' she said angrily, building his absence into a monstrous betrayal.

'Was it too much to ask you to wait for me?'

'Why should I? What would I have gained by waiting?' Her sharp, brittle beauty hurt him, her harsh words wounding his mind.

'You knew I loved you,' he said quietly.

'Love?' she laughed. 'That has nothing whatever to do with it!'

'So what did you want – what *do* you want?'

She looked away from him.

'Security,' she said at last.

'You have a passion for respectability!' he sneered.

'I am tired of living like this,' she said angrily. 'You never think of the effort it requires. You don't know what it feels like to wake up each morning remembering one is nothing!'

Her words startled him. He seemed to have heard them somewhere before.

'You have changed,' he said.

'I am older.'

She lit a cigarette with trembling fingers, her angry outburst over.

'So you see,' she said and smiled, 'neither of us are the same people Ahmet. All that time you were away, I had to live.'

She'd never be able to speak to him of the loneliness of life without him, of the frigidity of Toto towards her, of long summer days with nothing to do, of Murat that winter day in the cinema. He might love her to distraction but there were things that she would never say.

'So you will not dine with me?'

'I can't.'

'It would mean so much to the boys. You would give our evening liveliness.'

'It is impossible.'

'Some quiet place perhaps, where there would be no danger of anyone seeing us?'

'I'm *not* afraid,' she said angrily.

'Then why do you refuse?' Her cruelty, her hardness, was inexplicable.

She stamped her foot in temper. 'I will *not* tell you!' she shouted at him. 'You have no right to question me like this!' Her eyes swept him bitterly. 'Go on, take your junior officers to dine,' she said, 'leave me alone!'

'You are too harsh,' said Ahmet.

Bowing stiffly, turning on his heel, he left, unable to bear any further rejection.

After he had gone Kamelya threw herself on a divan and wept.

'Rana!' she screamed after a time. 'Bring me some cognac and hurry yourself, damn you!'

Chapter 22

A<small>T THE</small> P<small>ASSING</small> O<small>UT</small> <small>PARADE</small> Murat marched puffed up with pride, resplendent in his smart new uniform and immaculate white gloves, sword at side.

The child Murat was gone. He was determined to consign the memory of his first, mysterious love to oblivion. In the space of a night he had altered. Even the lines of his young face had changed. He was a responsible citizen now with men under his command, and a monthly salary to spend as he liked, and he knew he would rise to the challenge. With Colonel Ahmet to kiss him on both cheeks and declare with tears in his eyes that this was the greatest day in his life too, Murat felt that he was no longer a nobody. He was Lieutenant Murat of the Turkish Army, with a glorious career stretching ahead of him.

***

Kamelya was in her flat already dressed to go out when she heard the sound of the military bands. Their gaiety drained her so completely that she was forced to sit down. She couldn't go into the crowded spring-time streets, couldn't bear to see the jubilant faces of the new officers.

Rana watched the parade from the windows of the salon but Kamelya stayed in her chair and refused to look out. As the bands drew nearer and the stirring strains of 'Old Comrades' invaded the flat she played with the fringes on her gloves and felt joy and despair sweep her together.

'Come and look at them *hanım*!'

'No, I don't want to Rana. I can hear them and it's more than enough.'

'I like this march,' said Rana. 'They always play it. I watch them every year.'

Mothers jostled in the streets, watching their sons in their new uniforms. Their laughing voices drifted up to the sunny flat. Why was military music and the sound of marching footsteps always so sad? It was terrible to be alive and not to be able to clasp her own to her, to see him in his young conceit, to be able to say proudly: 'My son!'

The telephone rang and when Rana said it was the minister she had to control her irritation. She went into the hall to speak to him. The sounds of the bands could not reach in there with the salon door closed. She leaned against the cream-washed walls and closed her eyes in despair.

'Yes?' she said distantly.

His voice came through thin and flat. His wife had just died. He thought she ought to know. Why had he thought such a thing? What was it to her when her son was marching through the Pera streets alive and gay and unconscious of her existence? What had the death of a woman she had never known to do with her?

'I am sorry,' she said formally. It was difficult to know what to say after that. 'You must be feeling... shocked...' she added lamely.

'Yes.'

But he sounded as if more than shock had happened to him that day.

'The children are in the house now,' he said, as if to explain his reticence. She felt pity wash over her. Perhaps if one had been married for a long time it was always a shock when one's partner died, even if you hadn't cared for them particularly. 'I shall not be in Istanbul for a while,' he said.

'But of course!' interrupted Kamelya swiftly. 'It is quite all right. I understand.' His wife would still have first claim on him. Maybe he felt bereft after so many years. Maybe he would remember her as she had been when he first knew her. One always thought politely of the dead. 'I understand,' she said again.

When she went back to the salon Rana turned from the window and said regretfully, 'They've gone now. It was a beautiful sight *hanım*. I watch them every year and every year they make me cry! They're so young, see?'

'The minister's wife is dead,' said Kamelya, who had not been listening to her.

'Well, what did he expect? She was old wasn't she? You can't expect to live forever.'

'Still, it's sad after so many years. Even if you hate a person I think it must make you sad when they die. It's so final… and there's no chance of making things right.'

She remembered Kara Kurt and shivered superstitiously. She had hated him. She had not felt sorry when the gendarmes killed him. Her eyes took on a far away look of fear. Why had she thought of him, today of all days? The bright flat seemed suddenly uneasy with his malignant presence. 'It's not right to talk of the dead,' she said, the fear still in her face.

'The dead can't hurt you,' said Rana, looking at her mistress, intrigued.

The grass must have grown high about him by now. Impatiently, as if trying to banish his persistent ghost, she said, 'I shall not go out after all. It is too late now.'

'When is the minister coming?' Rana asked.

'How can you talk like that Rana, with his wife only just dead!'

'No use being sentimental here,' said Rana without embarrassment.

Kamelya looked at her haggard, wicked old face. It was difficult to believe now that *she* had ever been young and pretty, or had a kind thought for anyone. 'Are you happy with me?' she asked impulsively. Rana looked surprised and suspicion crept into her currant-black eyes.

'Me?' she asked incredulously. 'Why *hanım* I'm happy anywhere where there's a good bed under me and enough food in my stomach.'

'Nothing else?' Kamelya asked regretfully.

'What else should there be *hanım*? I do what you tell me. I'm as well off here as anywhere else I dare say.'

She continued to look suspicious. What a funny question to be asked after all these years! Was there anything going on behind her back? Was Kamelya going to dismiss her and get someone else?

'I'm all right,' she said sulkily.

'I just wondered,' said Kamelya. 'It was nothing else but that Rana.'

***

Kamelya was married to the minister a few months after his wife's death. She was delirious with happiness and blazed with the passionate beauty of an Indian summer.

'Here is security at last and respectability!' she said to Toto gaily.

'Well, you've looked for it for years!' replied Toto drily. 'You're a very lucky woman!'

'It's not often that a man marries his mistress,' said her mother with a sigh and Toto looked at her sharply.

'He's old,' she said. 'He thinks Kamelya will keep him young.'

'And he's ugly,' said her mother with a chuckle. 'When they're young and nice-looking they marry someone else.'

'I don't care why he's married me,' said Kamelya. 'I just hope he won't die too soon!'

Pleased as a kitten with an unexpected bowl of cream, Kamelya seemed to purr contentedly. The minister was besotted with her. He'd known her for years now and, apart from that one doubtful episode when she was younger, which he had taken steps to deal with, he'd heard nothing against her. To marry her and secure her for himself for ever seemed the only course. His house, cluttered with furniture his wife had chosen, depressed him. Everything he touched bore the impress of her personality. Even from the grave she seemed to reach out and bully him, her ghostly voice demanding a dozen times a day what he thought he was doing when he moved a fanciful chair or table out of it's accustomed position. His children didn't want him. They had their own troubles – though of course they were always very glad of any financial support he could give. In a frenzy of loneliness he fled from his cluttered home to the cool elegance of Kamelya's.

***

In the second year of their marriage, they were invited to attend a racing function at the Officers' Club in Harbiye. Kamelya was enchanted. How soothing it was to be invited to such important events as a respectable woman! She took her time riffling through her closet, choosing exactly the right suit for the occasion. She remembered some kid gloves in a shade of violet which she had bought at Toto's the previous season. Where had Rana put them? Feeling towards the back of a drawer, her hand came into contact with an unexpected, cold, hard object. Her gun! Why was it still here, this memento from her distant past?

'Perhaps when we were moving into this flat Rana put it here,' she thought in confusion.

The bullets were still there as well. Two had been used she remembered, shivering despite the warmth of the afternoon, and one of them had killed a man. Nevertheless she found herself touching its smooth cold metal with fascination. Despite its neglect, it seemed very clean. Coming to her senses, she slammed the drawer shut, all thought of gloves vanished. She took down her hat and closed the wide doors to the closet with hands trembling as if she had the palsy.

'I'll throw it away!' she said desperately. 'It has nothing to do with me anymore!'

'You look so very beautiful,' complimented the minister when she went into the salon where he was waiting for her. She could not help smiling at his tremulous old face. She knew she was beautiful, and the tremor in her hand would soon pass. Spring suited her, she thought. She felt young and a scent of white lilac filled the flat.

As she stepped into their car she could not help wishing she was young again. She imagined herself going off to meet her lover. How tempting to escape old age once in a while!

By the time they reached the Officers' Club she was all rippling animation. It was so warming to be received in state like this, a lady of consequence, the minister's wife! How everyone made way for her! How the men stared obliquely! Looking remote, she swept into the long reception room, chic and silky, and full of devilment.

Walking past the bar, she recognised the silhouette of Ahmet, and the unease of earlier returned to her. With the minister so close beside her, she barely glanced in his direction. He watched her charm everyone and once, catching her eye, he winked. She looked offended and turned her back on him but after a time he managed to edge his way into the circle surrounding her.

'May I congratulate you?' he said, in a voice just loud enough to make her fearful someone had overheard.

'You may do as you please,' she said viciously and smiled at a gouty old general who was talking to her husband.

'If it was only marriage you wanted, you could have had me,' murmured Ahmet more softly. 'Why didn't you tell me?'

His smile was malicious and overbearing. She felt she would choke with fury at his presumption, and turned to walk away.

'If you go, I shall follow you,' he threatened and she looked at him pleadingly.

'Please!' she said.

'Not at all. Am I not permitted to talk to you?'

'*Go away*. You're attracting attention.'

He looked round him and said, 'My dear, I know you're usually the centre of attraction, but I assure you there is nobody looking at us at the moment.'

'Even so, go away Ahmet! I don't want to talk to you!'

She moved over to where her husband was standing and Ahmet's mouth twisted wryly.

***

Murat first caught sight of her when the minister was presenting the race trophies.

'My God!' he said and stared at her in amazement.

'What's wrong with you?' demanded Celal, who had not yet seen Kamelya.

'Nothing,' returned Murat in a surly voice.

He could not take his eyes off her. It must have been three or four years since last they had met. He had put her out of his mind but, now that he saw her again, impossible thoughts vied for attention. He watched her drinking sherry and sparkling with vivacity. She shone like a light, so elegant and self-assured. It seemed as if the corsage of flowers at her breast were actually blooming.

'Well, well, your girlfriend certainly moves in high society,' observed Celal, who was astonished at seeing her here.

'She's the wife of the minister!' said Murat.

Celal stared at him. 'Are you sure?' he asked.

'Yes.'

Something in his voice caught Celal's attention.

'You don't still think about her do you?'

'No. Why should I? I just remembered her when I saw her here, that's all.' But he knew she had always been somewhere in the back of his mind.

'She's a lovely woman,' said Celal carelessly. 'I wouldn't blame you if you thought of her occasionally. I tell you brother, I wouldn't mind spending a night with her.'

'She's old,' said Murat taking particular pride in attacking her.

'She's young enough.'

Kamelya, serenely unaware that her son was watching her, sipped her drink and tried to avoid Ahmet's eyes.

Down at the lower end of the room Murat drank his sherry like water. After a while he felt reckless enough to brave disapproval and break through the smart crowd of people surrounding the minister's wife.

'Don't be a damned fool!' said Celal. 'Do you want a first-class scandal?'

She would not look his way at all. She looked at everyone else but never at him.

'I'll go and give her back her hundred-lira note,' he joked.

'You'll go and put your silly head under a cold water tap instead,' said Celal grimly.

***

The party showed signs of breaking up at last. Through blurred eyes Murat saw the minister whispering something in Kamelya's ear. He saw her smile and then turn to a general who bowed to her. There seemed to be an awful lot of bowing going on and a great military clicking of heels with the ladies smiling like mad. Murat wanted to burst into derisive laughter.

Kamelya, looking like a brilliant butterfly in the sun, went off with the minister.

'And that's that!' said Murat savagely, taking another glass of sherry.

He drained the glass quickly and slammed it on an empty table beside him with such force that the base of it splintered. Murat grinned drunkenly. I've a good mind to smash up the whole place, he thought.

'What's wrong with you?' Celal demanded with irritation.

He didn't know what was wrong. It was something to do with that damned smile of hers. It never meant anything at all, although there were lots of fools who no doubt thought it did. Once upon a time he himself had thought so too.

Chapter 23

K AMELYA MOVED RESTLESSLY to the window, watching for Ahmet to come.

The novelty of being a respectable wife had worn off. Seeing Ahmet at the Officers' Club had agitated old passions. He'd taken a flat behind the Pera Palas Hotel and here they would meet occasionally when the minister was known to be safely in Ankara. Less frequently he would come to Kamelya's apartment. Their relationship was back to its familiar footing.

She drummed her long fingernails against the glass and thought about him. She'd come to rely on him so to assuage her loneliness. There were moments, when they were especially close, when she had to exercise an iron will not to blurt out to him about herself and Murat. Yet, despite the loneliness of her loveless marriage, she had no wish to go back to the makeshift life of earning her own living, or working in Toto's salon.

The women of her social circle made a point of excluding her. 'Loneliness is terrible,' she reflected to herself angrily. 'No one ever comes to see me. They all look at me as if I am nothing at all. But what can I do?' She heard a ring at the door and turned quickly. Whilst she'd been musing, Ahmet must have come along the street unseen by her. But when the door of her salon opened it was young Neriman who was shown in by Rana.

Kamelya was annoyed by the intrusion yet forced a smile of welcome to her lips.

'How nice to see you Neriman!' she said without warmth. 'I quite thought you had forgotten me!'

Her eyes directed a furious message to Rana who, she felt, should have known better than to have admitted her.

'Sit down,' she said.

'I've been busy lately,' Neriman said as she lowered herself into a chair. 'And since you married I hardly like to visit you. I never know who I may find here!'

'What nonsense!' said Kamelya lightly.

She could have replied with perfect truth that generally she was alone, but preferred to keep up the grand illusion that her afternoons were occupied entertaining the society of Istanbul.

She moved back to the window, ostensibly to pull a fold of curtain into place. There was still no sign of Ahmet. Perhaps he would not come after all.

'You do not look well,' she remarked, coming back to Neriman. 'What have you been doing with yourself?'

'Nothing at all.'

'Oh, come now, you can't lie to me! I know! You've been dining and dancing and making love every night for a month,' she laughed gaily. 'Nothing else would put those dark circles under your eyes Neriman!'

'You know how strict my father is. He doesn't let me go out at night!'

Kamelya assumed a little face of disbelief. 'You don't escape sometimes?'

Neriman smiled faintly. 'How can I?' she asked, reclining back and spreading her hands over the arms of her chair. 'It's not that,' she said harshly.

'Then tell me what it is.' Kamelya lit a cigarette impatiently. She hoped she would not stay too long. At any other time she would have welcomed Neriman's gossip but with Ahmet expected at any moment she could not concentrate properly.

'What is it?' she asked again smilingly, making an effort to be interested.

'I'm going to have a baby,' said Neriman.

Kamelya felt her face paling. She could hardly believe the utterance, so matter-of-fact yet loaded.

'You're *what*?' she asked incredulously.

'I'm going to have a baby,' repeated Neriman and this time her voice sounded defiant and desperate. 'It's true,' she said. 'Don't look at me as if I were making it up!'

'I can't believe it!' said Kamelya.

She looked at Neriman with dilated eyes and felt a flutter of warning in her brain.

'Do you think I'd bother to make it up?' said Neriman contemptuously.

'But what are you going to do?'

'I don't know – I – I thought perhaps you could help me.'

'*I*?' Kamelya asked, all her coldness rising to the surface in an instant.

'I can't tell them at home. My mother would only cry and my father would beat me to death,' her voice broke into a sob and Kamelya stared at her with loathing. 'I shall kill myself first but I shall never tell them!' she said.

'Come girl, pull yourself together!' Kamelya said sharply.

'You must know about these things,' said Neriman stubbornly. She looked tender and pathetic with her frightened eyes and her sleek hair combed primly back from her face. Kamelya stared at her with terror. She didn't want to be involved in anything unpleasant.

'I know nothing,' she said, 'and even if I did I wouldn't tell you. These things are dangerous.'

'You mean you won't help me?' Neriman's mouth folded in a red sulky line and she surveyed Kamelya bitterly. 'I thought *you'd* be certain to help,' she said with emphasis.

'How could you let such a thing happen to you?' Kamelya demanded angrily, her voice high and shrill with strain. 'You're too sentimental. You appal me Neriman! To be so careless... not to think...'

'It's done now,' said Neriman interrupting her. 'What's the use of talking like that to me now?'

'What about the man?'

'He's married. He can't help.'

Kamelya rang the bell beside her chair.

'We'll ask Rana,' she said despite herself. 'She'll be sure to know of something you can do. We'll ask her when she brings the coffee.'

If Ahmet should come now, she fretted, Rana would send him away again. Their afternoon would be spoiled! She wished Neriman would go! Why did she have to come here with her troubles? What did she expect? A cold hand clutched her heart. Rana had always warned her against having anything to do with Neriman.

'She'll bring you trouble, mark my words,' she'd said over and over again.

'You're a fool to have anything to do with her!' Toto had said.

But she had refused to listen to either of them. There was something about the girl that she could not resist. She reminded her so strongly of someone.

'Rana is so wise,' she said aloud.

'Oh, I hope she can help!' said Neriman, misinterpreting her meaning.

But Rana shook her head when she heard the story. 'How would I know anything?' she asked woodenly, shooting Neriman a bitter hostile look. 'I always made it my business to keep clear of things like that,' said Rana and poured coffee.

'All right Rana, never mind now!' said Kamelya nervously. 'I expect something will be found for *bayan* Neriman.'

'Shouldn't think it's likely,' said Rana as a parting shot and went out of the room.

'She doesn't like me,' said Neriman pathetically.

'Rana doesn't like anyone!'

'She knows but she won't tell me! I could kill her!'

'It's a difficult situation. Perhaps she doesn't know, or perhaps she thinks you're too young to be in this mess.'

Neriman's mouth curved scornfully. 'I'm nearly nineteen,' she said.

'You should have married.'

'Who would marry *me*?'

'You didn't try hard enough.'

'Anyway, that's irrelevant now! Don't you see I've got to get this over with, now? I thought you'd be sure to know, I really did.'

Kamelya twisted her wedding ring on her finger.

'I'm sorry,' she said.

'You don't care!' Neriman exploded viciously. 'You're secure, nothing like this can ever happen to you, damn you – d-a-m-n you!'

'Stop it! Pull yourself together Neriman. Drink some coffee and wipe your eyes. You can't go out looking like that.'

'Who said I'm going out looking like anything? Are you trying to make me go?'

'Of course not! Don't be absurd! You can stay here as long as you like.'

The afternoon was already ruined, it didn't matter now. Perhaps Ahmet had already been and Rana had told him that she was engaged. How would she ever be able to get through the long evening alone?

Neriman touched her eyes with a screwed up handkerchief and then hiccoughed. 'I can't really believe it's true!' she said.

'We'll think of something for you,' promised Kamelya falsely.

Neriman sipped the scalding coffee. 'I should like a life like yours,' she said, taking time to look at Kamelya narrowly. 'It must be nice to know you've reached the top, to be safe ...'

'None of us are very safe Neriman.'

'I think you're quite wonderful,' said Neriman, ignoring her. 'I've always admired the way you kept your past so secret. Wouldn't the minister be surprised if he knew where it was we first met!' She gurgled with laughter. 'Aren't you ever afraid someone will knock on the door and walk right in and tell him everything about you?'

'Certainly not!' Her eyes were wary. 'Why should I be?' she asked.

'If I were you I'd be afraid. I should never be able to carry things off the way you do.'

'Don't be silly!'

'You must have the strength of iron not to be afraid.'

'Do you think my husband would believe such things about me?'

'But that is why I think you are so wonderful – to have made him believe in you and not to care about those things.'

'The past doesn't alarm me Neriman. Nowadays I'm a very ordinary person indeed.'

'Are you? Honestly?'

Kamelya looked at her sharply.

'Of course,' she said, with a too final flick to her voice.

'Still it really must be *very* nice indeed to be you.'

Kamelya felt her heart beating very fast.

'I don't think I quite understand you,' she said.

Neriman looked around the elegant room.

'Well, all this for a start,' she said, waving her hands vaguely. 'You've such a lovely home and servants to wait on you and a husband who is important so that everybody looks at you when you go out – and then... there's your child too of course.'

'Child?'

'Yes. Haven't you a child somewhere?'

'I think you're mistaken Neriman. I have no child.'

Neriman's eyes opened wide in astonishment.

'Haven't you?' she asked. 'I thought you had.'

Kamelya felt the skin tightening across her cheekbones.

'What made you think *I* had a child?' she asked.

'Fitnet told me.'

'*Fitnet*? But you never knew Fitnet. How could you know her?'

'Don't be silly! Everybody knows Fitnet, at least everybody in our profession...'

'Our?'

'*Our* profession I said. Didn't you hear the first time?'

She laughed at the expression on Kamelya's face. 'Surely you didn't think you were the only one to know Fitnet? She was *very* interested when I told her you were married to the minister. She said she'd come and see you sometime.'

'Did she now?'

Her shocked voice was no more than a thread of sound.

'Yes. She told me she knew you when you were young and I told her I'd met you at Madame Toto's home.'

'What else did she tell you?'

'Oh... I can't remember everything I hear. But she said you had a child and that you left it in the streets so that you could have a better life.'

'I did nothing of the sort,' she wanted to cry out, but restrained herself in time.

'You're making a mistake,' she managed to smile. 'Fitnet must have confused me with someone else she knew – after all my name is not uncommon!'

Neriman looked nonplussed.

'She was very certain,' she said.

She leaned forward and helped herself to a cigarette from an ornate gold box.

'Why do you look so frightened?' she asked.

'I'm not frightened.'

'You are. Your hands are shaking!'

'Don't be a bloody little fool!' said Kamelya angrily. 'D'you think you can come here and frighten me with your silly tittle tattle Neriman? What can *you* possibly know about me?'

'Fitnet said many things.'

'I don't care what Fitnet said!'

'So you have no child?'

'No.'

'What a pity! It sounded so romantic when Fitnet told me.'

She stood up and smoothed her dress over her hips.

'But we have got away from the subject of *me*,' she said meaningfully.

'I'll see what I can think of…'

'Yes, do! I'll come round again one of these afternoons. If I don't go now my father will ask questions. He's simply a devil, an absolute *şeytan*. He knows when lectures are over at the university. It's quite useless trying to hoodwink him!'

'Yes?'

Neriman sighed affectedly.

'You have no idea how stern he is!' she said.

She touched Kamelya's rouged cheek with her hand.

'You look so frightened,' she said playfully. 'There's no need to be afraid of me Kamelya. But, remember, I've only you to depend on.'

'Try depending on marriage instead,' advised Kamelya acidly.

Neriman's eyes glimmered with hatred.

'We cannot all be so fortunate.'

***

Ahmet tried to get rid of Murat at Taksim.

'I have a call to make,' he said firmly.

'Well I'll walk as far as your house with you,' said Murat.

'But really there's no need!'

'I'm in no hurry,' grinned Murat, 'and it's a lovely day for walking.'

'Well, please yourself!' replied Ahmet in a slightly ruffled voice and quickened his pace.

Outside Kamelya's block of flats, a black iron-grilled glass door separating cool marble from the dust of the street, they stopped.

'Here we are,' said Ahmet.

'In that case, I'll see you at the club tomorrow night, sir,' said Murat and saluted. 'It was very good of you to see me this afternoon.'

'That's all right. I'll do my best about your posting anyway.'

He turned away but Murat still lingered.

'I say, sir!' he called urgently. 'Doesn't the Minister of Trade live in one of these flats?'

'Does he?'

'Believe so. Lucky old devil to live here! Well, goodbye sir.'

Ahmet and Neriman passed one another at the entrance. She flicked him a quick look of approval, for she liked to see a handsome man even if he was a bit old. She clattered down the steps noisily, high heels like daggers, and Murat woke from his daydream of the minister's wife.

Time enough to think of *her* later.

Squaring his shoulders and adjusting his cap at an angle, he walked after Neriman.

Chapter 24

'YOU LOOK TROUBLED,' said Ahmet, releasing Kamelya.
She tried to look natural.

'I'm all right,' she said, smoothing back her hair from her forehead, 'I thought you weren't coming, that's all.'

'I was delayed. Murat came practically at the last minute. I couldn't not listen to him ...'

'No, of course not.'

A pang shot through her that Murat would always have first claim on him. It had not mattered that she sat alone and waited for him to come.

'Everything was all right?' she asked.

'Yes. It was nothing but a matter of his posting. He's anxious to stay here now he's back again and I said I'd do what I could.'

He laughed suddenly.

'It was very funny,' he said. 'He insisted on walking here with me.'

'Here?'

'Yes. He didn't know whom I was visiting of course but downstairs he said to me "Isn't this where the Minister of Trade lives?"'

'And what did you say?'

'I think I looked vague.'

Kamelya turned away, remembering that Neriman had been leaving at the same time.

'Is there something the matter with you?'

'No. No.' She couldn't say that Murat had passed this way before. That they had met in the street several times with his eyes begging her to smile at him. That from her windows she had seen him staring upwards from the pavement below, his figure foreshortened by distance. How could she tell Ahmet all this? Unless she told him the whole story he would never understand.

'Anyway, I'm glad you came... really,' she said and smiled at him. Some half-felt sadness within her moved him to catch her hand impulsively and lift it to his lips.

'You've been alone all the afternoon!' he said with remorse. 'I knew that but I couldn't not see Murat, could I?'

'But of course not!'

She switched on a little Venetian Tiffany lamp and moved to draw the curtains across the windows.

'It's almost night!' she said wonderingly, as though amazed at the swift passage of time.

***

Murat walked jauntily after Neriman.

The autumn afternoon had grown chilly and the leaves from several dejected looking plane trees pattered to the ground like whispering, frightened old ladies. People hurried past him, their faces dim and mysterious with the gathering dusk. In apartments lights were being switched on and curtains drawn. Neriman walked quickly, her expression worried and desperate, her spirit broken.

Her earlier mood of defiance was no more, Kamelya forgotten in the urgency of her own impossible predicament. She was unaware of the tall cavalry officer who chinked behind her.

She noticed him only at the tram stop, where he appeared to bump into her. She heard his charming voice apologising and looked at him curiously.

'It's nothing,' she said on impulse, and smiled because she'd had time to see he was good looking.

'A stupid accident,' he was saying deferentially. 'I didn't hurt you did I?'

He was wondering what he could do to prolong the conversation. She was so much prettier than he had thought.

'It's quite all right,' said Neriman still smiling. 'Really, it was nothing at all!'

A brilliantly lit tram swayed and lurched towards them.

'This is my tram,' she said softly.

'Really? Such a coincidence! Mine too!'

'How odd!' said Neriman, blushing.

Having boarded the crowded tram together it seemed perfectly natural they should remain together. Their talk was desultory but when Neriman made to alight Murat followed her.

'You don't mind?' he asked anxiously.

'No.'

But when they reached the corner of her street, all too quickly, she cautioned in a small voice, 'Please don't come any further with me lieutenant. If anyone should see me perhaps they might tell my father. He is very stern and I have never walked with a young man before…'

Murat was enchanted with her demure air.

'May I see you again?' he asked.

She stared up at him and then lowered her eyes quickly, her voice barely audible.

'It is very difficult.'

'But could you not try? I'm only in Istanbul for a short time.'

'Are you on leave?'

'Well, not exactly, but pretty soon I'm bound to be transferred to some forgotten place at the end of the world. Couldn't you take pity on a poor, lonely officer who knows nobody?'

'Well, perhaps one afternoon I'll try,' she sighed with feeling, 'but my father is very stern.'

'Of course, what do you expect?' He smiled down at her but could not quite catch her eyes. 'Shall we meet tomorrow then?'

She hesitated for so long he thought she was going to refuse.

'It will be difficult,' she murmured.

'In Pera no one would know you.'

'Very well then, I'll meet you tomorrow at the tram stop.' She looked at him, wondering if it would be worth keeping the appointment. What would she get out of meeting a penniless young officer?

'Are you sure?' Murat kept on going, urgently.

She decided she would meet him. She might as well enjoy her last few weeks of freedom.

'Yes,' she said with a smile, 'I'll be there.'

'What is your name?'

'Neriman.'

'Mine is Murat. Well, goodbye Neriman! Until tomorrow.'

'Goodbye,' she said gravely and watched as he saluted her.

Young and cheeky, he was rather nice perhaps. She was troubled for a moment, in the uncertain glow of the evening, by a likeness in his smile to someone she knew – but then as he moved and the lamp light fell across his face the resemblance was gone. She hurried down the dark street to her home feeling unaccountably exhilarated.

***

They met many times.

Kamelya was forgotten again and now it was Neriman who disturbed Murat's dreams, keeping him at fever pitch, the pretty innocent creature with her trusting eyes and the confiding way she had of tucking her hand through his arm. He felt old and wise, so strong he could push a mountain over, and now and then she let him kiss her chastely.

She grew reckless and stayed with him later and later, somehow escaping her stern father. It was difficult to tear themselves away from one another, they were so young and so full of emotion. Murat was caught in a web of infatuation; Neriman thought the feeling might be something deeper and was disturbed because she had never experienced anything like this before.

They went to the cinema, in the dark cheap seats at the back because Murat never had enough money. They walked up and down the Pera streets, time and again. Neriman wondered how she had ever let herself be dominated like this. They watched the boats, leaning over Galata Bridge together, talking about themselves vociferously, enchanting one another with their good looks and their nearness, he manly, she fragrantly lissome. Neriman was scornful of herself but could not help being touched. She'd be sorry in a way if he left Istanbul… Murat swore to himself that this time his feelings were different. No other girl had ever captured his imagination in quite the same way. The face of the minister's wife flashed for an instant, yearning and seductive, but was gone before he could properly recognise her. He asked himself how he could be faithful to a love he had never known.

Neriman decided to marry him.

He had come in the nick of time, perhaps life was going to be good to her after all. Desperate with her secret knowledge, she wondered how she could do it. Loving him a little, it appalled her he should be cheated; loving herself more, she told herself she would never again have the same chance.

Aching with self-pity, she would press herself against him, driving him to a frenzy. She would bite her lips to keep back her tears when she thought of a future to be faced alone. If only she could get out of this terrible mess she would be good for the rest of her life! Could she not do it somehow?

Then fate offered her the chance casually, so casually that she almost let the moment slip by.

Murat asked her if they could not meet during the evenings. 'Only sometimes,' he begged, his eyes glazed with desire and frustration.

The moment hovered – and almost passed.

'But what would I tell them at home?'

Her hands were clasped in a little attitude of supplication. How could she do such a thing as this, her eyes seemed to be asking him.

'We could go to a casino,' persisted Murat. 'We could have dinner there and perhaps dance – oh Neriman, Neriman please!'

He was winning her over. The moment settled and she looked at him with blazing, excited certainty. She was sure she could get her own way now.

'Yes,' she acquiesced, breathless with her own daring thoughts, 'Yes, I'll manage something!' The blaze died out of her. 'But don't forget it will be difficult,' she said, suddenly prim, all the while her body arching towards his in a gesture of surrender. He kissed her, then bit her ear in an excess of emotion.

'But not impossible?' he whispered. 'Ah you! Teasing me! Of course you can manage something!'

Chapter 25

Neriman tried to plan but the plans would not come right. All the way home she tried to plan what she would say. She needed time for this, but she had just two days. What could she say? Could she say there was a party – someone she knew at the university was having a party? They would never suspect it was not the truth, after all she had never stayed out late before.

She thought of Murat and dinner in the casino and desire burned through her. Perhaps he would not be so very difficult after all. He was young, he had a sense of honour. Afterwards she could blame him.

In bed that night she could not sleep. The long moments pulled the grey dawn closer but sleep refused to come. She lay there in despair. Could she do it? How could she do it? It would not be difficult to make him believe her innocent. Had she ever given him any reason to suspect otherwise? Even though there had been times when she had ached to twine herself into his strong arms, she had held herself back. She'd be good to him. 'Oh, God! You know I'll be good to him! I'll never look at another man again if You get me out of this mess!' she implored. Feverishness evaporated at last. She became alert and calculating, she had to plan, she must be *quiet*.

'Be quiet!' her taut nerves screamed, so that the whole of her little room became full of their clamour. In a minute everyone would hear their noise! Was she really screaming or was she only imagining she was screaming? If only there was someone who would help her! Images rose to monstrous proportions in her brain – Toto, Kamelya, Fitnet, but they were all useless. They would never help her, she would have to go through this alone.

'Help me! Help me!' she babbled and let herself be carried away on the sound of the words. After a time their meaning was lost and they were nothing but noise. Her teeth chattered with cold but she still went on saying 'help me!'

Throughout the day she could not concentrate. How could she study when her whole life must be decided before tomorrow night? In a fever of impatience she hurried home from lectures, her mind a blank.

'Why so early today?' asked her father pulling out his watch and regarding it attentively. 'Why aren't you here at this time every day?'

'A lecture was cut *baba* – I think the professor was ill ...' She stared at him offhandedly, trying to be normal.

'I wish he was ill every day,' she said and laughed. She could feel the edge of her mouth twitching. Then it seemed like a terrible jerking, pulling her face out of shape. 'Let me make some *kahve* for you,' she said hurriedly, stooping above his chair and running her hand through his greying hair. 'Just to show you how well I can make it'.

'Well, don't waste the sugar,' he said sourly.

The warmth of the kitchen made her sick in the pit of her stomach. She felt so sick she thought she was dying and she could not control the twitching muscle in her face.

'You look very flushed,' said her mother as she came into the sitting-room with the tray of coffees.

'I'm all right,' said Neriman faintly. 'It was bending over the fire that's all.' She could feel her head swimming. 'It was so hot out there,' she said in confusion.

'You must be starting a cold,' said her mother. 'Hot? Why it's freezing today child!'

'I'm all right.' But if she did not sit down in a minute she would faint. 'I shall go to bed early,' she said. 'With the party tomorrow, there won't be much sleep you know!'

'What do you want with parties?' her father asked, glaring at her unpleasantly.

She remained quiet. She was afraid he might do something at the last moment, perhaps he'd stop her going out... She grew ice cold with hatred.

'But I can't not go now *baba*,' she said striving for calmness. 'You promised me I could go!'

He gave her a piercing look.

'So, have I said anything?' he asked roughly.

She got away from them at last. Her room was bitterly cold but she was alone at last, they would not disturb her here. She could not bear to think about Murat. She would muddle everything if she began to think about him now. She closed her aching eyelids and gradually everything grew further and further away. This was like being drunk, no it was better than being drunk because the bed stayed still. By this time tomorrow night, perhaps, she'd be safe.

Tears squeezed from under her closed eyes as she thought of being safe again.

Chapter 26

Neriman's mother said anxiously, 'I hope you won't be cold in that dress, it's so thin! Oughtn't you put on something heavier?'

'Oh, no mother!' said Neriman impatiently. She twisted herself round so that she could see her reflection better. 'I want to look nice,' she said. She shrugged herself into her winter coat and pulled a little woollen cap over her sleek head. How pretty she looked with her pink cheeks, sparkling eyes and her tremulous red lips, the very picture of a desperate young adventurer out to sack a city! How could she fail tonight if she went on looking like this?

'Will you be late home, Neriman? Don't you think *baba* should fetch you?'

'I've told you, mother! If it gets very late, I shall stay the night there. I don't want *baba* coming out in the middle of the night.'

'Well, if you're coming home, don't be too late. You know how cross *baba* gets. Perhaps he won't let you go another time!'

Neriman smiled into the glass. 'Perhaps I shan't want to go again,' she said.

'Oughtn't you to leave us the address, just in case?'

'Oh, stop fussing mother! I don't know the address properly anyway. I'm meeting Suna and she will take me there.'

'You look so pretty!' her mother sighed wistfully.

'Yes.' She searched for her gloves feverishly. 'And now I must go,' she said.

It was cold outside with a hint of rain in the air. The pavements were still wet from an earlier shower and reflected the tall yellow street lamps. The last of the leaves tossed madly in the wind, exciting Neriman. What a wild night it was! Her eager feet hurried to meet her lover, ablaze with excitement, well muffled in last winter's coat. Murat waited at the corner, half in shadow. 'I'm here!' she said breathlessly, giggling with relief. He took her hand in his and squeezed it tightly.

'I'm so glad I got away all right,' she said and looked up at him with her mouth half open. She was all dewy freshness like a rose. He thought he had never seen her lovelier.

'Was it very difficult?'

'They think I'm going to a party,' she said with laughter bubbling inside her like a spring that could not be stilled. 'It was the only thing to say.' She looked away from him with a strained expression. 'I've never told them a lie before,' she pouted. Her face crumpled into laughter as she remembered her mother's anxiety, and she took Murat's arm confidingly.

'Isn't it lovely to be out at night?' she said.

'I thought we might go to Bebek, to the casino there,' Murat said as they walked along. 'Or would it be too cold for you Neriman?'

'Oh no.' She smiled into the darkness. 'I've never seen Bebek at night,' she said.

'Let's be rich and take a taxi,' Murat suggested.

'That'd be lovely!'

In the taxi they held hands tightly, stealing kisses now and then. They were delighted by their nearness to one another, the long happy evening stretching ahead of them invitingly. 'Isn't it fun?' said Neriman excitedly, her white teeth flashing in the light of a passing lamp.

'I've been looking forward to it all day,' said Murat. Kamelya's face flickered before him, took shape, then died away again. He'd seen her that morning in Pera. She'd had a big white dog on a lead and had looked as if she were going to speak to him at last. He had raised his head expectantly. But she changed her mind. He saw her call a passing taxi. Then she and the big dog had been whisked away.

He sighed.

'What's wrong?'

'Nothing.'

Because she had been his first love, the magic would never leave her entirely. Whenever he saw her, nostalgia would sting him. He resented her mystery. If he had known her, the enchantment would have faded by now. She would have meant less than Neriman.

'You're so quiet Murat!'

He squeezed her hand lovingly. 'I'm thinking about you,' he said.

At the casino, just as they had seated themselves comfortably, Neriman said urgently, 'Murat we can't stay here!'

'What's wrong?'

'One of my father's friends is sitting over there – that officer with the woman in blue...' She sheltered behind Murat while he glanced across at the officer. 'If he sees me he might tell my father!' she said in panic. In fact, she was afraid because the officer might tell Murat who she was. 'Let's leave,' she said urgently.

Her whiteness alarmed Murat and he hurried her outside, into the protective darkness. 'That was a terrible moment,' she said, leaning against him weakly with her teeth chattering, 'I'm so glad he didn't see me!'

'Where shall we go now?' He felt despondent, her nervousness had affected him too.

'Anywhere you like,' she said, quickly smiling at him, anxious to make up for the bad start to their lovely evening.

He said hesitantly, 'There's a place I know in Arnavutköy. I don't know whether I can take you there or not. They have private rooms,' he said. 'Do you think you could come to such a place with me Neriman?' He looked at her sideways, trying to gauge her expression unawares. 'You would be quite safe,' he added nervously.

She felt hysterical with exhaustion. The day had been long. Had it only led to this?

'If anyone saw me I should be very compromised,' she replied. 'But if you think it's all right?'

'You can't be seen in a private room anyway.'

'All right then,' she said, trying to control her voice. 'I'll leave it to you.'

She was thinking that even if she had not seen that officer she would have invented someone. It had been in her mind all day. Was Murat going to ruin everything now?

He looked at her with indecision and after a time said: 'Very well then. Let's go to Arnavutköy!'

They took another taxi, with Murat reflecting sorrowfully that most of the money Ahmet had given him seemed to be going on transport. Neriman rubbed her chin against his shoulder.

'You're so quiet tonight!' she complained.

'You're only imagining it.'

'Anyway, I'm happy,' she said and sighed blissfully. He clasped her hand, fingers entwined, but made no reply and she wondered what had changed his mood. Was it because she would not stay in the Bebek casino? Her heart began to beat heavily and nervously. He *was* a little in love with her wasn't he?

Trying to compose herself, she nevertheless felt herself frowning. What did she know about him or what he did with his other evenings? Did he take other women to casinos? Was he in love with someone else? She shivered, defenceless in her need. How could she compete with the unknown women in his life? There must have been others before her? Perhaps there had even been one who had meant something special. There were moments when she felt him far away from her.

'You're the quiet one now!' he accused smilingly.

'I'm all right,' she said in a muffled voice. She felt inadequate and childish in her silly dress. She ached with a sense of loss.

At Arnavutköy it was easy enough to engage a private room. It was late in the season, the nights were chilly, and couples preferred the warm bright lights of public restaurants. The room overhung the sea and Neriman went to the window and looked out on the dark heaving face of the water. The moaning noise it made alarmed her and she turned back to Murat, her young face grave and her eyes dilated.

'Cold,' she said and shivered in her coat. 'The sea, I mean.' She paused, 'It looks so lonely out there.'

He put his hands on her narrow shoulders and she longed to feel his arms about her and to sob out her sorrow on his breast. He looked so dependable. She smiled at him wanly. 'It's the time of the year,' she said weakly, 'it makes me stupid! I'll be all right presently.'

'You're hungry,' said Murat and kissed her eyes. He rang for the waiter while she took off her coat and her gay woolly cap. 'What are you going to drink?' he asked, looking up from the menu he was studying.

The waiter came into the room as she tidied her hair back.

'Nothing,' she said.

'Oh, you must drink something,' said Murat and she felt the surprised, sardonic eye of the waiter turned on her.

'No, nothing really,' she persisted obstinately.

'Just a sip of something, eh Neriman?' Murat was smiling at her, coaxingly, innocent of her intentions.

'Oh… whatever you like!' she said hurriedly and looked away from them. She felt she was doing it all wrong, and was spoiling the happy mood of the evening before it had begun. Murat ordered *rakı* and when it was brought in she grew reckless and said, 'Let me taste some Murat, perhaps it will warm me!' She caressed her bare arms, lovingly rubbing warmth into them. Murat looked at her with his eyebrows raised and she ached with emotion. How had it happened? She had never meant to love him like this!

'Well, it's very brave of you,' he was saying as he poured a small glass for her, adding water. 'I only hope your head will stand it, that's all!'

He held the glass to her lips and she sipped then coughed as the hot, fiery liquid went down her throat. She didn't like it but it was warming her already. If only she could go on feeling like this, everything would be all right. She stooped and kissed his sleeve impulsively. 'Sometimes you're nice, aren't you?' she remarked with a tremor in her voice and he tilted her face upwards.

'What's this?' he asked. 'Tears, Neriman? Why are you crying?'

'It's nothing. You mustn't take any notice of me! I'm happy that's all. It was so difficult to get away from home with everyone fussing and mother asking questions.' She looked at him through a haze. 'Perhaps that's all it is,' she said and went on talking. He must not know there was anything wrong. She took another sip of *rakı*. It had brought colour to her cheeks and her face burned as if she were on fire but her body was icy cold.

'Have some meze!' said Murat and speared a stuffed olive with his fork. 'Open your mouth!' he said.

She did as she was bid.

'And that's the way to close it,' he said, leaning forward to kiss her.

'You're so nice to me Murat! I wish I could stay here forever!' To be able to catch the shining moment and hold it fast, never to let it go again! She felt her eyes misting with tears she could not control. 'I shall miss you,' she said huskily. 'When you go away I mean…'

'But I haven't gone yet,' he said in mystification. 'Have another drink – you're all on edge tonight!'

The *rakı* was lovely – horrible, horrible taste but how warming! She was warm all over now. Why didn't he kiss her again?

'Can you hear the music from downstairs?' he asked with his head a little on one side in listening attitude. 'I wish we could dance.'

'Let's dance here.'

'It wouldn't be the same.'

'Oh, Murat! Do let's dance, it may never happen again – look, let's put the light out and dance here!' For all the excitement in her voice there was sadness too. It pulled at his nerves, disturbing him. She jumped up and went over beside him. 'Come on!' she said with her hands around his head and holding him so close he could hear the beating of her heart. 'Let's dance near the window! We can hear the sea from there. Can you hear the noise the waves are making under us?'

'Yes, they're making me feel cold!'

'You're so unromantic,' she said and laughed into his face, her eyes level with his. 'I shall put out the light!' she said.

'There'll be a moon presently. The Bosphor will turn silver.'

In the half darkness he took her in his arms. 'I can't see you properly,' he said, 'Who are you, mysterious stranger?' A memory stirred with savage pain, a face hurt him with it's cool look of indifference.

'There's the moon now!' said Neriman. 'Look Murat! It's just coming over those mountains there, isn't it lovely?'

'I believe you timed it,' he teased her.

'Oh, you!'

'Ah, I can see who you are now! You're sweet Neriman with the stern father. Will you dance with me Neriman?' He held his arms wide.

'They're playing a tango,' she said rapturously. 'I'm sure you tango beautifully!'

'You're not bad yourself,' said Murat after awhile. He bent forward and kissed her long pale throat. 'Like a girl in a dream,' he said with urgency in his voice. 'I don't believe you're real at all!'

She danced with her eyes closed and a little smile on her passionate mouth. 'Silly!' she murmured. Each time they passed the loaded table they bent forward to drink from the *rakı* glasses.

'The music isn't loud enough,' said Murat.

'It's your heart,' said Neriman. 'It's terrible the way it's pounding against me!'

After a while she broke away from him and flung herself on the wide divan under the window.

'You can see the moon much better from here,' she beckoned in a small voice.

Murat stood in the middle of the room where she had left him. His head was whirling – he didn't know if it was the *rakı* or her nearness.

'Come over,' she called. 'You're so far away I can't see you properly. Come along Murat!' she said, her nerves tingling with impatience.

He moved slowly.

'Let's put the light on,' he said uncertainly.

'We don't need light! It's lovely here. We can put the light on later. Come and rest.'

He sat down beside her and felt her hip warm against him.

'Isn't it lovely?' she said.

He kissed her and her mouth closed over his own with finality. Who was she? Did it matter that she did not wear the face of love? She was beautiful just as she was, with the moon outlining her hair and the delicate contours of her face. He kissed her with urgency and she did not resist. His mouth travelled down, across her throat, lingering for a while until it dared upon her tender young breasts.

She might have been any woman put there for his desire.

Chapter 27

THUNDERSTRUCK, AHMET SAID, 'Did you say marriage?'
'Yes.' Murat shuffled his feet and looked defiant. This was one of the times when Ahmet intimidated him. 'Damn it!' he said irritably. 'You needn't look so surprised about it! Hasn't the possibility ever occurred to you?'

'I never thought about it.' He looked at Murat keenly.

'Who is the girl?' he asked. 'Do you know anything about her at all?'

'Naturally,' Murat's mouth curled with nervous contempt. 'I shouldn't be marrying her if I didn't. She's at the university and her people are quite respectable. Her father's a civil servant.'

'Have you met them?'

'Of course,' Murat shook his shoulders with impatience. 'It's all all right,' he said with emphasis, 'but I thought you ought to know.'

'Very kind of you,' said Ahmet drily and flung himself into an armchair. 'You make me feel old,' he said looking up at Murat, 'hearing you talking of marriage.'

'I'm twenty-four. What do you expect?'

'Well, I'm glad you had the sense to choose an educated girl anyway. Where did you meet her?'

Murat looked haughty and uncomfortable. 'I met her by accident,' he said.

Ahmet said sharply, 'Look here! Is there anything wrong about this? I don't understand this secretiveness.'

'There's nothing wrong,' said Murat loudly. 'What the devil do you mean by "wrong"?'

'You are remarkably nervous,' said Ahmet mildly. 'If you can't discuss the thing civilly let's leave it altogether.'

'You mean you are not interested whether I marry or not?'

'I'm very interested but I'm more interested to know why you're hedging. Did you come here to ask for my congratulations or is there something else?'

Murat stared at him miserably.

'I can't say you look like an excited bridegroom,' said Ahmet in the same even voice. 'I suggest you sit down and stop looking fierce and tell me what's on your mind!'

Murat opened his mouth to speak then seemed to change his mind again. He picked up a shiny magazine from the table and studied the cover intently. After a time he said slowly, 'There's nothing else to say. You wouldn't understand.'

Ahmet stood up and put his hands on the young man's shoulders. 'Put that thing down,' he said, taking away the magazine. He stared at Murat deeply. 'Now tell me what it is I wouldn't understand,' he said.

Murat gave a guilty half smile. 'I'm in a mess,' he said.

Ahmet released him and turned away. 'Would you like to tell me about it? Perhaps I can help... you know.'

He sat down again and motioned to Murat to take the other chair.

'I don't know what you've been up to,' he commenced, 'but there's not much use telling me part of the story. You thrust yourself on me uninvited, announce you're getting married, and then that you're in a mess and obviously expect advice on something I know nothing about!' He smiled to take the harshness from his words, 'Now tell me!' he said.

Murat leaned forward and put his head in his hands. 'It's difficult,' he said in a muffled voice, 'when I know I can't get out of it.'

'Out of the marriage?'

Murat nodded.

Ahmet frowned. 'Have you been coerced into this?' he asked sharply. 'Did you get drunk or something and promise the girl's parents?'

Murat raised his head. 'It's not quite like that,' he said bitterly. 'I got drunk all right but I knew what I was doing when I asked her to marry me.' He took a deep breath. 'I may as well start from the beginning,' he said nervously.

He told Ahmet the whole story and at the end Ahmet said in bewilderment, 'But Murat *canım* what sort of girl is she who would let herself be taken to a private room in a casino?'

'She didn't know.'

'Are you sure she's as innocent as you think?'

'Quite sure.'

They looked at one another for a long moment. 'I see,' Ahmet said uncomfortably.

He looked away from Murat. 'Was it wise to go so far?' he asked stiffly, 'with a young girl you were convinced was a virgin?' His stiffness stimulated Murat to anger.

'You asked me to explain,' he said.

'But were you mad?' Ahmet turned on him with a face of blazing contempt. 'Didn't you know what you were doing? Why in heaven's name did you take her to a private room in the first place? Why did you let her drink with you?'

'I didn't think. It didn't occur to me...'

'If her family were so concerned about her why did they allow her to stay out at night?'

'I explained to you! They thought she was going to a party!'

'Who was the man, the officer, in Bebek?'

'How the devil do I know? She said he was a friend of her father's, and we couldn't stay there after that! Somehow or other I just thought of the place in Arnavutköy.'

'And now you want to get out of marrying her?'

Murat raised his head sharply. 'I didn't say that!'

'Then what are we doing here discussing it?'

'I didn't want to discuss it,' said Murat passionately. 'I came here to tell you I was getting married. You forced the discussion!'

'You bloody young fool! Hadn't you any better sense? What're you going to do now?'

'I shall do what I intended to do all along. I shall marry her because I have no alternative.'

Ahmet's eyes swept him bitterly. 'I was so proud of you,' he said witheringly. 'What d'you think you're going to live on at your age? Has she any money?'

'No, but we'll manage I expect.'

'I won't give you a goddamned penny!'

'Nobody asked you to!'

'I might have known something like this would happen one day! You're so impossibly weak!'

'It's not weakness to marry a girl you've ruined. What do you expect me to do? I've no case to take to law but she has. There was a waiter at the casino. He knew what was going on.'

'Look, if you went to law you'd be finished anyway. At your age the scandal would be the end of you.'

Anger dropped from Murat. 'I know,' he said bitterly. 'Don't you think I've thought of all this myself?'

The sophisticate in Ahmet forced him to say, 'We place too high a value on virginity.'

Murat looked surprised, 'Yes, well…' he said unhappily and then stopped, uncertain how to go on. 'There's nothing we can do now,' he said angrily.

Ahmet looked at his dejected stance. 'Has everything been arranged?'

'Yes.'

'Her parents are delighted of course?'

'Of course.'

'They should have guarded her a little better. Do you want me to go and see them?'

'No. There's no need. It's done now.' He stood up and paced around the room. 'I shall ask for a transfer,' he said. 'Do you think you could do anything about it for me, sir? I'd like a transfer as soon as I'm married.'

'You're going to leave her in Istanbul?'

'Yes.'

'I'm very disappointed,' said Ahmet, scowling at him. 'I never thought I'd see you marrying like this, my boy. You realise if you get a transfer you'll have to support two homes?'

'Who cares?'

'Is she going to continue at the university?'

'I have no idea.'

'Well your attitude is surely admirable for a young man going into marriage!'

'It needn't have been like this.' Murat's face settled into sulkiness.

'Quite. But you were apparently sufficiently attracted to this girl from the beginning?'

'Does one have to marry every girl one is attracted to?'

'May I ask does one have to seduce every girl one takes out? You weren't entertaining a prostitute.'

'There's a woman in Pera,' Murat said slowly. 'I don't know why it is but I always have the feeling she is somehow responsible for all this.' He paused, looking bemused.

'A woman in Pera? Murat, please… what are you trying to say now?'

'I don't quite know. It's hard to explain. I don't know her or anything about her and yet in a way I *do* know her. I met her a long time ago when I was in Harbiye, earlier even perhaps. Celal and I used to meet her in the street sometimes. She used to look at me as if she wanted to speak…'

'Someone trying to pick you up?' interrupted Ahmet with a frown.

'Yes. Celal used to say that too. I don't know, I never thought so somehow. She… she used to look at me as if she… well as if she liked me.'

'But what has this to do with your getting married?'

'I don't know, I tell you!' said Murat angrily. 'I only think perhaps it has – I still see her sometimes in Pera when she's shopping.'

'You sound infatuated!'

'I don't think it's that,' said Murat carefully, trying to control his anger, 'excepting that I found myself thinking about her that night at the casino – she kept coming into my mind and…'

'Are you trying to tell me you seduced the girl because you were thinking about this woman?'

Murat looked muddled. 'I don't think I meant that,' he said, 'but now you've said it I think it's just possible. I saw her that morning. She had a big white dog with her and I remember she stopped a little when she saw me and I felt certain she was going to speak…'

'A woman with a white dog?' interposed Ahmet quickly. 'What was she like?'

'Very beautiful,' said Murat and looked nonplussed. 'Just very beautiful,' he said helplessly, at a loss to describe her.

'Yes, yes, you've made it very clear,' said Ahmet acidly. 'I would recognise her anywhere by such an excellently detailed description!' He stood up feeling suddenly disquietened. 'But what is she *like*?' he persisted. 'Do you know her name? Is she dark or…'

'She has red hair,' said Murat, 'if that's all you mean. She is married to… well, to someone rather important.' Ahmet felt coldness settling over him. 'You mean you're talking about the wife of the Minister of Trade?' he observed in a clipped, compressed voice.

'But how do you know that, sir?'

Ahmet felt jealousy rising in him. Was Kamelya deceiving him behind his back, the way she had deceived the minister for years? 'She is very well known,' he said stiffly. 'She also parades Pera with her aristocratic white dog, she has red hair, and is very beautiful. She is probably the best known woman in Istanbul.' He turned away, feeling hatred for Murat. 'You say she has known you since you were in Harbiye?'

'She has been aware of me – hardly known me sir, for we have never spoken to one another.' He remembered the time she sat next to him in the cinema and his mouth creased in a smile.

'I forbid you to have anything to do with this woman,' said Ahmet who had seen the smile. 'Do you hear me?' he asked angrily.

'You have no right to forbid me anything at all!'

'I have every right you idiot! You've got yourself involved in an unfortunate marriage and now you tell me some fantastic story about a minister's wife!'

'I would have said nothing at all if I'd not thought you would understand.' Murat was as white as Ahmet. They glared at one another with suspicion and the glimmerings of enmity. 'What is it to you?' Murat asked softly.

'Never mind!' said Ahmet in a rage of wounded vanity. 'But keep away from that woman that's all!'

'You're afraid I shall be involved in scandal?'

'*You*? Do you think she'd look at you or involve herself with *you*?' Ahmet stopped speaking as he saw the superior amusement on Murat's face. 'Blast you!' he said thickly. 'You insolent jackal! You and Celal parading the streets like clowns, discussing a respectable woman like dirty schoolboys – have you no decency?'

He saw the white, surprised face of Murat through a red mist of anger and distrust.

'You great fool!' he said contemptuously.

Murat continued to look at him with blank astonishment.

It was the last thing the colonel saw as he lunged blindly towards him.

Chapter 28

KAMELYA WAS DRINKING her after-lunch coffee when she heard the sound of argument in the hall.

'What is it?' she said hurrying to the door.

Rana stood there looking truculent whilst Neriman argued with her.

'What is it?' asked Kamelya again. 'Oh! It's you Neriman!'

'She wouldn't let me in,' said Neriman jerking a finger in Rana's direction.

'I said the *hanım* was busy.'

'You said nothing of the sort you old witch. You said she was not at home!'

'Well, there's no need for all this argument,' said Kamelya crossly. 'You'd better come in now you're here Neriman.'

She led the way back to her drawing-room.

'How she hates me!' said Neriman, pulling off her gloves. 'Twice in the past week I have been here but she always refuses to let me in!'

'There wouldn't have been much purpose,' said Kamelya calmly. 'I have been in Ankara with my husband. I only got back yesterday.'

'Oh, I see.'

Neriman sat down in a chair and Kamelya poured coffee for her. 'So, what have you been up to?' she asked as she handed her the coffee. 'You look mischievous!'

Neriman chuckled happily.

'I have so wanted to see you,' she said.

Kamelya sat down and lit a cigarette. She felt somewhat apprehensive and hoped Neriman was not going to repeat one of her scenes.

'Is everything all right with you?' she asked diffidently, partially reassured by the happy look of expectancy on the girl's face.

Neriman made a little mouth. 'Oh *yes!*' she said. She leaned back in her chair. 'I'm going to be married.'

'Married?' asked Kamelya and her eyes crinkled into relieved amusement. 'Are you really serious?'

'Yes,' she clasped her hands together like a child and said gently, 'I'm so happy I can't believe it's true!'

Kamelya stared at her with amazement. 'I really believe you are serious!' she said, standing up to go to the buffet to open a bottle of Château d'Yquem Sauternes. 'This calls for some sort of celebration.'

'How did it happen?' she asked, as she returned to her chair with the tray of glasses balanced delicately on one hand. 'Can you stay and have dinner with me? I shall be quite alone?'

'No,' said Neriman half regretfully, as she took a glass of wine. 'There is a small party at home tonight. I wish I could have asked you but you would hate it.' She raised her glass. 'Toast me!' she said.

'To your happiness,' said Kamelya, sipping the wine.

Neriman giggled. 'You're responsible in a way,' she said.

'I?'

'Yes. Once you told me I ought to try marriage, don't you remember? Well, perhaps you wouldn't... but I didn't forget.' Her face sobered into seriousness. 'Really, though, it wasn't so much what you said, it just happened in the right way.' She looked pensive. 'He's an officer,' she said, 'a lieutenant... he's nice...' She blushed, looking away from Kamelya's interested gaze, adding slowly, 'He knows nothing about me.'

'Well now, my dearest, I hardly suppose he would!'

'We used to meet sometimes and go for walks or to a cinema and then one night we went to that casino in Arnavutköy, the one where they have the private rooms.' She grinned self-consciously. 'Oh, you know!' she said impatiently.

Kamelya could not help smiling. 'Is he very young?' she asked.

'Twenty-four.'

'Young enough to be deceived,' said Kamelya and drank more wine. Laughter touched her pretty eyes. 'Oh Neriman!' she said explosively.

Neriman looked shy suddenly. 'He's... he's very nice,' she said lamely, looking down at the glass in her hands.

'You're in love with him!'

Neriman's mouth curved downwards. 'Yes,' she said sadly. 'That's why I was sorry I had to deceive him. But it was the only way. There was nothing else for me to do.'

She finished her wine quickly. 'But it's all right now,' she said defiantly. 'Everything's arranged.'

'So you are going to be good now?'

'Yes. I shall be so good to him you can't imagine!'

'And what about his parents? Will you have to live with them after you marry?'

'No, there aren't any parents. Only some old guardian, some man, who won't interfere.'

'How very convenient!' said Kamelya drily. 'In fact, he's just ready made for you. You won't have any formidable old mother-in-law screaming at her neighbours that you weren't a virgin on marriage!'

Neriman winced. 'Must you?' she asked.

'I'm sorry,' said Kamelya impulsively. 'Really I didn't think you'd mind. How all this has changed you my dear!'

'I want to put everything else behind me,' said Neriman slowly. 'He's the first person I've ever been able to believe in. You can't imagine what that means!'

'Are your parents pleased?'

'Naturally! My father is so pleased he's paying for everything.'

'Well, I expect that pleases your young man,' said Kamelya brightly. 'He's not rich is he?'

'No. How could he be rich? He was orphaned when he was a child. For years he was brought up in a *konak* until he was sent to military school. He's no one to give him money.'

Kamelya changed colour with such rapidity she thought she was going to faint.

'Why, whatever's the matter with you?' cried Neriman in alarm. 'Are you all right?'

'Nothing's the matter,' said Kamelya, making an effort to remain normal. 'Go on.'

'There's nothing else to tell, I've told you everything I know.'

'What's his name?' Kamelya interrupted harshly. Neriman looked uncertain. What *was* the matter?

'Murat,' she said. 'He is a cavalry officer, a lieutenant.'

'I...' said Kamelya, but she could not go on.

'What is it?' said Neriman. 'Shall I call Rana? Are you ill?'

'I'm perfectly all right,' said Kamelya in a hard cold voice. 'Do you… I mean have you his photograph?'

Neriman rummaged in her bag. 'But of course,' she said with an attempt at lightness. 'What do you expect?' She handed the photograph to Kamelya. 'Isn't he good looking?' she asked proudly. She watched Kamelya as she looked at the scrap of card in her hand.

'All my friends at university envy me,' she said shyly.

Kamelya looked at her with piercing hatred. 'When are you getting married?'

'Tomorrow. That's why I wanted to see you before.'

'You will never marry him,' said Kamelya, ignoring her placatory smile. She stood up and moved nearer to Neriman. 'Did you hear what I said?' she asked. 'You will never marry him.'

'But what's it to you?' Neriman stammered, intimidated by Kamelya's high cold look and the daunting whiteness of her face. 'Why do you look at me like that Kamelya? My God! What's wrong with you today?'

'Did you hear what I said?' Kamelya repeated venomously. 'You will never marry him, never. Now get out of my house immediately, you damned bloody whore!'

Neriman watched her with fear. 'You're… it's… What the hell are you talking about?' she asked in a shrill girlish voice. She was too amazed to be angry.

'Listen, you slut, this boy is too good for you!' Kamelya's voice tore the air savagely. 'I know him well,' she said. 'He's…'

Rage gripped Neriman. 'Damn you,' she cried. 'Who are you to call me names? Who are *you* to interfere in my life?'

'I wouldn't have expected anything better from you than this,' said Kamelya. 'But you'll never marry him, I'll see to that. Never, never.'

'Who are you to talk like this?' Neriman interrupted, her voice crazed with hatred. 'What's he to…' She suddenly stopped talking, her mouth half-open in a way that made her look half-witted, 'I know!' she said softly. 'I know now who you are! Fitnet said before, I didn't think. How could I think? You're his mother, aren't you? I didn't think. I saw it before in Murat. I remember now… that look of someone I knew.'

'Stop trying to invent!' said Kamelya contemptuously.

'I'm not inventing anything, I remember now!' She laughed stupidly. '*Of course* you're his mother!' she said. 'Yes, that's it. I saw your name on the wedding papers when we went to Eyüp Sultan. I didn't think then, there are so many Kamelyas. You came from Eyüp Sultan didn't you?' Her voice cracked with fatigue. 'Oh... what's the use of asking you that?' she said. 'You'll only deny it.' She approached Kamelya, pleading. 'How could I know?' Her face was hideous with despair. 'You'll never stop me!' she said. 'I'll kill you first. You wouldn't dare!'

Kamelya took hold of her and shook her shoulders until the girl's teeth chattered against one another. 'Did I sacrifice him for this?' she asked wildly, all caution gone from her in an instant. 'Did I leave him to his respectable life only to see him marrying a cheap little prostitute like you, opening your legs at the drop of a lira?' She shook her wildly in her own wild agony. 'Did I cut him out of my heart for *you*?'

'Well, whatever, I'm a good deal better than you,' said Neriman, twisting herself away from the terrible shaking arms and pincer-like fingers. 'You left him on the streets and went away with a man. You're a bigger prostitute than I am! I love him, do you hear? I *love* him.'

'You? Love? You're not fit to kiss his boots. I'll never let you marry him, damn you! By Allah I'll disgrace you in public, I'll...'

'You'll do nothing of the sort! You'd be too afraid of disgracing yourself and your precious minister. You never cared about Murat. You let him grow up with strangers while you made love and enjoyed yourself. You didn't care what happened to him as long as you were free.' She was half crying with rage and emotion. 'I'll be better to him than you ever were,' she cried, and then laughter swept over her so that she could hardly speak. 'I'll be a respectable wife just like you!' she whispered, exhausted.

'You'll never marry him I tell you!'

'You can't stop it. You're years too late Kamelya! You should have looked after him better. Why didn't you help me get rid of my baby? You didn't want to help, did you? You and old Rana, you're both the same. You were glad I was in trouble! You were afraid of scandal! "Try marriage," you said. Well, I took your advice, damn you! I took your advice!' She was laughing and crying at the same time. She saw Kamelya's icy face, distorted with passion, through a veil of tears. 'Try and stop me,' she cried, leaning against the back of a chair to steady her aching back. 'A prostitute's son for a prostitute wife. Excepting that I love him...' She put her hands over her face and sobbed. 'I love him!' she cried in an access of terror. 'Can't you understand that?'

'Get out!' said Kamelya, keeping control of herself. 'Get out and *never* come here again. You'll never marry Murat.' She made a soft forward movement and the girl watched her with dilated eyes.

'Don't touch me!' she whined in a high childish voice. 'Let me go!'

'I would not dream of touching you,' said Kamelya with scorn, standing aside to let her pass.

She saw Neriman wrench open the door, heard her pattering steps on the stairs, and then she leaned her head on the cool marble of the mantelpiece.

No matter what disgrace she brought, she would never let Murat marry that girl. She was a soft-faced streetwalker who had tricked him into believing she was innocent!

'I'll kill her first!' she said, to an astonished Rana in the doorway.

She pushed past her and went into her bedroom. She opened the massive mahogany doors of her wardrobe and felt under a pile of gloves until she found her gun. 'Have I cleaned it regularly all these years for this?' she asked her distraught reflection in the long glass. 'Was it only for this?' She looked at the little gun with fear and loathing. 'Am I a murderer?' she asked aloud. Leaving the wardrobe doors gaping wide she went back to the sitting-room where Rana was clearing the dirty coffee cups and the empty wine glasses.

'Isn't there some other way Rana?' she pleaded as she put the little gun on the mantelpiece, partly pushing it behind a tall vase of flowers.

'I don't know *hanım*,' said Rana, looking terrified.

Kamelya ruffled her red hair with a manic theatrical gesture.

'Get me the Officers' Club on the phone,' she said to Rana. 'Quickly! Leave all those things now. I must speak to Colonel Ahmet at once!'

Chapter 29

A HMET WAS NOT at the Officers' Club.
    'Do you know when he'll be back?'

'I couldn't say *hanım*,' said the faraway, impersonal voice at the other end of the line.

Kamelya felt she would scream with frustration.

'Would you like to leave a message?' asked the voice persuasively.

'No. No thank you. I'll ring again later.'

Kamelya put down the telephone and looked at the clock on the mantelpiece. Almost five o'clock! Where could Ahmet be and why had he not been to see her since she'd come back from Ankara?

She paced restlessly up and down the room feeling caged, almost choked with nerves.

'Time is so short!' she said and beat her hands together in agitation. 'Something must be done immediately!'

She rang the club at half-hourly intervals but still Ahmet was not there.

At seven o'clock a new voice told her that Colonel Ahmet was at Haydarpaşa on duty.

'Is he – is he expected back soon?' she asked faintly.

'I really couldn't say *hanım*,' the voice replied, disapprovingly.

She bit her lips and then said desperately, 'Do you – I mean – is Lieutenant Murat at the club?'

'Will you please hold on *hanım* while I see?'

The minutes she waited seemed the longest in her life, but after a while she heard the low, diffident voice of her son asking who it was who wanted him.

For a long moment she was unable to answer him, but then she put her lips to the telephone. 'Kamelya… Kamelya,' she said.

***

Ahmet returned to the Officers' Club a little after half-past seven. Leaving the two gouty generals he'd escorted from Haydarpaşa Station for a few minutes, he went over to Celal who was drinking alone.

'Where's Murat?' Ahmet asked him.

'He left here a few minutes ago, sir.'

Ahmet frowned. He had particularly asked Murat to wait until he returned from the station. He looked at his watch with impatience. Surely he'd left early for his dinner appointment with Neriman's family? 'Do you know where he went?'

Celal hesitated and then said, 'I don't, sir, no.'

Ahmet sensed he was lying but time pressed and the Generals still awaited him. He could not hope to be released from their company for at least another half hour.

'Look here!' he said angrily. 'You've got to tell me where Murat's gone!'

Celal stood to attention in front of him and did not reply.

'God damn it, are you dumb?' Ahmet demanded irritably. 'Surely he said where he was going?'

Celal said sulkily, 'A lady telephoned him, sir, and he left here almost immediately afterwards.'

'A lady?' Ahmet felt his face flame with suspicion. 'Do you know who she was?' he asked.

'No sir.'

There was no use questioning Celal any further. It was obvious he would say no more than he had already and Ahmet went back to the generals and ordered drinks. As he sat in his comfortable chair talking about regimental matters, he could feel the blood drumming behind his temples. Had Kamelya telephoned Murat? Remembering his last conversation with Murat, he did not think that anyone else could have acted on him with the same urgency. Part of him answered with mechanical precision the questions the generals put to him. Another side harangued Kamelya. He was in the grip of a jealousy he'd never known before. The minutes could not pass quickly enough for him. He hated Murat with a passionate destructiveness. At eight o'clock he was able to take his leave. Distraught with mounting suspicion, for Murat had not returned, he went out into the street and hailed a passing taxi, American-made.

Dark Journey

***

Half an hour earlier Murat had paid off his cab and tried not to hurry up the marble-faced steps to the apartment where Kamelya lived. With his finger pressed on the whirring electric bell he remembered his dinner appointment with Neriman and her family. 'Oh, well,' he murmured inaudibly, and pressed the bell harder. 'There's not much I can do about *that* now!' He shrugged away responsibility. This was his last night of freedom. Must he spend it with Neriman?

Rana opened the door to him, her poker face creasing into a smile of welcome when she saw him standing there. She had never seen him in her life before but he was so good looking, so tall and straight with his cap tilted at that rakish angle, he quite fluttered her wicked old heart.

'Come in, sir,' she said and opened the door wider to him. 'The *hanım* is expecting you.'

He put his cap and his gloves on the hall table and followed Rana to the salon where Kamelya waited for him.

He saw at once that it was a large room lit by a bright fire burning in an English-style fireplace and the lesser light of a floor lamp in one corner. It looked rich and elegant, with large spaces of polished floor between glowing Sparta rugs. There were a few Moorish coffee tables and heavy, cream silk curtains were draped across the windows. Murat was impressed and somewhat nervous.

Kamelya moved forward to greet him, giving him her hand over which he bowed formally. He straightened himself and his smile shook her heart with its brilliance.

'It was good of you to come so soon,' she said, and stood back from him.

She was so beautiful! But what did she want from him? She glowed for him, all traces of anger gone from her face, leaving it smooth and clear as a young girl's. Calm, elegant, a little bit nervous of his nearness – what chance had another woman?

'Please sit down, won't you?' she said and sat down herself. She waited as he lowered himself into an armchair opposite, and then she said carefully, 'You must be wondering why I telephoned you?'

194

She tried not to look at him too much. It was such bliss to have him here at last in his rightful place. Yet, despite it all, she tried to keep both her head and her heart.

'You sounded as if the matter might be important,' said Murat. Now it was *he* who could not look at her, except in sly, sidelong glances. She was so achingly lovely and the touch of her cool hand had almost undone him.

Kamelya smiled. 'It was,' she said. Was? Wasn't it so any longer? He caught her eyes and she looked away hurriedly, pushing a cigarette box towards him, taking a cigarette herself and busying herself with lighting it. She could not help thinking how handsome he was. She wished she had the ordinary rights of every mother to kiss his cheeks, touch his worn uniform, and run her hands through his thick, black hair which, she saw with a pang of dismay, grew back from the widow's peak like her own. Busying herself with little things, trying to act normally, she poured wine from a decanter.

'I hope you will like this wine,' she said in a formal voice. 'My husband gets it from France. I believe it is very good...' She handed him a glass, 'a connoisseur's wine.'

Murat sipped self-consciously, but it tasted like any other wine to him. What had he expected? He was no connoisseur. The glass in his hand gave him confidence. He could lean back in his chair at ease now with his long legs in their shining riding boots thrust carelessly before him. He became aware of music from somewhere behind him. A radio was it? He did not care to look to find out, staring instead at Kamelya with near insolence. She had invited him here this winter evening, what would the next move be?

Kamelya, sitting with one silk-stockinged leg crossed over the other at the knee, tantalised him to the point of foolishness. She wore black, with a fantastically large diamond pinned to the low neck of her dress just where a cleft of mysterious shadow divided her breasts. She was too disturbing. She should have known better than to invite a stranger to her home, he was thinking.

She said abruptly, 'I understand you are getting married tomorrow, lieutenant?'

He looked at her with raised eyebrows. 'You know that?'

'But yes! I know your – I know Neriman well.'

'I see.' What had they said about him? He finished his drink quickly. 'Yes, I am getting married tomorrow,' he said nervously.

Kamelya leaned forward in agitation, her dress parting at the centre with her abrupt movement. 'You have not much time,' she said.

'No.' He remembered again his dinner appointment.

'You will think it very impertinent perhaps if I tell you that… that I know of reasons why you must not marry this Neriman?' she spoke rapidly, twisting the base of her glass round and round in her hand.

Murat raised his eyes to her face. 'What do you mean?' he asked frowning.

She stared at him over the rim of her glass, her face half in shadow, seductive, infinitely sweet, an old tenderness shaping the nervous lines of her mouth. 'It is hard for me to say this,' she said, 'and, if you love her, perhaps it's unforgivable of me to interfere.' She paused and her silence seemed to be asking if he loved her.

Murat was astonished by her seriousness, a little angry, and all his senses warned him to leave and put an end to this ridiculous conversation. 'What are you trying to tell me?' he asked gravely. Should he stay? Should he listen to her? The face of Neriman flashed for an instant – did she beseech him? The face was gone almost before he had time to recognise it. How could Neriman have any power over him? Feeling hot and uncomfortable, he said stiffly, 'Please explain yourself *hanım*.'

God, how she stared at him over the rim of her glass! He moved nervously. What was she trying to do to him? Drive him mad?

She said carefully, 'Neriman was not innocent when you met her lieutenant. If that fact makes no difference to you, then I shall say no more, but a great deal of importance is usually attached to it.'

'It's impossible!' said Murat, sitting up straighter. If he went now, it would still be all right! He had no right to sit here and listen to stories about Neriman. He made a movement to rise but Kamelya held out a detaining hand.

'No!' she said firmly. 'Please!' Her eyes beseeched him to stay. 'Please,' she said earnestly, 'you must believe me. I have evidence in my hands to prove she isn't what you think. I can see you are startled. You do not want to believe me because her innocence was something you were certain of.'

'I won't listen to any more,' said Murat in panic. 'You've no right to... no right...' He stopped. He had listened already. It was too late now to go away with this tormenting half-knowledge and he had ached for release from this travesty of a marriage anyway. Should he remain? Could anything this woman said make any difference now?

'I have every right to say what I will,' said Kamelya and lifted her chin arrogantly. 'You *must* listen to me.' She poured more wine with fingers surprisingly steady.

'You are wrong,' he said coldly. 'I know Neriman well.' He had to stop. How could he explain himself to a stranger? Kamelya took one of his hands in hers, unnerving him again with the intimacy of the gesture. She leaned towards him so that he was aware of nothing but her enormous eyes looking into his.

'The girl's a prostitute,' she said. 'You must believe me! She's having a baby by somebody else.'

He pulled his hand away as though it were burning. 'How can I believe you?' he asked jerkily and stood up. A girl was singing on from the radio – soft, husky, sensual. Why didn't she stop it? 'You ask me to believe the impossible,' he told her, dispassionately feeling he had the advantage now he was standing.

'You *will* believe me!' declared Kamelya with passion and stood up too. 'You... you...' She wanted to say 'fool' but this was not the time to antagonise him. She stared at him wildly. 'Perhaps you will believe it when she gives you a child within six months!' she said disdainfully.

'May I ask by what right you interfere in my affairs like this?'

'You are so young.' She looked downwards so that her long silky lashes touched her cheeks. 'It's not right that a young officer with his future before him should be deceived by a wily prostitute like Neriman!'

He stared at her disbelievingly. He thought she was only jealous. 'What interest do you have in me?' he persisted with a half smile just touching the corner of his mouth. 'Was it for this you called me here so urgently? Wouldn't it have been wiser to have let me find out for myself?'

'No, no, you are so easily deceived! You are so chivalrous!'

She was looking away from him now but he would force her to look at him again! How dare she? He found himself shaking with anger. 'Why should I listen to *you*?' He took a step forward and forced her face upwards with his hard hand, his own face deathly white. 'Why, tell me!' he said.

She pulled herself away pettishly. 'It isn't difficult to prove,' she said in a matter-of-fact tone. 'There are brother officers out there who could tell you more than I – lustful men who've had her without thought. She's rotten. She's been visiting a rendezvous house for years. Hadn't you anyone to warn you?'

'I didn't need any warnings and I am quite ready to accept my responsibilities *hanım!*'

'You have no responsibility towards her. She tricked you because of her baby! Why do you deceive yourself? If you love her you would have left here the moment I started to talk about her! You couldn't have listened to me!'

'You take too much for granted!' said Murat, very pale. 'You should have thought of all this before *hanım*. I'm marrying her tomorrow. Isn't it a little late now?'

They glared at one another, the hatred of shared blood at boiling point.

'*Please* listen to me!' Her voice had changed again. Now it pleaded with him to hear her out. Every movement she made, every rustle of her dress, sent perfume rising between them. 'You are an honourable officer,' she said. 'She'll ruin you Murat! She's bad!'

'Shut up!' he said savagely. She'd hurt his pride. Couldn't she see? 'I don't believe you,' he said rapidly. 'I won't listen to any more. You're making it up for reasons of your own *hanım*! What is it you want with me?'

'I'm telling you the truth! Everyone knows what she is. Even my maid knows ...'

Murat stared at her wildly, desire shaking him so badly he could scarcely understand what she was saying. He thought crazily: what does it matter what she says? 'Who are you?' he asked, coming closer to her. 'You've disturbed me on and off for years, ever since I was in Harbiye and you used to look at me in the streets. What did you want with me? What do you want now?' He pulled her close against him, her astonished face looking up at him. 'You're the most beautiful woman I've ever seen,' he said. 'And I don't care what you're saying to me. I don't care, do you hear me?' He shook her a little in his excitement. 'I think perhaps if I care about anyone it's you. Do you hear that *hanım*?

You've spoiled me for everyone else, although I didn't know that until someone else pointed it out to me the other day.'

He heard Ahmet's words again. 'You sound infatuated!' Ahmet had said. But he thought it was more than infatuation that had kept him aware of her so long. 'I can't get you out of my thoughts,' he said to her. 'What have you done to me?'

She pulled away from him in panic but she was not quick enough to escape the invasive touch of his lips on hers. 'Oh!' she said, hand to her mouth, her eyes stricken with something like despair. 'Oh, I didn't *know!*' she said fearfully. She burst into tears. She felt his strong arms around her and the urgent beating of his heart against her own, but when the first violence of her crying had run its course all she could remember was that he had given her the passionate tribute of a lover.

'I'm sorry,' said Murat.

'Will you please go lieutenant?' she asked with a dignity he found almost unendurable. 'I didn't ask you here tonight for this.' Her hands were twisting and untwisting themselves in agonised appeal. 'I tried to save you from an unfortunate marriage, that was all. There wasn't anything else, I swear!' She was almost crying again. 'There wasn't anything else,' she repeated.

They were too engrossed to hear the ringing of the hall door and voices outside the salon.

'Please understand!' said Murat helplessly, barely able to hear anything above the thundering of his heart. He moved towards her again. 'Don't be alarmed,' he said as he saw apprehension leap to her eyes. 'I wouldn't harm you. I love you.' It was said at last and he paused, considering it. He thought it might possibly be true.

'No, no!' said Kamelya. He caught her fluttering hands in a grip that hurt and she stared at him with wide, tormented eyes.

The door of the salon crashed open. Neriman stood framed against it. She looked reckless and a little drunk and she halted when she saw their attitude of passion. There was a moment's startled silence.

'What a pretty tableau!' said Neriman, a crazy laugh creeping into her voice. 'Oh, *such* a very pretty tableau for mother and son!' Paroxysms of laughter shook her shoulders, and Murat let go of Kamelya's hands.

'Neriman!' he said. He remembered the dinner appointment. 'How did you know where to find me?'

'How could I help knowing?' She tried to master her demented laughter. 'We waited and waited at home but you didn't come. I telephoned the club but they said you'd gone out so I knew you were here.' She turned to look at Kamelya with an almost frightening detachment, 'I knew *she'd* have you...' She trailed her scarlet fingernails along the polished top of a table. 'I knew you'd get him first you bitch! You... old... used up... *nothing... nothing!*'

'Stop it!' screamed Kamelya as Ahmet walked through the door, surprising everyone.

***

'So, you're all here!' said Ahmet in a clipped voice. His eyes swept over Murat's white face. 'What is *your* business here, if I might ask?'

'I might ask the same of you,' retorted Murat furiously. 'You seem to have the right of entry, when and how you will!'

'Please!' said Kamelya faintly. 'Wait a moment please, let me explain.'

'Are you *another* of them?' Neriman said to Ahmet. 'I remember passing you on the steps one day. I didn't know you were visiting *her!*'

'Stop it!' said Kamelya bitterly. 'I can explain.'

'What's there to explain?' Neriman enquired idly. 'Isn't it obvious he's your lover?' She looked across to Murat. 'Has she told you yet?' she asked him. 'Has she told you I'm a prostitute like she is?'

Ahmet interposed angrily, 'What are you all trying to say? Hasn't this farce gone far enough?' He could not look at Kamelya and he turned in Murat's direction. 'Get out of here!' he said, 'And take this girl with you!'

'Mind your own business,' sneered Neriman. 'I'm not going anywhere! I'm staying here. There are things I have to say too!' Her eyes swept them viciously. 'You're fools!' she said to the two men. 'You know nothing about her at all. She's deceived you the way she's deceived everyone else – the beautiful Kamelya with her prim face is the greatest old bitch you'll ever meet!' Hysteria shook her voice and she said to Murat, 'Has she told you she's your mother?'

There was a movement from Ahmet as he thrust her aside roughly. 'Are you mad?' he asked her.

'It's true,' said Neriman scornfully. Murat looked stupified. 'Look at yourself in the mirror,' said Neriman moving over to him. 'Do you remember the registry papers at Eyüp Sultan? Well, this is Kamelya your mother, the one who abandoned you, the one you thought was dead.'

'Leave it,' said Ahmet, a flicker of fear in his heart. He put a hand on Kamelya's arm protectively. She was so ashen he thought she was going to faint.

Neriman thrust her face close against Murat's. 'If you don't believe me,' she said, 'ask old Fitnet the brothel keeper. She told me. She knows all about it.'

'Fitnet?' asked Murat with stiff lips. He looked across at Kamelya. A memory stirred of a woman with red hair, a woman who'd been to Fatma's house many times, a woman who'd told him his mother was dead. So long ago? He shook himself to escape the fierceness of the memory.

'Don't keep looking at her like that!' said Neriman impatiently. 'It's the truth! Fitnet knows. She'll tell you all right if you ask her.'

'Shut up!' shouted Murat, his eyes suddenly ablaze.

Neriman looked uncertain for a moment or two, then she started to cry, her head drooping on to her chest. 'It's true,' she kept repeating. 'She'll never tell you herself but she knows I'm telling the truth. She left you so she could have a good time without you. She didn't care a damn about you, she never did...' Her voice trailed off into sobs and Murat went on staring at Kamelya as though he'd never seen her before. Ahmet still held her arm, feeling closer to her than he had ever felt before, and aching with pity for Murat who had come here for something else.

'She tried to stop you marrying me,' said Neriman through the sobs which choked her voice. 'What's it to her? She's no better than I am.'

'My mother died when I was a child,' said Murat, trying to drag his heavy eyes from Kamelya's face.

Ahmet's hand tightened as he felt Kamelya's head stiffen. 'Murat – I *am* your mother,' she said. He saw Murat look at her with fear and wonder, before the young lines of his face sagged into shock.

'I have no mother,' he said harshly. 'My mother died when I was a child.'

'Murat, listen to what's been said, she *is* your mother,' said Ahmet, his heart breaking for them both. He tried to smile at Kamelya and then went to Murat's side. 'It's difficult for you now,' he said and wondered why he had never seen their likeness before, 'but you have to believe it my boy.'

'You are my father and mother in one,' said Murat, kissing his hand in passionate gratitude. 'I can only remember you. I have no one else.'

Ahmet saw the tears well up and overflow in Kamelya's eyes. How could he comfort her? He didn't know.

'Old bag!' said Neriman, hating her with a loathing beyond words.

Kamelya came to life tempestuously. 'Shut up!' she cried in rage. 'You've done enough damage for one night. You thought you'd get away with it! You didn't think I'd do anything to stop you – you with your baby inside you and your innocent face.' She squared up to Neriman, panting a little in her anger. 'You'll never have him!' she cried, beside herself with emotion. 'Damn you, you'll *never* have him, d'you hear?' She ran across to the fireplace and reached for her gun but Murat got there first.

'Are you crazy?' he asked, his eyes raking her cruelly. He could feel his mouth jerking with nervousness as he put the gun in his pocket.

'Why did you take it?' Kamelya wailed.

'Now, all of you, let me speak for a change!' Murat commanded harshly.

The women looked at him in astonishment. It had been their battle. What had he to do with it? Ahmet folded his arms and watched Murat as he turned towards Kamelya. 'I don't know who you are,' he said. 'I've heard so many things here tonight that I can't believe any of them, yet. But what I want to say to you is this: whether you're my mother or not makes no difference to me at all.' He looked at her pretty face with derision. '*My* mother!' he said and managed to laugh. 'Anyway, no matter now! You're quite dead for me, do you understand? You left it too late to interfere in my affairs, to protect me I suppose you'd call it. I needed your help when I was that child under Galata Bridge with nowhere to go. I can take care of myself now. I'm dependent on no one. I don't want you, do you understand that? You've ruined my life although I don't suppose you'd see it that way.' His eyes moved away from her, looking back to yesterday and the long road of childhood he had travelled alone, a nobody always, just a charity boy of no importance.

'I'm all right now,' he said, looking back to her ravished face. 'I don't need you now or ever again.' He saw Kasım Ağa and the ghost of the wretched child who'd been locked in the coal hole.

'Why did you come back? You weren't wanted.' His hurt eyes pierced her like hot pokers. 'Making me think of you in another way was the worst thing you ever did to me. *That* will last long after you're gone.' His mouth quivered and he stopped talking.

'Murat! Murat! My son, don't look at me like that, don't judge me too harshly until you know the story!'

'I wouldn't presume to judge you at all! You're nothing to me I tell you, you...'

He remembered that Neriman had called her a prostitute and that Ahmet was her lover. Well, it didn't matter really one way or the other now. There was nothing for him. How could he hold up his head again with all this knowledge in his heart? Where could he go to escape Ahmet's sympathy and the laughter of others? He saw the faces of his friends mocking him. They trooped past him in weary procession. What a joke! A nobody who thought he was somebody! The son of a Pera prostitute, the minister's wife, infatuated with his own mother! Celal knew. Celal had known since the Harbiye days. How could he look at him again? He bent his head in shame and felt tears hurt his throat.

'I wish I'd never been born,' he said bitterly.

Neriman ran across to him, her face aged and wise with the pity she felt. 'Don't say that!' she cried urgently. 'Don't say that Murat! It was all my fault, I shouldn't have told you.' She tried to steady her wildly shaking voice. 'Look, you're quite free,' she said. 'There's no need to marry me Murat! Don't go on looking like that, please. I never meant...' She fell at his feet, her heart breaking for the look of tragedy on his face.

He felt her soft childish face pressed against his leg. Her hands held him tightly and she cried with a terrible, ancient bitterness that had nothing to do with the Neriman he knew. He bent down and touched her sleek head. 'Don't cry!' he said and raised her to her feet. He saw her with compassion, touched with the tremulous ghost of love. 'Maybe we could have been happy enough,' he said wonderingly, 'if she had left us alone. Perhaps it wouldn't have mattered after all about the baby. Perhaps you couldn't help it, I don't know.'

She released herself from his hands. 'You're too harsh on her,' she cried, with heavy tears chasing one another down her face. 'I know you are Murat! She's right in a way – none of us know the truth, only her. Perhaps there was nothing else she could do for you.' She pressed her hands over her stomach in a gesture of unconscious tenderness. 'I'd do the same for my child too,' she said. 'Then I'd hide myself the way she did. I can't bear to think of it now, but I know I'd do the same. I wouldn't have him grow up to be called names. It'd break my heart.'

'Stop crying!' said Murat and pulled her hands away from her eyes so that her face was revealed in all its hideous despair. 'It's difficult to understand all this woman's talk. I can only see her from the angle of my childhood and your child will do the same one day. You're not going to leave him Neriman! We'll look after him, you and I! It's better to have a name than to be nameless.' He kissed her wet eyes with a passion of pity. 'He'll need you when he's a child,' he said. 'A child looks for its mother everywhere.'

'Let me go!' cried Neriman. 'I want to go home, I won't listen to you. You don't know what you're saying.'

'I'll take you home.'

'No,' said Kamelya and he turned to look at her with surprise. He had almost forgotten she was there. 'Don't go with her,' she said wearily.

'Have you no pity?' Murat asked. His eyes took in every little detail of her. They swept her blindly – hating her, loving her, tortured by her. 'You had no right to interfere,' he said.

'Leave it now,' said Ahmet sharply. He had been silent for so long it was a shock to hear his calm voice. What right had he to witness these things?

'Don't come,' said Neriman. 'I don't want you with me. I never want you ever again. Let me go!' She ran to the door. 'I shall be all right,' she said and held up her head with pride. 'There's no need to worry about me.' Murat ran after her but she would not wait for him. 'Go back!' she cried shrilly. 'Go back and leave me alone.'

He stood staring after her into the darkness. With a sort of weary wonder he thought that it must be late. Something had gone wrong. The tinselled evening already behind him mocked him with its false promise. He remembered that Ahmet and Kamelya still waited for him in the salon. 'Kamelya!' he said to the empty street. His brain was tired, numb with exhaustion, yet something stirred faintly, warning him. He could hear nothing but her name, repeating itself over and over like a worn-out gramophone record. It deafened him with its monotonous insistence. She had betrayed him into being foolish. She didn't care about him at all! She was his mother! No, no! She couldn't be that! That was just some childish nonsense Neriman had talked. He'd never live again, he was already dead and looking back at this exhausted night. He was so tired he couldn't think.

He went back up the steps and into the quiet hall. She was in there waiting for him, in her elegant salon with her lover beside her to give her comfort. She'd been in places like this all the years he'd starved in the gutters and been kicked by old Fatma.

'Murat!' she said, as he appeared in the doorway.

She was standing by the dying fire and Ahmet sat in an armchair with his head in his hands. Now that Neriman was gone it was their turn to talk. How could he bear any more talk? Like a wounded bird he limped across to her, his legs stiff with exhaustion.

He looked at her tender radiant face, the face that had haunted him since before time. Kamelya the stranger, the woman in the streets of Pera with her white dog for show. He wished he could concentrate a bit better. All his thoughts were running into each other making him feel muddled. What was it he had been trying to think? Was it about the face? Yes! That was it – the face! So lovely, selfish and ruthless, so tender. The face of his mother!

The tide of emotion which had held him all night surged to a crescendo. Presently it would have to break, break and fall... His eyes met hers in a look of utter love. He took the gun from his pocket. Was it her gun or was it his own? No matter! But how surprised she looked, surprised and silly with her painted mouth wide open! She was foolish. She'd tried to do something to him, he'd remember in a moment, but first it was necessary to obliterate that evil face. How could he think when that face went on smiling at him like that?

'You fool!' shouted Ahmet's voice from a far-off distance. Murat saw him leap towards him but he had already fired.

He watched her fall even though Ahmet's strong arms imprisoned him and he was interested to see that she still looked surprised. He turned his blank, witless eyes on Ahmet. 'Doesn't she look silly?' he said, half laughing, half crying.

A tango on the radio. An ember from the fire, spluttering and chinking… Murat gazed down at the face of his dead mother, his lips stretched in a smile of crazed pain.

Afterword

Dark Journey is one of those books that's always been with me – yet never for very long at any one time, having for the best part of sixty years been relegated to an assortment of boxes secreted away in lofts or damp barns, gathering dust and mildew, the tattered pages of its typescript a home to mice and silverfish. On my father's death in November 1970 it trailed me around the English home counties and East Anglia before finally coming to roost in France, in Ambronay among the foothills of the Rhône Alps. In the autumn of 2007 it resurfaced from within the remains of an old leather attaché case, itself a reminder of father's grander, more opulent days as an air force captain at the Turkish Embassy in wartime London. Coffee-stained and foxed, tied up with string, several of its pages in disarray, others with alterations or alternatives, the torn label of a literary agent peeling off its turquoise cover, it lay crushed among an assortment of manuscripts including some short stories and another novel, no longer complete, called *The Strangers*. I put it in a drawer, along with some family photographs and memorabilia. Then one cloudy winter afternoon a while later, sitting by a stove burning cherry and to a soundtrack from Maria Tănase, a vista of snow-covered Essex fields spread before me, I got it out, poured myself a glass of Tekirdağ *rakı* ... and began to read.

When it was written isn't clear (the typescript is undated and no corroborative material has survived). But in all probability it was drafted in London, in a rented room at 35 Inverness Terrace, Bayswater, a Greek house, some time in late 1950 or early 1951, following the publication of my father's memoirs, *Portrait of a Turkish Family*. I have a distant recollection of it being among the various rejections my parents received during the late summer of '51 – by which time we had moved to Blackrock, County Dublin. We never learnt why publishers refused the book. Most likely the story – a young Turkish woman's descent towards moral annihilation, set in localities few in Britain or America would have then recognised, with an added Oedipean counterpoint, tensions of enslavement and fallen women, and discords of empire, republic and religious policy – was out of chime with the general post-war climate and perceived comfort needs of the West. Maybe the agent, Spencer Curtis Brown, for all his influence and connections, didn't try hard enough. Whatever, it did the rounds and got nowhere. My father was disappointed. Similarly my mother, Margarete, whose terse phraseology, percussive at times, and finer turns of English tacitly permeate the pages.

Father's published books all drew on personal experience, each in the process offering varying degrees of autobiographical insight. So too with *Dark Journey*. Why Fatma, his autocratic grandmother in black, should ever have seen fit to recount such a fraught story to small boys, as recounted in the foreword, is odd. But she did, and the bardic telling of the tale was hers. Reworking it, father translated it into his own time, embellishing situations and inventing people, 'filming' in sepia a place, period and society in transition between Empire and decay, Republic and rejuventation, Islam and secularism, the orient and the occident. The book masquerades as a novel. And a morality – that no good will ever come of hypocrisy and double standards. But behind its façade there's enough to suggest that it might also in part be social documentary, touching unapologetically on dimensions, attitudes and prejudices of early 20th-century Turkish life more usually side-stepped. When the reader is joltingly reminded that the main protagonists of the drama, Kamelya and Murat, widow and son, were people who'd once lived, we are invited to cross the line into reality. In the updated form in which they are presented, were they known to him? (On occasion Kamelya and his own mother share more than just the usual dilemmas and choices faced by their Istanbul sisters in 1915 bereaved by war or destroyed by economic collapse – their efforts to command French, for instance, and their unveiled aura and recognisability around the fashion houses of Pera.) Were he and Murat shades of the same person? (Murat, a little older than father's frail brother, Mehmet, could conceivably have been a younger peer at Kuleli.) Later in the narrative could he

himself have been the source of Major Ahmet? (Ahmet's transfer
to the east of Turkey, 'the very furthest, most desolate point they
could find for me, the sort of place they send unruly officers to
cool off,' strikingly mirrors his own banishment to Diyarbakır in
1945 following his London posting and liaison with my Anglo-
Irish mother, not then his wife.) Other parallels are for the seeking.
Kamelya keeping her pistol hidden among her accoutrements isn't
so far removed from father keeping live bullets in a drawer until at
least the early fifties. I know, I played with them as a child.

From its timeline, 1915–33, to the setting of the principal
action in Istanbul, the book shares many resonances with *Portrait
of a Turkish Family*. Similar characters crowd the pages. Here
again are the black servants and Bekçi Baba the night watchman
patrolling the streets of cramped wooden houses, keeping an eye
on neighbourhood respectability. Kuleli and Harbiye troop their
military colours. Those who are special smile the same 'brilliant
smile'. A name occasionally leaps off the page. Was young Neriman's
friend Suna the flighty Suna of the 'gay red dress' for whom father
had fallen as a cadet in 1925? 'Why should a war in Europe make
any difference in our lives?' barks my great-grandmother in *Portrait*.
She lived to see the error of her flippancy. Yet, to some extent, such
sentiment was the colour of my father's childhood. In *Dark Journey*,
as in *Portrait*, the bloodshed of war is once removed, impinging
little on day-to-day life sewing and laundering for a few coins in
infested backstreets. Women got on as best they could. Sometimes
their menfolk came back, mostly they didn't. What mattered was to
maintain a semblance of family life, to protect their children from
the sights and sounds of demonstration and strife, to give them
food if not fun. On that spring morning in 1915 when we first meet
Kamelya and Murat, nothing would have been further from her
mind than the Armenians being deported from Istanbul, nor those
who would be strung from the gallows in Beyazıt Square weeks
later. And as for my father, so too with her: whatever the bitterness
of the moment, the massacre-fields far away, it was invariably better
to get on with Greeks than hate them, to have Madame Toto as
friend rather than foe.

Women of a certain exotic place and time shaped by pragmatic
necessity, women wanting liberation who are yet judged morally

and socially by the men whose company they need or keep – husbands, protectors, clients – women who are survivors whatever their warp, are among the pervasive subtexts of *Dark Journey*. Kamelya runs the gamut from the moment she is conned by Cemal *bey*, and then abducted by Kara Kurt – Black Wolf – who makes her his second 'harem' woman. Responsible for her destiny and desires, she flirts, she dabbles, she's kept by an ageing political grandee who then marries her, she takes a handsome lover from the army, she becomes the beautiful quasi-courtesan of the city, hovering at the edges of prostitution. 'Light women' had a place in father's heart. A liberal-minded man, never one to preach, he neither passed judgement nor denigrated their calling. Maybe in his Istanbul youth, in the brothels and *pensions* off the gas-lit lanes of Tünel down the Grand Rue de Péra, his forays had embraced friendships and loves beyond lust. Maybe the consummation of Murat and Neriman across the moonlit Bosphorus from Kuleli, the frustrated young officer and the desperate girl with child, had been a life awakening he'd similarly gone through, hence his particular handling of the scene.

Seeing this book into print, I am grateful as always to the patience, editorial eye and discernment of my publisher, Rose Baring. And to Barnaby Rogerson for believing in it. A special word of thanks, too, to my Bulgarian friend, the pianist Nadejda Vlaeva. She will know why.

Ateş Orga
Great Yeldham, Essex
Arcueil, Île-de-France
Summer 2014

Glossary of Turkish & foreign words

Ahmak Dolt, goose, idiot, simpleton, term of derision.
Allah God.
Anne(m) (My) mother, mother-in-law.
Baba(m) (My) father, old man.
Bayan Lady, madam, miss, mistress, honorific title.
Bayram Feast day, holiday.
Bekçi Baba Night watchman, warden, district elder.
Bey Gentleman, mister, squire, honorific title.
Börek A savoury pastry of Ottoman provincial origin, frequently triangular in shape (especially among Albanian or Armenian communities), made with paper-thin layers of unleavened dough, filled with white cheese, meat or vegetables, seasoned with herbs, then lightly baked, boiled or deep-fried.
Canım My life, lifeblood, soul.
Çarşaf A black dress or 'sheet' enclosing the body from head to foot which attained fashion in the late-19th century during the reign of Abdülhamid II, 'Emperor of the Ottomans, Caliph of the Faithful' (1876–1909), before being discouraged, along with the abolition of the male *fez*, in 1925. In the decade between the Balkan Wars (1912–13) and the declaration of the Republic (1923), foreign correspondents in Istanbul noted a progressive misuse and abuse of the 'Muslim veil'. 'In spite of or perhaps because of the veil, [clandestine prostitution] is said to be rather frequent in some Moslem quarters' (*The Times*, 13 March 1914). 'Appreciating the allurement of the unseen, [most prostitutes] now wear the veil, either in its old or modified form. In consequence, the relinquishment of the veil among respectable women has been accelerated' (*The Washington Post*, 6 May 1919).
Çay Tea.
Cezve Pot for making Turkish coffee, traditionally in copper with a long brass handle.

Dark Journey

Cucumber (Hıyar) Term of derision, sexual slang.
Efendi Lord, master, sir, honorific title.
Eşek Ass, donkey, term of derision.
Gendarme (Jandarma) Armed constabulary, from the French.
Hamam Turkish Bath, a gender-segregated public place of cleansing and a forum of gossip where, amongst women, eligible girls could be appraised and marriages brokered.
Hanım Lady, madam, miss, mistress, honorific title.
Helva A dessert made with sesame paste, semolina or flour, studded with slivers of almond, pistachio nuts or pine kernels, high in sugar and butter content. Traditionally associated with, but not only, births, circumcision feasts, weddings, deaths and holy days.
Hoca Religious master or teacher, wise man.
İmam Leader in a Sunni mosque and community, spiritual mentor, upholder of moral values.
Kafes Lattice or grill window; originally the 'Golden Cage' of the Imperial Harem where claimants to the Ottoman throne were immured indefinitely to await their fate.
Kahve Coffee
Konak High status mansion or villa, surrounded by gardens and fountains, distinctive of the late 19th-century vernacular architecture of Istanbul (*see* June Taboroff, 'The wooden houses of Istanbul', *Unasylva* FAO, Vol 35, 1983).
Kuruş (Piastre) Ottoman billon coin, 1/100th of a *lira*, introduced in 1844.
Lira Ottoman gold coin in circulation from 1844 to 1927. The First Issue of Turkish lira notes in denominations of 1, 4, 10, 50, 100, 500 and 1000, printed in French and Ottoman script, with medallions of Atatürk on the 50–1000 bills, became legal tender from 5 December 1927.
Mama Franco-Turkish version of mother (*anne*). (French was the preferred language of Istanbul's upper class, valued in some circles higher than English or German. Despite Republican attempts to Turkify, the custom for Pera shops and *haute couture* houses to address their clientele in French lasted well into the 1930s.)
Mana Greek version of mother.
Meze Appetiser, an assortment of dips and delicacies.

Müezzin The one calling the faithful to prayer, of honest character and mellifluous voice.

Muhallebi A milk, cream, starch and sugar pudding, served with rose water.

Nightingale Lamp Egyptian-derived copper and waxed linen candle lantern.

Old Comrades (Alte Kameraden) Prussian march written by Carl Teike in 1889, indelibly fixed in father's memory.

Padişah Ottoman Sultan, royal title.

Para Generically 'money'; specifically an Ottoman coin, 1/40th of a *kuruş*.

Pezevenk Pimp, ponce, procurer, son-of-a-bitch, sexual slang – father's most recurrent swear word.

Pilav Turkish-style rice, the long grains pre-coated in butter or oil (to ensure separation), boiled briefly in stock or water, then 'rested'. Served plain or mixed with pine kernels.

Rakı Aniseed spirit served with iced water, related to French *pastis*, Greek *ouzo*, Italian *sambuca* and Levantine *arak*.

Şeytan Satan.

Simit Sesame-coated bread ring akin to a bagel, popular throughout the Balkans and Middle East, baked and sold in Istanbul since the early 16th century.

Sokak Street.

Tango Lascivious South American/Balkan/Turkish dance. Semi-obsolete Turkish slang for a prostitute or 'dolled-up' woman.

A.O.

Lexicon of people and place

Arnavutköy Wealthy Bosphorus neighbourhood between Ortaköy and Bebek – the 'Albanian Village' – notable historically for its mixed ethnicity (Greek pre-Great War, Jewish before that).

At Pazarı The old Horse Bazaar in Fatih district, between the Golden Horn and Marmara.

Bebek Affluent Bosphorus quarter in Beşiktaş between Arnavutköy and Rumelihisarı.

Black Ottomans (Afro Turks) From Nubia, Abyssinia, Sudan and the remoter regions of Central and East Africa, black slaves, rank-and-file soldiers and servants, such as the one employed by Saadet *hanım*, were a part of Ottoman life for more than four centuries (*see* Alan W. Fisher, 'The Sale of Slaves in the Ottoman Empire: Markets and State Taxes on Slave Sales, some Preliminary Considerations', *Boğaziçi Universitesi Dergisi* Humanities, Vol. 6 [1978]). At the Imperial court the Chief Black Eunuch – in charge of the Harem – was customarily African, fearsome of manner, highly informed, and politically influential. Despite the closure in the late 1840s of Istanbul's Slave Market and the eventual outlawing of the trade, covert trafficking through male and female dealers continued well into the early 20th century, with an estimated 10,000 black slaves – cheaper to acquire than whites from the Balkans and Caucasus – being imported annually between 1860 and 1890 alone. As a boy my father was brought up by a 'coal black' nursemaid, İnci, whose mother, Feride, widow of a former palace servant at Dolmabahçe, worked for the family 'upstairs'. Tales of a dark Abyssinian beauty marrying into the Orga line, purportedly one of father's 'aunts', pervaded my childhood – how closely related she may have been, however, and what her name was, he never revealed.

Bosphorus The Istanbul waterway separating Asia from Europe and joining the Black Sea and Marmara – the 'Bosphor' of my father's idiosyncratic spelling.

Bursa Bursa, in the south Marmara region, was the capital city of the Ottomans during the 14th and early 15th centuries.

Çengelköy A neighbourhood on the Asian side of the Bosphorus. The boat station is the local stop for Kuleli.

Eyüp, Eyüp Sultan An Istanbul district at the head of the Golden Horn, which takes its name from Ebu Eyyûb el-Ensarî, companion of the Prophet, who in the early 670s lost his life here during the first Arab siege of the city. Several centuries later Mehmet the Conqueror had a marble tomb (*türbe*) erected above his grave, and commanded the building of the Eyüp Sultan Mosque, completed in 1458 – turning the vicinity into a site of pilgrimage. On acceding to the throne, Ottoman sultans traditionally received the Sword of Osman at the mosque. Eyüp Cemetry, a place of royal, civic, religious, military and common burial, is among the largest and oldest in Istanbul.

Galata A neighbourhood of Pera, on the northern side of the Golden Horn, with strong Eastern Roman, Byzantine, Genoese, Venetian and Jewish associations.

Galata Bridge Meeting place and departure point for millions, Galata Bridge, opened in November 1845 at the mouth of the Golden Horn, symbolically connects civilisations and cultures – the imperial palace and grand mosques of the Muslim 'Old City' and the non-Muslim 'New' with its foreign diplomats, Levantine merchants, ethnic minorities and 'painted women'. The cobbled, tram-lined bridge Kamelya and Murat walked was a German-built floating design completed in 1912. Pedestrians paid a toll of 5 *para* and horse-drawn carriages 100 *para*. Military personnel, essential services and clerics went free.

Gemlik By Kamelya's time this once famous naval dockyard in an olive-growing region on the southern shore of the Marmara not far from Bursa, mountain-locked on three sides and close to the ruins of ancient Kios (Prusias on the Sea), was little more than a motley of neglected buildings and impoverished communities. Out of nearly 39,000 inhabitants identified in the 1891 Ottoman census, 43% were Armenian, 39% Turkish, and 17% Greek. By 1920 the population had dwindled to 5,000.

Golden Horn Estuary of the Alibeyköy and Kağıthane rivers feeding into the Bosphorus, separating Old Istanbul and the Seraglio Point (Sarayburnu) from the rest of the metropolis.

Dark Journey

Hacı Abdullah Ottoman restaurant established in 1888 with a personal licence from Abdulhamid II. Between 1915 and 1940 it served clientele from the ground floor of Rumeli Han on İstiklâl Caddesi, the trammelled Grand Rue running through Pera from Taksim to Tünel.

Hacı Bekir Confectioners famous for 'Bonbon Turc' – *lokum*, Turkish Delight – established in 1777.

Haydarpaşa Station A neo-classical German-designed building inaugurated in 1909, Haydarpaşa, the St. Pancras of Istanbul, situated by the sea at Kadıköy on the Asiatic side, was the western terminus of the *Anatolian Express* connecting Istanbul and Ankara nightly from 1927.

Harbiye Military Academy Founded in 1834, in keeping with the reforms of Sultan Mahmud II, this was the elite finishing school of the Ottoman/Turkish officer corps, located until 1936 in the Istanbul neighbourhood of Harbiye. Atatürk graduated in 1902, my father in 1931. The 'racing function' described in Chapter 22 relates most probably to a meeting run elsewhere at the Veliefendi Race Course in Zeytinburnu, constructed by German equestrian specialists in 1912–13.

Haseki Hospital During the period leading up to Kamelya's day, this 16th century complex in Fatih provided care for widows and orphans as well as 'needy women and prostitutes' (*see* Nadir Özbek, 'The Politics of Poor Relief in the Late Ottoman Empire, 1876–1914', *New Perspectives on Turkey*, Fall 1999).

Istanbul University Between the Sülemaniye Mosque, Beyazıt Square and Grand Bazaar (*Kapalıçarşı*), founded by Mehmet the Conqueror in 1453. Its Republican resurrection – the university Neriman knew – opened its doors in November 1933.

Kuleli Military High School Occupying the old twin-towered Cavalry Barracks in Çengelköy on the Asian shore of the Bosphorus, this was founded by Abdülmecid I in September 1845. During the Allied Occupation of Istanbul (13 November 1918–23 September 1923), denuded of its iconic towers and under the American flag, it served as an orphanage for Albanians, Arabs, Armenians, Kurds and others. Witness to forsaken souls, to the fallout and indignity of war, to the remnants of an Empire crushed and a city ravaged, my father, not yet eleven, was offered a place in 1919 – at a time when a handful of indigenous Turks were still being admitted to the 'Military School' for juniors housed in the 'grey, ancient building on the hill' which used to stand behind the 'white shining palace' that was the 'Military College' for seniors. He graduated ten years later, his friends and peers having included İrfan Tansel, a future commander-in-chief of the Turkish Air Force, and the poet Fazıl Hüsnü Dağlarca. What it was like to become a man during this volcanic period, a first generation Republican transcending Monarchy and Occupation, was to permeate his memoirs.

Mısır Çarşısı The covered Spice or Egyptian Bazaar by the New Mosque off Galata Bridge, dating from the 17th century.

Papatya Sokak A *cul-de-sac* in Pera.

Pera The cosmopolitan 'New City' district of Istanbul – modern Beyoğlu – immediately north of the Golden Horn, referred to by its occidental/Greek name from the Middle Ages to the formation of the Republic.

Pera Palas Hotel Istanbul's *belle epoque grande dame*, built in the 1890s to receive passengers disembarking the *Orient Express* at Sirkeci Station in Eminönü. Following a neo-classical design by the Frenchman Alexander Vallaury and owned originally by the Ottoman–Armenian Esayan family, the hotel welcomed a galaxy of wealthy, celebrated, legendary and infamous 20th century figures – from Atatürk and Edward VIII to Mata Hari and Trotsky to Agatha Christie (she plotted *Murder on the Orient Express* in Room 411), Graham Greene, Ernest Hemingway, Pierre Loti and Greta Garbo. In December 1926 the management hosted Istanbul's first catwalk show western-style, *The Istanbul Fashion Revue*, with guests treated cross-culturally to hookah pipes and fountains of champagne.

Prostitution A prostitute, Ottoman law defined, 'is a woman who offers herself for the pleasure of others and in this way has relations with numerous men, for the purpose of monetary profit'. Under the 1915 *règlementation* 'owners of brothels [madams only, men were not permitted] were required to record the name [nickname], age, origin, nationality, and [addresses]' of their workers. Following hospital examination, 'registered women were required go have [an] identity booklet at all times [for which, in addition to a photograph, they paid 5 *kuruş*], both inside and outside the brothel' (*see* Mark David Wyers, '*Wicked Istanbul': The*

Dark Journey

Regulation of Prostitution in the Early Turkish Republic [Istanbul 2012]). Legally, prostitutes had to be eighteen or above – though, as Neriman 'the schoolgirl' was to shock Kamelya, the rule was often flouted – and it was forbidden to solicit for business by leaning out of windows or loitering in doorways. During the Occupation years the number of registered women working Istanbul's vice districts was estimated (conservatively) at between one and two thousand. By 1933, according to a German report, the number had dropped to less than 300. Clandestine activity, however, at all levels of the social chain, was rampant. Resigned to a seemingly endless journey of displacement, deprivation and hardship, many 'virtuous' girls of breeding, widowed by war or cheated by hollow promises, unable to make a living from sewing or laundering, turned to prostitution for survival. Their life, such as we know of it, was a sleepless one of 'cheese, lemonade, rice and bread' ... unheated rooms and loveless hours, *rakı* and rage, violence and murder, abortions and miscarriages ... disease ... desperation.

Süleymaniye Mosque Commanding Istanbul's Third Hill, the resplendent Süleymaniye comlex dates from 1558. Ravaged at various times by fire and earthquake, its courtyard was used as a munitions depot during the First World War, with inevitably disastrous consequences. The tombs of Süleyman the Magnificent, his Ukranian consort Roxelana and Mimar Sinan, the mosque's architect, lie within a whisper of its minarets.

Tahtakale Neighbourhood in Fatih.

Tırnava A south-east Bulgarian/North Thracian village near Yambol and the modern Turkish frontier, an autonomous part of the Empire until 1908. According to my father's foreword, his grandmother was born here (in around 1872), though received family wisdom has it that she was of Macedonian stock from Skopje.

Tokatlian Hotel Second only to the Pera Palas and Gümüşsuyu's Park Hotel on İnönü Caddesi (a favourite haunt of my parents) – and as consciously European – the Tokatlian on the Grande Rue de Péra next to the Flower Arcade (Çiçek Pasajı), opened for business in 1897. Following vandalism during the Armenian purges of the First World War, it was acquired in 1919 by a Serbian businessman, Nikolai Medovitch. Notwithstanding the Allied Occupation, Medovitch brought a fresh lease of life to the place. Among Istanbul socialites in

218

the early Republican years, to entrepeneurs on the up, it was *the* locale of the moment. Here Atatürk, indulging his weakness for liquour and women, hosted grand balls and afternoon teas *à l'anglaise* – and smashed an occasional mirror. The real and the imagined played out nightly in its rooms and corridors. On a ley line between the Balkans, Soviet Russia and the old Ottoman Near East it was a place where secrets were made and secrets were kept.

A.O.

ELAND

61 Exmouth Market, London EC1R 4QL
Email: info@travelbooks.co.uk

Eland was started thirty years ago to revive great travel books that had fallen out of print. Although the list soon diversified into biography and fiction, all the books are chosen for their interest in spirit of place. One of our readers explained that for him reading an Eland is like listening to an experienced anthropologist at the bar – she's let her hair down and is telling all the stories that were just too good to go in to the textbook.

Eland books are for travellers, and for readers who are content to travel in their own minds. They open out our understanding of other cultures, interpret the unknown and reveal different environments, as well as celebrating the humour and occasional horrors of travel. We take immense trouble to select only the most readable books and therefore many readers collect the entire, hundred-volume series.

You will find a very brief description of some of our books on the following pages. Extracts from each and every one of them can be read on our website, at www.travelbooks.co.uk. If you would like a free copy of our catalogue you can request one via the website, email us or send a postcard.

ELAND

'One of the very best travel lists' WILLIAM DALRYMPLE

An Innocent Anthropologist
NIGEL BARLEY
An honest, funny, affectionate and compulsively irreverent account of fieldwork in West Africa

Jigsaw
SYBILLE BEDFORD
An intensely remembered autobiographical novel about an inter-war childhood

A Visit to Don Otavio
SYBILLE BEDFORD
The hell of travel and the Eden of arrival in post-war Mexico

Journey into the Mind's Eye
LESLEY BLANCH
An obsessive love affair with Russia and one particular Russian

The Way of the World
NICOLAS BOUVIER
A 1950's roadtrip from Serbia to Afghanistan

The Devil Drives
FAWN BRODIE
Biography of Sir Richard Burton, explorer, linguist and pornographer

Turkish Letters
OGIER DE BUSBECQ
Eyewitness history at its best: Istanbul during the reign of Suleyman the Magnificent

Two Middle-Aged Ladies in Andalusia
PENELOPE CHETWODE
An infectious, personal account of a fascination with horses, God and Spain

My Early Life
WINSTON CHURCHILL
From North West frontier to Boer War by the age of twenty-fivet

A Square of Sky
JANINA DAVID
A Jewish childhood in the Warsaw ghetto and hiding from the Nazis

Chantemesle
ROBIN FEDDEN
A lyrical evocation of childhood in Normandy

Viva Mexico!
CHARLES FLANDRAU
Five years in turn-of-the-century Mexico, described by an enchanted Yankee

Travels with Myself and Another
MARTHA GELLHORN
Five journeys from hell by a great war correspondent

The Weather in Africa
MARTHA GELLHORN
Three novellas set amongst the white settlers of East Africa

The Last Leopard
DAVID GILMOUR
The biography of Giuseppe di Lampedusa, author of The Leopard

Walled Gardens
ANNABEL GOFF
An Anglo-Irish childhood

Africa Dances
GEOFFREY GORER
The magic of indigenous culture and the banality of colonisation

Cinema Eden
JUAN GOYTISOLO
Essays from the Muslim Mediterranean

A State of Fear
ANDREW GRAHAM-YOOLL
A journalist witnesses Argentina's nightmare in the 1970s

Warriors
GERALD HANLEY
Life and death among the Somalis

Morocco That Was
WALTER HARRIS
All the cruelty, fascination and humour of a pre-modern kingdom